Cheap Lives

Cheap Lives

ANTONY SHER

With five drawings by the author

LITTLE, BROWN AND COMPANY

A *Little, Brown* Book

First published in Great Britain in 1995
by Little, Brown and Company

A CIP catalogue record for this book
is available from the British Library.

ISBN 0 316 91450 9

Typeset by Palimpsest Book Production Limited,
Polmont, Stirlingshire
Printed and bound in Great Britain by
Clays Ltd, St Ives plc.

Little, Brown and Company (UK)
Brettenham House
Lancaster Place
London WC2E 7EN

For Greg

ACKNOWLEDGEMENTS

As this book developed, invaluable contributions were made by my partner, Greg Doran, my literary agent, Mic Cheetham, and my editor at Little, Brown, Philippa Harrison. At Little, Brown, I'd also like to thank Alan Samson, Tim Holman and the art director, Peter Cotton. In London, excellent work was done by my research assistant, Sue Powell, and the South African lawyer Michael Richman. In South Africa, I'm greatly indebted to Edwin Cameron, prominent human rights campaigner, lawyer, and now judge; Andries Nel, formerly of the Lawyers For Human Rights, and now an MP in the new government; Laurel Angus of the Centre For Applied Legal Studies; Robert and Paula McBride, who granted me an interview; as did Zonga Mokgatle, of the Upington 14; and Oupa Seheri, who was on death row when I visited him (his sentence has since been commuted to life). Other research included visiting Isandlwana with Zulu War experts David Rattray and Chris Harvie; and travelling through Sabi Sabi Game Reserve with the Executive Ranger, Leo Frankel. Thanks also to three tour guides, Vic Schulze, Arthur Thiele and Peter Uhlenhaut; and some members of Cape Town's Coloured community – William Goliath, Lovetta Bolters, Charmaine Oosthuizen, and the actor Ivan D. Lucas. In terms of published material, I found Phyllis Naidoo's document, 'Waiting to Die in Pretoria', and Lawrence G. Green's book, *Karoo*, very useful. Finally I must thank some members of my family for their help: Randall Sher, Joan Silver, Verne Borchardt, and my nephew, Dean Borchardt, who was my expert on surfing!

NOTE

This story is a work of fiction created in the mind of the author. The events are fictitious and, with only three exceptions, the characters who feature in the action are fictitious. The three exceptions are Robert McBride, Dimitri Tsafendas and Barend Strydom.

I. LETTERS

ONE

83143118
Pretoria Maximum Security Prison
Private Bag X45
Pretoria 0001

Mister.

You ask what it was like to kill you. I'll tell you later.

It's very quiet around me. Night, I think.

The light in my cage is kept on all the time. He's always up there, my sun in a bottle. Night and day and also day and night. Same thing. The one called night is just a bit longer. This big bright fat thing you'll never climb over.

So it's down to the man himself. Round and round himself he goes. What's there? Hair, nails, skin. An option of spit, seed, shit, grey matter.

Combinations of the aforementioned substances can cook up emotions. So the night passes.

I'm an intellectual by the bye. Prison has opened doors for me.

So I've changed from the person you met on what could be termed THAT fateful day.

In here the books are spy stories, cowboys and crooks, and suchlike trash. But the other prisons had full libraries. There you could also keep books on a long-term loan in your cage.

Like my best one, which was called BOTH A DICTIONARY AND AN ENCYCLOPAEDIA.

Here the only book on a long-term loan is the Bible.

The one they gave me was in Afrikaans. This I regard as an intellectually inferior language. I complained, fully expecting my words to fall on deaf ears. In here even the kaffir warders speak Afrikaans. It is the prison language.

But miracle of miracles they gave me another Bible in the queen's English.

When I was growing up in Bonteheuwel I spoke a kind of stew. English, Afrikaans, our own coloured sauce, some Malay spice, even a little black pepper.

Haai ou pél, happy new year and salaam alaikom, vat jou piel en byt hom, lets jol on down through the streets of smoked-up dronkie coons an' impis doing the kwela, an' there by Gawa's shebeen, there we'll have us a doppie or two, squash the top so you drink to the bottom, till kyk nou there's only empties left, amen an' sweet dreams.

Those days are bygones, once upon a time junk.

When I was wise without reading any books.

But I can still think with my nose.

So what I'm saying is this.

Watch out, you hear?

On the day a man arrives here, he's given the rules. Strict rules. He can write letters but not about the following subjects.

Prison conditions.

Politics.

Sex.

It gave me no heartsore, these rules. I didn't plan to write letters, I didn't plan to get any. But then one day a nun came to call. Afterwards she wrote me a letter on the subject of thin air. I wrote back on the subject of her immaculate organ.

I don't know if they censored my comments but I never heard from her or anyone again.

Then this morning I'm brought back to my cage from the showers, and there lying nicely on my bed is

A letter.

I walk back and forwards. Looking at it.

No stamps or nothing.

I pick it up and sniff.

Clean paper smell.

4

I tear open a corner and I'm in for a surprise.

You inside.

YOU reminding me who you are. That's a laugh. YOU saying how we can write to one another. Without censorship. YOU telling me to leave my reply on my bed during shower time. Or during exercise.

I put you back in your envelope. I put the envelope back on the bed. I move round. I watch. I keep my distance. I stay on the tips of my toes. I think, what's up?

Listen, I know there's bribery and corruption on these corridors. I see Sergeant Fourie with the half-jack of whisky in his top pocket. I see him lean against some cage doors. I see the straw going through a small hole the guys have stabbed in their mesh with a Bic. I see those guys sucking on fat Fourie's tit like puppies. So fine, they've bribed and corrupted him. Or their friends on the outside have. Booze, buttons, dagga. That's what bribery and corruption buys.

But I've never heard of it buying this.

Freedom of speech.

As the bloody COMRADES might say.

It isn't just our letters that are censored in here. Also our tongues. Unless the warders ask a question, you keep your trap shut. Can only talk in talking time. Through our closed doors. From about maybe 4 to maybe 6, hard to tell what's the bells. We're not allowed to wear watches. A person could choke to death on a watch. And they don't like death here. It's fine in that room up the 42 steps, the stairway to heaven, but not here. No death on death row.

No death, no darkness, no watches, no talking.

Break the rule of silence and it's SPARE DIET. Five days of the same food for breakfast, lunch, supper. Pap without sugar, salt, milk. It's like a clump of wet toilet paper. Doctor van Zyl checks you out during these five days. He also doesn't want you to die on death row.

In short, they all just want me to shut up. And wait for the big day.

All except you. You're asking me to speak.

Don't know what I feel about this. Suppose I feel fuckall. Numb. From brain to bum. Sitting here without a clock. I just want the big day to dawn. I just want them to carry out my sentence. I want it because it's MINE. Like MY smell, MY shadow.

And you know what I'm talking about.

Only you came back from the dead.

Dumb cunt.

Yours Faith Fully,

83143118.

The above appellation is how you must address me. Not what you put in your letter. Kindly address me properly if you write again.

TWO

The Johannesburg Towers
Jeppe Street
Johannesburg 2000
Room 2707

Fri. 15th Sept. 1989

To 83143118,

It's difficult to describe the impact of your letter: the impact of being in touch with you again, and the feel of that *touch*. Your handwriting; the envelope you'd licked. Like you, I lifted it cautiously, opened it cautiously, surprised that it only felt like paper. I was expecting something more like, I don't know, something softer, hotter; something more like flesh – I think that's what I'm trying not to say. And I expected an odour, but when, like you, I held it to my nose, there was only a faint municipal whiff ... disinfectant on cement ... (so prisons smell like city halls) ... just a letter, just paper. Yet it was like touching you again, and it's sent a terrific shock through me.

I've locked myself up here in my hotel room for the evening, with a bottle of Nederburg Paarl Riesling, unchilled. There's no mini-bar in these rooms; there's not much of anything. A plastic cactus on the table, one sachet of shampoo and one wrapped tablet of soap in the bathroom. In the sink, drainage is slow, clogged with a thousand hairs: blonde Germans, grey Britishers, ginger Australians. The lock on my door has been busted open and crudely repaired. What happened in this room? ... no, *rooms* ... I see torn locks and

7

gouged door frames all round the country. The bellboy only needed a key to get into our room, yours and mine, after our encounter. That hotel was not dissimilar to this one; both part of cheap 'n' cheerful groups dotted across the country – this one being a little cheaper, which is why my firm uses it. (I've also changed since we met – I'm now a tour guide, or tourist courier as head office would have it.) Business isn't great in these hotels at the moment. The air conditioning sends an icy breeze down the quiet corridors, over vacant tables in the Carvery, into empty lifts, which float up and down, playing the theme tunes from British and American TV shows, which we've never seen . . .

I pick up your letter again, I gently press the envelope, feeling the fullness inside; it's substantial, yet I can balance the whole thing on two fingers. I put it down again, I line up one corner to the corner of the table, admiring the exactness of both objects, their perfect, machine-cut angles. Then I swivel the letter, I slip one finger into the torn slit, I touch what's there – my hand jerks away. I stare at my trembling fingers, trying to smile.

I wasn't expecting to feel like this. Although I was warned by one of the people involved in . . . don't know what to call it . . . our chain of communication. He told me that this arrangement was made once before, and broke down when one of the correspondents, the person at liberty, became terrorised by what they described as 'dangerous words'.

It always surprises me that our most dangerous words are full of pleasure, tenderness, vulnerability . . . our bodies.

I've always found comfort in words, and I'm seldom at a loss for them: a compulsive diarist and would-be travel writer . . . that's me as fantasist . . . the actual job of tour guide requires no delicacy or insights when it comes to words; they just have to spill out in non-stop narration, round-the-clock patter, oral musak.

Roll up, roll up, folks, roll up and tune in, I am your showman, your DJ and your sing-a-long host. Pay attention now, shush, stop what you're doing, I am also your scout master and schoolteacher. I am going to instruct you about South Africa's flora and fauna, its climate and geography,

8

industries, distances, temperatures, shopping hours and stamp prices. When these things threaten to bore you, I shall relate interesting tales from history, colourful tribal folklore, and, if I can't think of anything else, humorous anecdotes from previous tours. The one thing I'll never do is stop talking. You'll only see the back of my neat but trendy haircut – to the left of the coach driver – but you'll hear me all the time. I'm the soundtrack on your TV documentary, I'm your bedside radio, your speaking clock, your 24-hour helpline. I'm parent, friend, nurse, interpreter, bodyguard, slave *and* master. Master? Oh yes, I'm going to do all your thinking for you. I'm going to choose your restaurants and shops, when and where you may visit these places, or sleep, or wake up, or empty your bowels . . .

(Maybe it's like being a warder in your place.)

So anyway, words are not normally a problem, but at the moment I don't know what to say to you. We've secured the freedom to write whatever we want, yet I'm at a loss as to how to use this freedom. Other than to ask the one, big, difficult question which I asked in my first letter – what actually happened between us in that hotel room four years ago? – and which you avoided answering; hinting that you might do so 'later'.

'Later' – there's a dangerous word. Does anyone dare use it here at the moment?

Leaning out of the window, I stare down at the streets twenty-seven floors below. Who would believe this was the centre of town on a hot Friday night? It's more like a ghost city, a city under curfew. Mile after mile of empty pavements, empty roads. It's so silent, you can almost hear the cicadas, the safe heartbeat of the northern suburbs. People say that a week ago even day-time Joburg was this quiet – because of the strikes and stay-aways around election time.

It's a relief now, when I hear a ripple of noises. A distant alarm bell, some guard dogs, a cop car showing off – 'Wow, wow, wow!' – an ambulance giving chase with a similar cry.

Sitting back in my chair, I'm suddenly struck by another feature of these rooms. They're covered in mirrors. Scratched and greasy in the corners, but flatteringly lit and angled;

designed to make holiday-makers look and feel good. I shy away from all the reflections of myself, and focus back on my TOSHIBA lap-top. My appearance has been something of a problem all my life . . .

It's odd: writing to you about something like that. It's not important, it's not what I want to say. I feel nervous, embarrassed. Never mind . . . forgive me, it's late, and I think I've drunk too much. Gosh, and I've got an early start; picking up a new 'brood' at the airport tomorrow.

I lift the phone, I tap in a system, 33, followed by my choice of time, 0630, then a voice says, 'Thank you, your wake-up request has been accepted, thank you, your wake-up request has been accepted, thank you, your . . .'

I'd better sign off. I don't understand why I'm not allowed to use your name. However . . .

Yours reciprocally,

A.H.

THREE

83143118
Pretoria Maximum Security

Hey, who's our postman? How does this system actually work?

I have to admit it's helping to pass the time.

The English poet, Browning, Robert, dead in 1889, says the following.

What's time? Leave NOW for dogs and apes. Man has FOREVER.

That's a laugh coming from a dead man.

The South African prisoner 83143118, not yet dead, but don't go away it's the coming attraction, he also has something to say on the subject.

Boredom is the real killer on death row.

I'm not allowed to write that. It's a description of prison conditions. I've already described some others in my last letter. Like talking time and spare diet.

What else am I not allowed to write about?

Sex.

You'd be interested in that.

There's a lot of interest in that. I hear it's big business on American death row. Those men get a lot of pen pals who want to marry them or just talk dirty.

By the bye, in your letter you said the following. MY APPEARANCE HAS BEEN SOMETHING OF A PROBLEM ALL MY LIFE. I remember you as good-looking. Or am I mixing you up with one of my others? Can't be. You're the only one who lived to tell the tale.

Anyhow, what else mustn't I write about? This is giving me a bit of a thrill.

Politics.

We've got some very famous political people in residence at the moment.

Whites and kaffirs and even some of my own people.

I've always thought it funny that my colour is called coloured. Just coloured. It's like they ran out of words. Or got embarrassed. Because it's the colour you find in underpants. A telling little stain. Specially in the underpants of mister whiteman and his kaffir fast-fucks.

Among our famous whites here there's one so white he's called WHITE WOLF. Barend Strydom. Who went for a stroll round Pretoria last year with a smile on his face and a 9mm piece in his fist, blasting random kaffirs to smithereens. I've never seen the WOLF. We're not allowed to mix with the whities. But I hear there's another one here who's even more famous. And who's not supposed to be on death row at all. I mean this is bigtime news. So maybe I better not mention his name.

Not yet.

Not till you've told me the full ins and outs of our postal service.

Among our famous kaffirs are the Upington 14. Yanked from that crowd, round that cop, in that tyre, with that fire. There's a guy called Zonga, who makes boats out of matchsticks, also an old man whose name I can't remember, also an old lady over in the women's section, who apparently weeps day and night, plus 11 others. Everyone feels sorry for them and reckons they won't be hung at the end of the story.

Among us coloureds there's Robert McBride. He did the Magoo's Bar bombing in Durban that blew away 3 white ladies. For a good cause he says. The ANC. So people reckon his sentence could get changed to life if Mandela really is released.

And then there's me.

Who should be the most famous of all.

I had a really fancy career. With only one problem.

I never made it political.

So people never noticed it. Until it bumped into you.

In considering my lack of fame, one must also take into account historical plus geographical plus sociological factors. We're in Africa. Death is as natural as breathing here. Famine, slave trading, malaria, wild animals, blah blah.

I picked the wrong spot to make my mark.

Nobody knows my score. Not even I remember it.

The guys in the other cages, they know their scores. They've got cops and newspapers and TV and courts backing them up. So the WHITE WOLF knows for sure he did 8 and maimed 16. McBride knows for sure he did 3 and maimed 89. The Upington 14 know for sure they didn't do no-one.

I care fuckall for politics. But I once heard some of the comrades in talking time, saying this. MAN IS BY NATURE A POLITICAL ANIMAL. Which is a funny thought. It means you've got no choice in the matter. Particularly if you're born in this country. And with a hue that's found in underpants.

The daily news isn't allowed into death row.

No death, no watches, no talking, no darkness, no news.

But all the same NEWS TRAVELS FAST.

After the elections last week, the news travelled in here bloody damned fast. During talking time it was noisy as a zoo. Hey, freedom's a banana. Anyhow, the comrades reckon this new president is maybe serious about reforms.

I'll admit something now, OK? It made me scared for the first time. I dream this dream, this cruel dream. It starts with a noise like when you smash in a car window. You break the seal, the vacuum thing, and the air comes out. POP. In my dream it's Mandela coming out. KING-SIZE POP. Then the floodgates open and every non-white prisoner goes toyi-toyi-ing away into a new golden morn. SNAP CRACKLE POP. In the end there's only the WHITE WOLF left in here and the other famous whiteman whose name I haven't told you yet. For security reasons.

And in this SNAP CRACKLE POP they free me too.

It scares me.

According to Nietzsche, Friedrich Wilhelm, dead in 1900, mankind is divided into the MASTER CLASS and the HERD.

13

I tried to be part of the former. Via a famous career. But I failed. It was, so saith the authorities, just my FANTASY.

Which is, by the bye, the dirtiest word I learned at school. I've already had 32 years of it. Living as trash in the herd. No more please.

Yours Faith Fully,

83143118.

FOUR

The Johannesburg Towers
Room 2707

Sun. 17th Sept.

To 83143118,

I'm pleased these letters are helping you to pass the time; that's good, that's very good . . . I'm sending in more paper and ballpoints; feel free to write as much as you want.

It still feels very strange doing this, doesn't it? Finding a way of talking to one another. What should I tell you about?

I had quite a time yesterday morning . . . rounding up the new brood as they arrived for our three-week 'World in One Country' tour. They come in on different flights, some of which were delayed, so it meant hanging round Jan Smuts Airport for hours. The place was very quiet – as usual. These days our only substantial tourism comes from Germany, and of course Taiwan. Expelled from the UN, and so from the sanctions issue, the Taiwanese have descended on our empty marketplaces like flies, and holiday here with the same frenzy, doing the whole country in one week flat, swarming on and off their coaches, cameras buzzing. Both they and the Germans need their own language guides. The English-speaking tours have a few Israelis joining in (with chips piled high on their shoulders – 'We're misunderstood too, *that's* why we holiday here!'); no Americans at all any more (their government advises them not to come); and then the ones which I mostly get – Brits and a smattering of Ossies.

I keep wanting the Brits to be like my paternal grandparents

15

(a clerk and a secretary in colonial administration), civilised, discreet and kindly – but instead they tend to be rude, crude folk, indistinguishable from the Ossies; a colleague of mine calls both 'our modern savages'.

At first glance, the gentlest Brits in this brood appear to be Mr and Mrs Moonje from Leicester – and formerly Uganda – who have relatives among the Indian population of Durban (explaining, I suppose, why they're holidaying in a country which isn't overly welcoming to them); and old Mrs Gill from Wickford, Essex, who actually *does* remind me of my granny. A retired librarian, Mrs Gill has a habit of licking the tips of her forefinger and thumb while she talks, as though forever turning a page.

Yesterday, once the full brood was assembled, I gave them a talk on security. I have to choose my words carefully. Where you are, your censors are the Department of Prison Services, out here mine is the Government Tourist Board, SATOUR. As soon as the election results were announced, a memo flew round with a new phrase – 'a New South Africa' – which we were instructed to plug. For some time now we've also been told/asked to avoid using a particularly *dangerous* word; the word which has tarnished South Africa's image for the last forty years . . . head office just calls it the A-word. SATOUR wants our homeland to be seen as a place that's safe to holiday, settle, and most importantly, invest in. But it's not easy for us in the field, believe me. I mean, you try guiding tourists around a State of Emergency! For a start, it's crazy to let them loose in *Joburg*, the world's most violent city. Yet I'm not allowed to say that. So I do what I can; I try and warn them, using a tone that's firm but humorous:

(Bear in mind we're also discouraged from using the b+w words.)

'This is a city where there's quite a gulf between rich and poor, so please take a little extra care when walking around on your own. As I like to say, a combination of common sense and cowardice is your best defence . . .' (I wait for chuckles.) 'Don't advertise your tourist status. Flaunting wallets, jewellery, fancy sunglasses, cameras, especially video cameras, is like carrying a sign saying, I'm a mug, you're a mugger, let's boogie.' (Wait for groaning chuckles.) 'For shopping expeditions, our hotel offers what they call *unobtrusive* security escorts, which means those bulges in their clothes are probably just muscles . . .' (A dirty chuckle or two.) 'If anyone is thinking of hiring a car, I'd say it's too risky, don't bother – you'll find our taxis pretty cheap. Actually, you're going to find everything pretty cheap here. Your sterling, Australian dollars and shekels are going to multiply like those proverbial bunnies!' (Laughter and cheers.)

On the drive back from the airport, one of the brood, Mr Webb, a London cabby, asked whether we have young men waiting at the robots (he calls them traffic lights) to dash forward and wash our windscreens? I just said no – I didn't mention that they'd be shot dead on the spot. When Joburg drivers approach robots, they wind up windows, lock doors, and start thinking through the drill they learned at last weekend's gun school.

This is precisely why I discourage my broods from hiring cars. How would they ever learn our (unofficial) traffic regulations fast enough? Before getting into your car check the back seat for stowaways; if ever in danger, treat a robot as no more than a go-slow junction; if you're hijacked, don't argue – run! – the worst will be if you're taken *with* the car.

(Sorry, but I'm suddenly aware how absurd this is: writing to *you* about these things . . .)

Anyway, my broods aren't remotely worried – they're determinedly, stubbornly, greedily *on holiday*. It's a kind of second childhood. They can do what they want; other people, responsible people, people like me, will make sure they come to no harm. The world – even South Africa – is safe and glamorous again, a place full of treats and games. They can gorge themselves on sweet, rich foods, or rainbow-coloured drinks; this is a world without ulcers or heart-attacks. They can play with one another's rude bits, or Charlie's (our coach driver), or the good-time gals in Sun City; it's a world without pregnancy or disease. Back at home, they wouldn't dream of spilling stuff on the carpets, ripping down curtains that stick, or using two, three towels when they shower. Nor would they drink through the day, cheat on bills, or make love framed by

17

a lit window. But here and now they think to themselves, it's alright, it's not me – I've 'gone away'.

I'm not knocking it; we all do it; 'Cheers!' (. . . said he, finding a bottle of wine at his elbow again).

In your letter, you're puzzled by why my 'good looks' (your words) should be a problem. Yes, people are surprised that I'm uneasy with a gift from heaven. An angel – this is how I've been described. At other times like a Greek god, a dumb blonde, or Ken, the male Barbie doll. This probably comes closest. A certain lacquered look is required by the job. Airline stewards and hotel receptionists have to fabricate the same thing. Anyway, here I sit, head turned away from all the mirrors in this room, mistrusting what's in the glass, yet often – mostly – unable to stop parading it, exploiting it rotten. It's a complicated cycle . . .

I wonder what you look like now? I can't even clearly remember what you looked like *then* . . . we met so briefly, and it's four years ago. There was the trial later, but I was so worried about people staring at me, and any compulsion I might feel to stare at you, that I devised a special way of coping – I left my contact lenses at home each morning, and never saw a thing.

Better get to bed. We've got a full itinerary tomorrow. A helicopter tour of Soweto (the only safe way of seeing the one place they've *all* heard about), and then off in the coach for an overnight at Sun City in Bophuthatswana.

Yours,

A.H.

PS. You ask about our 'postal system', and who our postman is, etc. Let me just check with my contacts, but I can't see why you shouldn't know. After all, we're both in this together; partners in crime as it were. Because of the Bophuthatswana trip, it'll take a day or two to check with my people, but I'm sure I'll be able to let you have all the details. In return, I'd greatly appreciate it if you could answer my questions ... particularly the one I asked you first.

FIVE

83143118
Pretoria Maximum Security

I liked some of your words. Like the following.
LET ME CHECK WITH MY CONTACTS.
PARTNERS IN CRIME.
I see something now.
We're cheating the system, bending the rules, breaking some commandments.
And that's a sweet feeling.
So sweet I'm half shivering as I write, half laughing.
So you normally wear contact lenses? Why? If you're SHY of your good looks. Wear glasses instead. I've got news for you. Glasses don't suit angels, Greek gods, dumb blondes, or this doll I've never heard of.
Second point.
My itinerary is just as HECTIC as yours, baby.
6 a.m. Bell rings. Voices shout in Afrikaans STAND UP STAND UP. It's a wave coming down the corridor. STAND UP STAND UP.
Last night I couldn't sleep. Only dropped off a while ago. Now I can't wake up. In the cage, my sun in a bottle, my sun eternal, he's blinding me. All the same I'm moving to the door doubletime.
STAND UP they're shouting THE MAJOR WANTS TO SEE YOUR FOKKIN FACE.
I put my face in the window of my door. I sneeze. Dust in the mesh. Major Steenkamp snipes me with one eye, counts another number, moves on.

Today they're starting shower call from my end. Another wave is already coming down the corridor. A metal wave. Click cluck click cluck. They're unmastering. The master key plus each cage's own key.

I'm climbing out of my clothes fast. My green fatigues, my vest, underpants. I sleep in all of them. Because why? Because of the high window up there. The slats are jammed open under the mesh. And mesh lets in the cold. Also mist sometimes.

The metal wave reaches my cage. Click cluck.

And now I'm through the door in my birthday suit. Blue from the cold, with my blue towel and my blue soap, everything to match. Two warders with sticks. Four other guys stripped and shivering too. Pissed off because they're waiting for me.

You'll want to look at their genitals.

All small in the cold. Except for the tall Zulu miner, Pepsi. He's got a morning glory on him. Either from sweet dreams or he's planning an act of gross indecency in the showers.

Nobody notices his morning glory. Nobody cares. We go doubletime to the showers.

The room is big, split by a row of bars. Showers along the walls. Concrete floors tilting down to the drains in the middle.

Okkie and Mandiba shower fast and shoot over to the shaving mirrors. While the warders are issuing them with blades, Pepsi pumps the kid Zeph in less than 10 seconds. This is pumping at doubletime. Those four must have planned it during talking time yesterday afternoon.

Now we've all showered and shaved and the blades have all been returned.

Now we're also returned. To our cages. Doubletime.

Click cluck and I'm back home.

The whole trip over in 5 minutes flat.

Two things.

One. Is there a letter from you on my bed?

No. Maybe you won't write again until you get this.

Two. Warm up. Get dressed fast, make the bed fast. 2 grey blankets. They carry the words DEPARTMENT OF PRISON SERVICES in Afrikaans. This is so you can't steal the blankets on the morning you check out. The pillow has no pillowcase. The stripes on it help you dream of prisons and prisons and prisons.

I light smoke number 1. I take 5 deep puffs. Then I nip it, and straightaway

I shit in my bowl.

This pisses me off in a manner of speaking. I'd much rather defecate BEFORE my shower. But this I can only do if they start shower call from the other end of the corridor. When they don't, like today, I'm forced to soil myself AFTER my shower.

Hygiene is imperative.

My ma-bitch always taught us her kids to keep clean. Here is an example. Many of us had to share a bed. So she wrapped each little body in plastic or cloth or newspaper. We were kept separate and thus clean.

After my shit, my ablutions. Scrubbing the hands all the way up to the elbows. Like my daddie used to do. Even after he became a lapsed muslim man. My small sink dips into the wall. You can't get your face in. They don't want you to drown. The water button only gives you a short squirt at a time.

Tooth brushing time. Like with the toilet paper, you've got to carefully ration the Colgate they issue. The tooth brush also says DEPARTMENT OF PRISON SERVICES in Afrikaans.

Now there's a wait for breakfast. Because we were first to the showers today.

I read from the Bible. My readings are taken at random. This is because I've been given an assurance from Freud, Sigmund, dead in 1939, that there's no such thing as accidents. So any passage chosen at random is meant for me and me alone. Today I get St Mark 13.

NOW THE BROTHER SHALL BETRAY THE BROTHER TO DEATH, AND THE FATHER THE SON; AND CHILDREN SHALL RISE UP AGAINST THEIR PARENTS, AND SHALL CAUSE THEM TO BE PUT TO DEATH.

Sigmund was spot on, bull's-eye.

Another wave is coming down the corridor. Keys, wheels, shelves, pots and liquid.

STAND UP. Click cluck.

The warder is one of my people. This coloured man called Adams. Nearly fifty but never got above the rank of Warder. He always stands very still. Arms by his side. Tense. Like Clint Eastwood at high noon. A home-rolled hidden in one hand. Legs in the army position of AT EASE. But this man is not at ease. He's standing still, but he's shivering. All over. Like a pool with flies. Adams' pool tastes of brandy. Morning till night. He doesn't like me. When he looks in my direction he sees what he might've been. One time he took his dick out and put it in my cooldrink. This gave me no heartsore. Outer hygiene is more important than inner. Show me a stomach with a window in it. I've lived on the road. Dicks in a cooldrink is nothing. Dicks in a prison cooldrink improves flavour.

The trolley boy is a new prisoner. He probably still thinks he can save his neck. By sucking up to the warders. Sucking and sucking like there's no tomorrow. But when tomorrow comes, the warders will hang him anyway and get themselves a new sucker. These new prisoners are prepared to do anything. Much more than just breakfast trolley duty. They'll even wash the hanging hoods.

This new guy now, he hands me a bowl of pap, and what's called a KATKOP. Half a bread loaf, one side red with jam. I hold out my plastic mug for a scoop of coffee from his big pot.

Door closes. Must eat fast. They'll go down the corridor, about-turn and start collecting the bowls. Eat, eat. Thick cold pap. My spoon breaks. Fuck mother, this plastic trash. Finish with my fingers. Not fast enough. Door opens. BOWL shouts Adams. I surrender it. Door closes. Breakfast over.

But I haven't touched the coffee or the katkop. I chew one corner slowly, like a civilised being, and sip at my coffee. They never put enough sugar in it. But lots of that green stuff to kill your sex drive.

Not that I need help.

I've got myself beautifully under control.

But some of the others, like Pepsi, their sex drive is stronger than this coffee. Their sex drive is so strong they defy regulations and stick pictures from Scope on their walls. With blobs of Colgate. The warders turn a blind eye. It eases pressure if a guy just gives himself a five-tackle-one. Means fewer shower fucks. Not with Pepsi, granted, but in general.

It's a pity Pepsi can't read. Because the library trolley could also help with his sex drive. Some books are specially planted there for this purpose.

Yesterday I made the mistake of choosing one such book. It was stiff and smelly with the lost loves and spilt milk of my brethren.

Hollywood Wives by Jackie Collins.

By gum there's some appetites running through this bitch. A fuck on every page in word or deed. She should be thrown in here. My brethren would love to make her acquaintance. She could then write of her experiences in the other Beverly Hills.

Did you know we call death row Beverly Hills?

Maybe because there's so many stars here. Stars of South African history. Or maybe because we'll all be seeing stars soon.

In any case, I'm a bit pissed off to be frank. Four years ago I came across the world of western culture and literature like a man from mars. I read and read. And now what's happened? I'm stuck on death row with the Bible and Jackie Collins.

Must be about 8 o'clock now.

I sit looking round my cage.

I'm in a sort of coffin. On its end. Narrow little floor. Very high white walls. I can't possibly reach my sun in a bottle.

Above my sun is a grill so the warders can look down on me.

They can also check me out from two sides. My door window with bars and mesh. My bed window with slanted glass, thick as a piece of pavement.

My bed is wooden and bolted to the wall.

Over one end of the bed is my table. Also wooden, also bolted to the wall. Like a shelf.

To write like I'm doing now, I must sit on the bed, and twist to the table.

To sleep I must stick my head under the table, with my blue towel wrapped round my face, arab style. Like the long-ago forefathers of my daddie. And so I score a bit of the most precious commodity on death row. Darkness.

Hey, on your travels do you go over the Outeniqua Pass to Oudtshoorn? Have you seen those fields of hops on the left? With the big spotlights above them? They're also kept shining through the night. Making the hops grow, grow, grow. Get to the end of their days doubletime. Then they're cropped and the farmer starts with a new lot.

Same principle here. In our bright, upright coffins.

I can feel myself getting fed-up. So I take it out on myself. Exercise hard. Not a lot you can do in an upright coffin, but I damn well do it. Jogging. Skipping without a rope. Press ups army style, with feet on the bed. Or on the table so it's almost handstands. Frog jumps. There isn't enough space, so my frogs look like they've got half slashed away.

At last I'm stinking with sweat.

Good.

Means ANOTHER wash. Every inch of me. With little squirts from the water button it takes a lovely forever. Reminds me of how I used to do it on the open road. Like a cat. With my tongue. Wherever it couldn't reach was cleansed with spit on the fingers. Licking and touching my strength. Licking my salt. Putting it back into me. More strength.

In your letter, you say you can't remember what I look like. So. Come on a tour while I wash.

My head. Its shape is like a monkey's. Or apish as poets might say. Or simian as intellectuals would have it. The brow juts. The cheekbones are flat. The nose isn't really there. Just nostrils. The mouth is a muzzle. Lips push forward and twitch. Very flexible. Can hold things. Eyes are deep set, plus piercing, plus wise. This was true even before I became an intellectual. This was when I was still just a monkey.

Skin colour is bright shitbrown as I've said before. Some bits are darker. Red-black like clay. The bits which the sun used to bake on the road. Hands, arms, neck and face.

My fair hair sits on top of my face like a kind of joke. You say your fair hair makes you look like an angel. Mine makes me look like the opposite.

It's the whiteman popping out. These days my fair hair doesn't get too much comment. Because it's shaved to the skull. But in my life on the road I wore it long and heavy like a lion.

Once somebody said my fair and dark looks made me like a kind of

Aborigine.

Which years later I looked up in the dictionary, and it means a kind of

Original person.

My fingers are moving down to wash my body now. I was born on the coast. I only grew five foot five inches above sea level. Small but good hey, my body? I come into a room hips first. I come to dance or pump pussy. Despite the drink, dagga, buttons, glue, and scoff from trash bins, I'm fit. If you grip my flesh between two fingers you can't take any away with you. On my right tit is the first of my green tattoos. A hawk on its way down.

You sure you can't do this from memory?

Neither intellectuals nor monkeys would describe me as hirsute. But vegetation reappears where my second green tattoo is. A snake on its way down. Into a bush that's more reddish than fair.

I'm washing down strong bow legs and smart feet. Grip anything.

I'm washing the soles and back up the legs.

I'm washing over and into an arse with hard curves and swerves.

Funny all the words for what I'm washing now, hey? Some of them DANGEROUS words. Piel, eel, dick, crack hunter, lob, oar, ram, shit stirrer, gun, chopper, jam knife, marmite drill, gash crasher, or blood-gorged fuck muscle.

One that suits me is dong. The whiteman gave me his fair hair, the kaffir his dark dong. Like my nipples, the colour of my dong is very dark. Bruise-black. Even when he isn't up. When he is up I don't call him my dong any more. I call him my temper.

My balls. Like my dong, my balls wouldn't look stupid hanging from a much taller man.

Get it over with, pal. Get it out, get it up, make your milkSHAKE.

Under my balls is the third and last tattoo. A spider with shivery legs. It must've hurt like hell to have him put there but I was smoked-up and the old bitch doing it was having the time of her life.

Today, as I wash, I look at the sun. The real one. It hangs halfway across the mesh of my high window and it's covered in dust. I gradually become cleaner than the sun.

Now. At last. I hear it.

Wood and metal like the breakfast trolley. But also a special bump bump bump. Half hollow, half full. Like cupped hands. Books. Applauding me. They know I'm the only intellectual they're likely to meet here in Beverly Hills.

STAND UP.

Click cluck. Door opens.

Warder Adams still on duty. With his brandy shiver.

He nods at me. This means I'm allowed to approach the door. I throw Jackie Collins back on the heap. Now I've got to choose fast. I've got my eye on THE DEVIL'S ALTERNATIVE by Frederick Forsyth or BILLION DOLLAR BRAIN by Len Deighton. The DEVIL is fatter but the BRAIN wins.

Click cluck. Door closes.

I read the first line.

IT WAS THE MORNING OF MY HUNDREDTH BIRTH-DAY.

So far so good. This guy's got a sense of humour.

But I'm not crazy about what is termed first-person narrative.

It means the hero is still going to be alive at the end of the story.

Which isn't like life.

I flick through to the last page.

Sure enough.

BEHIND HIM I COULD SEE A TINY BLUE PATCH THROUGH THE GREY CLOUD; PERHAPS SPRING WOULD BE COMING SOON.

The other good reason for checking the end straightaway is this. It might be missing. These books are read so much and so fast, bits fall out. Or they're ripped out for sending messages. Or when people run out of toilet paper.

27

And it can really make me cross to read a book and find no end.

That's not like life either.

But all seems well here.

I read.

Time goes away.

Now it's lunch. Maybe about 11 o'clock.

STAND UP.

Door opens.

Today's lunch is small pieces of pig plus pap. And orange cooldrink in my plastic cup.

Door closes.

Eat fast.

Door opens.

BOWL NOW.

Door closes.

Lunch over.

There's never enough. A person's always hungry. That's why I ration myself to one shit a day only. Keep as much inside as possible.

Eschewing the temptation of having more of my katkop, I go instead for smoke number 1, second half.

The shop trolley only comes about once a month or so.

Selling smokes, writing paper and suchlike. It's lucky you're sending in paper with your letters, because I've got no bucks. I get sent a small charity donation from that nun I told to go fuck. With this donation, I buy my 2 packs of smokes and then I must make them last.

40 smokes into 30 days

Has turned me into a mathematical genius.

Wait. I'm hearing a new wave going down the corridor. A wave of names. SEHERI, ZUMA, JANTJIES, MOOI and others. It's visiting hours. The names smarten themselves up and are taken away. The wave passes. Followed immediately by another one.

EXERCISE.

They often do this. Use visiting hours to exercise us who haven't got visitors.

Off we go doubletime. Me and a bunch of others. Big tall baby-faced McBride is among us. Him who planted that bomb in Magoo's Bar in Durban.

I must tell you this. I'm not crazy about him.

A fellow coloured man. Fighting for the ANC.

I want to say to him, and one day will, you fool. We've spent our whole lives being non-white. So what now? The chance to be non-black? You fucking fool.

Also I want to tell him I'm not impressed by this bomb he planted. Anyone can plant a bomb. A person doesn't have to get his hands dirty. But try doing what I did. Then see what you get on your hands. Then come tell me which one of us should be famous.

Anyhow, its funny they're exercising him now. He's almost always got a visitor. Usually his Paula. He met this lady in the visiting room here in Beverly Hills. What's more, they let him marry her back in May. What's more, she's a WHITE lady.

Maybe she's overseas again, campaigning to get his sentence commuted.

At the entrance to the exercise yard, they frisk you. And they use this as a chance to bugger you round a bit. Kick your feet apart, bang your balls as they search for banned goods. Specially the young warders who've seen too many cop flicks. Or want to settle scores. The older ones, they just leave it to the state executioner. Anyhow, this frisking is part of life here.

Though not for everyone.

Not for McBride.

A while ago he started fighting back.

And since then, fuck me, it's THEM who's backed off.

Something IS going on out there. I promise you, my cruel dream IS coming true. The prison gates are threatening to open. SNAP CRACKLE POP.

A year ago, the warders would've cared fuckall for McBride's white wife or her friends overseas.

The exercise yard looks like everywhere else. Cement floor, white walls, mesh across the sky. Here the warders carry rifles instead of sticks. You mustn't stand, sit, smoke or talk. You must EXERCISE.

Fine by me. This is no breeding ground for intellectuals. I let the monkey in me go for a good old scamper. Round and round and round and round.

Today, 5 minutes in, a voice among us shouts LISTEN.

Sergeant fat Fourie shouts SILENCE.

But we've already stopped in our tracks and we've got our faces lifted to the mesh.

Sometimes you can hear traffic.

I can sometimes recognise what car it is. I know their different sounds. Their engines. Doing cars was my trick for a while.

Today it's a plane.

The voice among us says the following.

It's coming down to rescue us.

We all want to laugh, but we're all smart enough not to.

The voice is found and named. It's Pepsi who had himself a fuck this morning in the showers. My glory, it must've been good to make him so reckless.

Fat Fourie says to him YOU'RE ON SPARE DIET.

Pepsi says, do what you want man, I'm cool.

We all drop our eyes and move away fast.

Pepsi is a dumb cunt, but I blame McBride. Everyone thinks they can copy him now, and defy the system. But Pepsi is like me. Not a comrade. When he lands neck-deep in shit, there'll be no helping hand from outside.

Our half hour is up. Back we go doubletime.

My door goes click cluck.

I look at my bed. Exercise time was my second and last chance today to get a letter from you.

And you missed it.

Now I feel bored. BAD bored. So bored I can burst.

I have smoke number 2. I don't nip it halfway through. I carry on to the lovely bitter end. I wouldn't normally, but fuck it. Everybody's defying the system. I'll defy my own.

But just before the lovely bitter end I regret it.

So then I let the lovely bitter end burn on. I don't smoke filters, hey? I let the small fire touch my lips. Touch them till I can feel the first bubble rise. I'm shaking all over but I let it go on a bit longer. And a bit more. The smell is the worst

30

thing. Right under my nose. Eventually my own lip-meat puts out the fire.

So there we are.

Punishment was in order.

That'll teach me.

Now I hear a strange wave come down the corridor. It's the guys who had visits. They were allowed to talk to their visitors. Talk talk talk. About this and that and all sorts. Talk talk. Now they creep back into our silence. Their stupid sad pain passes among us.

I say this. Better not to have had visitors in the first place.

I'm getting fed-up again. So I grab mister Deighton.

It's good. Listen to this.

IT WAS A DEAD HAND, WAVING A TINY, POSTHUMOUS GOOD-BYE.

Page 135 already. My god I must beware. Or it'll be over before you know it.

I look at the book itself instead of its messages. It's grey and soft. Like its been through something's stomach a few times over. The smell is old, old. I'm thinking of all the dead men who've looked in here. Or been in my clothes. Or my blankets and pillow. I'm wearing ghosts, I'm sleeping with them.

STAND UP. Did I drop off? Door opens. Supper already. Door closes. A cob of corn and pieces of meat. Can't tell what kind of meat. Pale and dry and half cold. Eat quick. Door opens. BOWL NOW. Door closes. Supper over. I'm starving.

Must be about 3, maybe 3.30, in the afternoon. The sun is on the other side of the mesh in my high window, and pointing down in a thin arrow.

By standing on tiptoes on my bed I can just reach.

I do this every day.

I've got one sunburnt finger.

I requested sunoil. But their thinking is very rigid.

Now it must be 4. Because the best wave comes down the corridor. Talking time. Tongues and teeth and spit. Babble bubble.

The main word is that Pepsi has got his notice of execution.

31

Good glory, it's like he knew.

Had himself a good fuck in the showers this morning. Defied the system in the exercise yard this afternoon. Moved to the Pot this evening. The Pot is where you go for your last week. The corridor with only 7 cages and only 7 days to go. Well, well, travel well, Pepsi-cola. People say he was a migrant miner. His family is far away in KwaZulu. They'll be sent a rail warrant so they can make their stupid sad last visit.

Everyone's talking about him so much, you can't hear what's being said. But, no sweat, the point isn't to hear, it's to TALK. This is exercise time for the throat. WHA WHA WHA. I march around singing from songs I know and love. MR TAMBOURINE MAN. OH DANNY BOY. My blistered lips sing till they bleed.

Now talking time is over.

Everything is.

Nothing more can happen today.

No meals, no letters, no showers, no visitors, no exercise, no library, no shop, not even a notice of execution.

Nothing.

It's about 6 o'clock. 12 hours to go till the next 6 o'clock with its bell and the first STAND UP of the new day. Until then, the stretch they call night. Silent night. All is bright. 12 silent bright hours to go.

You know who I am? ONE BORN OUT OF DUE TIME. 1 Corinthians 15: 8.

I should've been here 4, 5 years ago. I heard Sergeant Fourie telling a new warder it was their heyday. They held the world record. At least one hanging every 3 days.

My corridor here was like a conveyor belt. Very lively, lots of singing. Kaffirs do an all-night vigil before a funeral, so they broke the rule of silence practically every night with their singing.

And when the warders knew they were going to be short-staffed, they worked extra shifts to clear stock. Like before christmas.

So I would've been through the system doubletime. No silent bright nights to get through. It's very inhumane. And yes I am the right one to talk. At least the people I did weren't

32

told months in advance. On some date soon you're going to be done. Now sit and wait. Everything came as a surprise to my ones. And some had a good time first. Some had the best times of their lives. As you can bear witness.

Instead of reaching for a black cap I'd like to see judges pull out a black revolver.

In any case, writing this has helped today pass. Time has flown, as they say. And I'm sure there'll be a letter from you tomorrow. With all the details of our postal service, all the ins and outs, blah blah. As you promised. So there's that to look forward to.

So tonight won't be too bad.

I've still got 196 pages of mister Deighton to go. Also three-quarters of my katkop bread. But not a single smoke. Because of this afternoon's misdemeanour, I badly buggered today's ration, and now must truly suffer.

Pity.

If only I could smoke through the night I'd die a happy man.

I wonder if you can help?

Think about it.

Yours Faith Fully,

83143118.

Six

The Pretoria Towers
Pretorius St
Pretoria 0002
Room 901

Tues. 19th Sept.

To 83143118,

I passed you on the roadside today. It stopped my breath . . .
I've been thinking of you non-stop after our first exchange of
letters at the weekend.

The brood and I have been up to Sun City in Bophuthatswana since then . . . 'Rising like an oasis out of this sparse
terrain, folks, here is a playground for grown-ups, here you will
rub shoulders with top international jet-setters . . . gambling,
golf, watersports, evening extravaganzas with gals, gals, gals . . .
all this is here for your entertainment!'

One overnight there, then the three-hour drive back today,
stopping at the Heia Safari Ranch for an early braaivleis lunch;
'In Afrikaans, ladies and gents, the word braai means roast or
grilled, and the word vleis means meat . . . hence braaivleis,
or braai as it's known – just like the Australians among you
shorten the word barbecue to . . . all together now . . . *barbie!*'

Afterwards, a short run to Pretoria; the brood drunk and
snoozing, self chattering away into the mike. The city had
just come into view from the R101, when I looked to the
left, and went cold. There you were. Or at any rate, the thing
that's become synonymous with you. Your address.

Is your wing, Maximum Security, visible from the R101?

34

Probably not. It's probably somewhere deeper in there; in that yellow man-made mountain, that blonde Afrikaner fortress. A race of farmers and cops, they love buildings like this; the colour of the stone like wheat, dust, sun, the thin mirrored windows like security men's shades. Those windows – are they the cells? Is any of them *your* window . . . with the open slats, covered by mesh . . .?

My mouth hangs open as we pass.

A little red-haired child is strolling out past the security blockhouse. He's carrying a tennis racket, and practises a shot over the swing-boom, which is about the height of a net. Now he breaks into a run and clambers into a station wagon waiting at the entrance. To the left, in the car park, two dusty combis have just stopped, and a crowd of blacks are clambering out. Relatives visiting prisoners, I suppose. They look like they've travelled far . . . from Upington maybe?

(If this was still visiting time, you might've been in the exercise yard . . .)

Above the prison, a flock of ducks, flying in formation, begin their descent, heading for somewhere inside the complex.

What's in there? Some open land? A park? A shopping centre for the warders and their families, with a bank, a cinema?

(Can you see the ducks through the mesh of the exercise yard?)

I must've passed Pretoria Central Prison a thousand times on these tours without really noticing it. Because usually I'm in the middle of one of my set pieces; the one which contains this tour's theme tune:

'. . . So Cape Town is our parliamentary capital, Johannesburg our commercial capital, Bloemfontein our judicial-stroke-agricultural capital, and Pretoria, which you can now see ahead, our administrative capital. You could say we've got four capital cities! Oh yes, South Africa is indeed a world in one country . . . so it's not a bad little slogan, is it? A world in one country. That's why I love the Republic so. Charlie our driver does too. Its different climates, its diversity, its physical build, its wildlife . . . we're just trying to harmonise its people at the moment.'

I overlay this last comment with one of my warmest chuckles, and that's the closest they'll hear me get to the A-word. Normally, that is. But this afternoon, passing you on the roadside, I was tempted to extemporise:

'And there on the left, folks, that giant yellow-brick appar- ition is – no, not the City of Oz – but Pretoria Central Prison, which contains our notorious death row. Sitting on it at the moment are some people you might have read about in your own papers, like Robert McBride, the Magoo's Bar bomber, and all of the Upington 14, and even a white man, known in fact as the White Wolf, Barend Strydom, a twenty-two-year-old member of one of our Neo-Nazi parties, who went on a shooting spree last November, killing blacks at random . . . this happened in Pretoria, now ahead of us, in Strijdom Square – no, not named after Barend himself – but after one of our prime ministers, Johannes G. Strijdom. I'll be taking you round the square tomorrow, and let's see if we can spot any bullet holes. Also incarcerated on death row at the moment is a gentleman whom you probably won't have heard about . . . our media called him the Fantasy Killer at the time of his trial, because although he claimed to have murdered up to fifty people, there was only evidence for one and a half. What's half a murder? Well yes, it's an interesting story . . .'

But, of course, I said none of this. For once I was completely silent as the coach sped past the prison. More than silent – holding my breath. You were so close . . . maybe just a hundred, two hundred metres away . . .

Look, thank you for your letter – it raises some difficult things:

I'm afraid I lied to you before – when I said I'd check with my contacts about letting you know about our postal system, our chain of communication. There's no need to check with them, because there's *absolutely* no question of you, or anyone, knowing the details of how this is being done. Right from the start, I had to give my word to the people involved; in fact, swear on the Bible – and I'm not joking. So I'm sorry, but you're just going to have to accept this. Please don't press me further on it. Just enjoy the freedom I've secured for us. Exploit it, use it; if it helps you get through the long days and nights, fine – use it like that.

The other thing is, you seem to be under the impression that my motive for writing to you is kinky, sexual somehow. I'm bewildered that you should think so. My motive is simple – I need to discuss our case. I've wanted to write to you every day over the past four years; to ask, and have answered, one question: *what happened?*

Something in your letter has increased the urgency of this, increased it terribly. It was your story about the man called Pepsi – the sudden arrival of his notice of execution. I had been told that it can arrive at any time, after prisoners have sat on death row for months or even years, but it was shocking to, in a way, witness it actually happen to someone. It seems such a haphazard system within such a rigid bureaucracy . . . like a deadly virus floating around your section of the prison . . . everyone's going to get it eventually, but *when?*

Look, forgive me if I put this clumsily . . . I actually don't know how to put it . . . but what if your notice arrives tomorrow? Or later today? Or now, as I'm writing? This frightens me. Yet you seem eager for it, impatient to get those last seven days started and finished.

I suppose I should say, well that's his business, that's certainly his business . . . but I can't.

I ask you again to relate your version of what happened between us in that hotel room four years ago – it's the only part of the case where the police found you unco-operative. You boasted about crimes for which they could find no evidence, but in this instance, where there *was* evidence, where there *was* a witness (albeit an unconscious one), you remained silent. I ask you again to tell me your side of the story, clearly, graphically; I shan't run away from any amount of 'dangerous words'. I just need to know what happened. Please.

Yours,

A.H.

PS. Just to remind you that, because my tour is currently in the vicinity of the prison, we can communicate very speedily, twice daily. The process will become much slower from Thursday, when the itinerary takes us to the Kruger Game Park.

PPS. You'll have found a carton of Peter Stuyvesant with this letter. You needn't ration them . . .

PPPS. Don't let me leave Pretoria without answering my question. Please.

SEVEN

83143118
Pretoria Maximum Security

People like you make me laugh.

You say there is ABSOLUTELY no way you can answer my question about our postal system.

It doesn't matter if I land in the shit. But you mustn't land in the shit. And your contacts who slap your palm with a Bible. They mustn't land in the shit.

On the other hand I must answer your question straight away. Our meeting 4 years ago. My side of the story. You want it and quick please.

PLEASE?

You pull this PLEASE over your question like a rubber. It's a torn rubber this PLEASE of yours.

GIVE ME AN ANSWER. This is what you're actually saying. It's not a question at all. It's an order. With one torn PLEASE pulled over it.

Your words are dangerous. Very dangerous. Full of tricks and traps.

You want my side of the story?

OK.

About a week ago I found a letter on my bed when they brought me back from the showers. It was from YOU and it was out of the blue. Saying let's write to one another without censorship.

That's my side of the story.

But you don't want to WRITE to me. You want to get the answer to one question. And then bugger off to the Kruger

39

Park. Back into the far blue yonder from whence you came. You think I can't sniff out the knowledge? I'd answer your question and then never hear from you again.

Your letters come into my cage like the tiny insects I sometimes find. Despite all the doors, the locks, the bars, the mesh, they've found their way to me. Nobody asked them in. But I pass the time with them, these insects, and they make the time go away.

I thought our letters could do the same kind of thing.

I was wrong.

Listen here. I don't know you. I never knew you. We met once. Who remembers someone they met once? And then we sat on the opposite sides of a courtroom for a while. Which one was you? There was a lot of strangers there.

Why should I tell a stranger something I never told the cops?

Hey stranger, go fuck.

Yours Faith Fully,

83143118.

EIGHT

To 83143118,

Today's tour was of the Voortrekker Monument and Museum near Valhalla ('Here in the Hall of Heroes, you'll see a frieze of the men who led the Great Trek from the Cape in 1838, to escape British rule . . . they were particularly disgruntled with the abolition of slavery'), and Pretoria itself: 'We'll view the stately Union Buildings, and we'll be going round Melrose House, where they signed the Vereeniging Peace Treaty in 1902, ending the Boer War, or Anglo-Boer War as we like to say these days. For those of you into nostalgia – wasn't *Room With A View* a marvellous movie? – well, Melrose House has that same lovely period furniture. Then on to Kruger House, which was Oom Paul's presidential residence . . . in Afrikaans the word "Oom" means Uncle, but is also used generally as a term of respect . . .'

We returned to the hotel at about 4.30 p.m.: 'Folks, as you probably discovered last night, Pretoria is a bit quiet after sundown, but have you tried the hotel pub, the Dubliner? It's very nice, and come six o'clock I'll certainly be in there, having a Guinness . . . we call it "stout" . . . so if anyone has any problems or queries about tomorrow's great trek to the Kruger Park, do please come and find me.'

As I walked into the foyer, the hall porter handed me your

41

letter of this morning, together with the (unopened) carton of Peter Stuyvesant. Strange to see him touching them.

Feeling eager, ashamed, worried (why were the cigarettes returned?), I hurried to my room and read the letter.

Then . . . pause for thought. Serious thought.

I'm replying immediately, by return of post. In other words, before going into the Dubliner for my stout, I'll get a taxi and deliver it personally to the prison. It'll be waiting on your bed when you return from tomorrow morning's shower. You could then leave your reply during exercise time. I will hold our departure to the Kruger. Charlie, the driver, and I have had to do this before (mostly because of Charlie's melodramatic love life), claiming the coach has mechanical problems. I'm not leaving until I've received your next reply.

So . . . where to begin now?

You'll remember that, when we met four years ago, I was a schoolteacher. A lot of tour guides were teachers first; others started out as actors; and then there are what I call the Railways Brigade – dour Afrikaner men whose knowledge of the country comes from working in one of the transport industries. They tend to be middle-aged, and wear pebble-dash spectacles with black plastic frames; they don't drink down in the Dubliner after working hours; they drink up in their rooms, seriously, and alone, except for a quick visit from one of the kitchen staff – a (black) girl in every port. Then there are also the part-time tour guides, the Housewife Brigade . . .

I'm gabbling, sorry. It's this job I do . . . press a button on any subject . . . and I'm nervous because I know you're angry. Bear with me; I'm giving you what you want.

I hated being a teacher (I dreamed of being Wilfred Thesiger, Paul Theroux, Jan Morris, Dame Freya Stark . . .!), but my father was determined – he wanted me to follow in his famous footsteps. Now retired, he was something of a legend in his day; a stubborn, belligerent, brave, lonely old warrior . . . actually more like a missionary, trying to convert the heathen, the barbarians – taking his beloved subject, English Literature, into the dark jungle of Afrikanerdom. Paul Roos Gymnasium in Stellenbosch. Where the boys all come from pedigree Boer families. Now and then, like once a decade, a pupil would respond to his labours. I remember, as a child, listening to him talk at supper one night – 'I finally found a way of helping Kobus hear the music of Milton' – and noticing that his eyes were bright, almost moist. The boy in question was Kobus Venter, who went on to have a glorious career in the police force, and is now Lieutenant General Venter, a deputy commissioner in the Department of Prison Services.

My father and Venter have corresponded over the years (Venter still invites Father to brush up his English), and two Sundays ago they finally had the reunion they'd been promising one another for ages. Venter came to our little house in Bantry Bay for a braai. We usually have these on the front lawn, overlooking the sea, but Venter's driver, also his bodyguard, wasn't happy with this location: there are tall building works across the road (what was he worried about – *snipers?*), so we had to move through to the backyard. No easy job, since the braai was already lit, and heavy; and poor Mum, sick with nerves over this VIP visit, had spent all morning carrying best cutlery, glasses, napkins, etc. through to the garden. (We don't have our maid on Sunday.)

Venter was very apologetic about all this fuss (a sweet chap, by the way: green eyes with a watery twinkle, whisky blooms on his cheeks; squat body kept in shape, except for the belly pushing down his beach shorts), and got stuck in, helping with the move.

Mind you, the 6' 6" driver, whose name we somehow never learned, looked like he could've carried the red-hot braai on his own, without gloves, and probably in his teeth. His great maw certainly wasn't designed for talking; more for clamping round a Scotch and soda. He drank even more than Venter during the afternoon, safe in the knowledge that if stopped for drunken driving . . .

I caught him staring at me several times, with a look which I used to get a lot – so *he's* the one from that trial! Pop stars and politicians must get this look too (and maybe McBride and White Wolf in your place): disbelief that one is actually flesh and blood, not just newsprint. At the height of all that media hoo-hah surrounding the case, 'the look' used to be tinged with something else, a kind of guilty, sweaty hunger.

They were dying to ask, 'Is it true what we read?' and 'What about the things they couldn't print?' . . . for a while, I held all the promise of a walking video nasty.

(After the trial, I changed my name – which made it easier to apply for new jobs, like this one – but really it was my *face* I needed to change. Someone at the office eventually recognised me, and told someone else, etc. But generally they've been very decent about it . . . I'm mostly out in the field anyway, with foreigners, who know nothing about the case.)

Anyway, Venter didn't give 'the look' – he's seen the likes of me too often. These top Afrikaner policemen, they're very comfortable with the world. As staunch Dutch Reformed Calvinists, they were brought up with the lowest possible regard for human nature, and everything in their life's work has confirmed their faith.

No, Venter just twinkled warmly at me: the son of a favourite teacher.

Absorbing his warmth, together with about a litre of Nederburg Riesling, I finally summoned the courage halfway through the afternoon:

'I'm thinking, sir, of corresponding with someone on death row – is that complicated to do?'

(Father was asleep under the umbrella, as was Venter's driver, and Mum was inside, loading the dishwasher. Venter and I were sunbathing, me simmering in a coconutty marinade of oil and sweat, him melting ice cubes over his powerful shoulders and chest.)

'Not at all,' said Venter, freshening his Scotch. 'Where's a pen? I'll give you the box number of Pretoria Max.'

'Will we be able to write freely to one another, this prisoner and I . . . about whatever we want?'

Venter paused, the bottle of Johnnie Walker atilt, filled more with sunlight than booze by now, then he laughed. 'Absolutely not. Letters are strictly, *strictly* censored.'

'Why's that?'

'Various reasons,' he said, signalling that the discussion was over. I let it rest for a moment, wiping my fingers dry of sunoil before reaching for my Rothmans, and offering him one.

'That's a pity,' I said, staring very directly at him as I

lit his cigarette, hoping not to have to say certain things out loud.

He held my stare, interested by something in it. Then he said, 'I mean, imagine if a rapist in there suddenly started writing to the woman he'd attacked. Imagine if we weren't censoring his letters. Imagine if she had to go through it all again.'

'But what if she needed to? Chose to. What if she felt she'd never get better again until she . . . talked to him?'

'Actually that happened, y'know. This particular lady, badly raped, badly traumatised . . . she felt she needed to write to the offender, and talk through certain things.'

I felt my heart rise. So it *had* been done before.

'You know what?' said Venter. 'She called a halt after about three or four letters. She said she just couldn't believe it . . . how dangerous words could be. How violent. But actually, as it happens, their correspondence would have finished anyhow. The man was served his notice of execution roundabout then, and hanged seven days later.'

I inhaled deeply on my cigarette, staring at Venter. Was this woman a friend of his, a relation maybe? Did *he* personally arrange for these letters to be exchanged? And when the woman became upset by them, did *he* influence the sudden arrival of the notice of execution?

'Hanged just for rape?' I said, trying to give myself thinking time.

'Ja sure, capital offence.' He added some more ice to his glass, and to each shoulder, just tensing those muscles, balancing the cubes as they started to melt. 'So listen, if you fancy writing to a death row prisoner, take my advice and choose one of the Born Again types. You're a tour guide, né – you can swop travellers' tales . . . he'll tell you about the road to Damascus, and you can—'

'No,' I said firmly, 'it's someone specific.' (I knew he *knew*.) Then I softened my features into an expression which works wonders . . . I become utterly lost, utterly innocent; an abandoned angel . . . or not so innocent – some people prefer their angels fallen . . . or an angel of mercy, if the person has some need I can help them with. Venter looked touched. I continued in a small voice. 'Sir, there's unfinished business . . .'

He interrupted. 'My name is Kobus.'

'Kobus.'

'Now show me where the lav is.'

I led the way, frowning to myself, suddenly wondering whether our locked gazes had been about something else. Why was there no *Mrs* Venter here today? Was the beefcake driver more than a bodyguard? Like that chap who Edgar J. Hoover always had with him? We passed the kitchen, where Mum was still clearing up. Surely Venter wouldn't try anything on with my parents so close. Would he? (He who was above the Law; he who *was* the Law.) We went on down the cool hallway; our nakedness – natural in the sunshine – now very indecent; Venter's gleaming shoulder hitting the wall now and again, the ice clunking in his glass. Why was he bringing his drink to the lav? I was desperate for the favour he could grant, but how far would I go?

(I've been chaste since you.)

We reached the toilet door, and I held it open, that arm outstretched; my body very exposed, the rest of me very unsure.

To my surprise, he pushed straight past and went into the lounge. Here Mum had half drawn the old wooden shutters, to prevent the roasting of her plants and magazines. The shadowy atmosphere, sliced with sunlight here and there, made me feel I was in an old Hollywood thriller.

Venter went to the bookcase, and stood there, his back to me, rattling the cubes in his glass like dice.

'What a fantastic library, hey!' he said. 'Your dad was the most marvellous bloody teacher! Have I told you that?'

'Only a dozen times, Oom Kobus,' I said.

He laughed. 'Ja, your dad gave me a respect for the English language . . . Milton, Shelley, Keats. And to my people, this interest I developed was a bit heretical, y'know. I felt naughty reading those poems . . . and excited. It gave me my first understanding of crime.'

He rattled the dice.

'I remember when I was still on the beat, once having

46

to search a distinguished playwright's house in P.E.,' he said, running his fingers over our book spines. 'And I remember paging through all the volumes he had there, all the great writers, and I remember saying to him, "Hell, in different circumstances, I'd so like to discuss these works with you!"'

Now he found a small, shabby book, and withdrew it from the shelves.

'Are you people churchgoers?' he asked. I realised the book was an old Bible.

'Regularly,' I lied. 'Anglican.'

'Anglican!' he laughed. 'No man, that's like this stuff they're putting in milk cartons these days. Skimmed. A person might as well not bother!'

I laughed.

He appeared to be offering me the book. I reached for it. He kept hold – collecting my fingers as well. His touch was hot, damp . . . something else *was* going on.

'I've forgotten the box number of Pretoria Max,' he said. 'Give me a ring tomorrow . . . if you're serious about it.' His fingers pressed mine into the surface of the Bible. His eyes had stopped twinkling.

At last I understood the intimacy. Not sex – religion. It *was* the angel in me that attracted him, but in its most Calvinist form: whiter than white, sweeter than sweet . . . like the condensed milk so loved by his people.

Now I became aware that the driver was standing in the doorway, filling it, Schwarzenegger-style, holding Venter's shirt.

'General,' said the driver, 'mustn't we make a move quite soon, sir?'

'OK,' said Venter, and then suddenly, with a wink, let go of the Bible.

I caught it.

They both laughed. I joined in, unsure of the joke. Was it just drunk, Sunday-afternoon-braai laughter? Or were they thinking: stupid kid, he thinks he's getting involved in big-time police corruption here!

Their laughter stayed with me through the evening, and I hardly slept. This thing was so insignificant to them, so important to me. Would Venter even remember it, in the sober light of day?

He did – putting me in touch with the man who runs Maximum Security, Major Steenkamp (whom you mention in one of your letters), and he, in turn, pointed me towards the person who would actually play postman; someone who works in your section . . .

I'd still prefer not to mention this last name; and surely it's irrelevant; surely, you now have enough information to protect yourself. Keep this letter, show it to them . . . if trouble arises. In addition, you can tell them that so far the exercise has cost me one case of finest Scottish malt whisky (for Venter), six bottles of ordinary whisky (for Steenkamp), and R25 per letter – for 'the postman'.

I hope we can now regard this matter as closed.

With regard to another point you make, I think you're correct – I probably had no real intention of *writing* to you in any full or proper sense. I probably just wanted my one question answered, and if you'd done so, yes you'd probably never have heard from me again.

So I have a new proposal. That we stop being strangers. That we do *write* to one another; about whatever we want, including the case . . . it would be dishonest of me to pretend I'll be able to leave that alone.

I'm offering to help you fill the long and difficult times which you've mentioned, like the nights, and I'm offering something more important, a sort of . . . and now I'll use the first truly dangerous word in this correspondence . . . a sort of *friendship*. Will you accept it?

Sincerely,

Adrian.

NINE

83143118
Pretoria Maximum Security

Adrian.

   Try me.

Yusuf.

II. TRAVELS

TEN

Dear Yusuf,

We've spent all today travelling over this beautiful earth; it
is coloured red, and holds the light with a kind of sheen, like
deep rust or the hide of local cattle. But you can travel over
it here in the Eastern Transvaal without noticing; after all,
it's only the dirt alongside the road. Look a little further, and
there's a landscape from your dreams: an ancient wilderness
of tangled bush and thorn trees, wooded valleys, deep
canyons, lichen-draped cliffs with caves and waterfalls, and,
towering above all, the horned peaks of the Drakensburg.

'This is the Africa of Rider Haggard and Sir Percy
Fitzpatrick,' I announce in a voice my brood haven't heard
before – hushed with excitement. 'The Africa where songs
of adventure and romance were sung in the shadow of the
bushwillow and the giant flaming aloe . . . the Africa of ivory
hunters, explorers and gold prospectors . . . here are places
called Pilgrim's Rest and Long Tom Pass . . . here are rivers
called Crocodile and Limpopo . . .'

In actual fact, those explorers and prospectors wouldn't
have found the area all that romantic; they lived in constant
fear of predators or disease; they'd have counted the hours
until they reached the sanctuary of the towns. These days
it's the other way round. The countryside, Africa herself, the

53

primeval wildland, is where you go to feel safe, and sane, while the towns are full of disease and predators. Waiting for your letter this morning, I *did* actually pace round Strijdom Square, hunting ground of the White Wolf, and *did* actually find myself looking for bullet holes in the walls, stains on the pavement . . .

Thank you for your reply. Exercise time must've been earlier today, because I had your letter by 10.45 – and so our departure was only delayed by about three hours. The brood were a little annoyed, but not seriously – just like kids; sulky and restless, without ever doubting that they were in safe hands . . .

Throughout the four-hour drive from Pretoria to the Kruger, I felt very high; I really enjoyed that mike in my hand, round my lips, like a singer. Actually, my rap is not unlike music these days, since I'm no longer alone – there's someone else talking all the time too, creating a kind of jazz improvisation with me, not altogether sweetly.

This other voice goes: 'How interesting . . . mh-hh . . . oh I see, bingo! . . . yes, yes, well bless me! . . . ah, mm . . . oh good fun, I love it! . . . ah-hah . . .'

It belongs to a thin, rather beautiful, forties-something lady from Cork, Ireland, an illustrator of children's stories: Ms Blanche Appleton. Despite my rule that the brood operate an informal system of seat rotation, Blanche has settled permanently into the best seat on the coach, just behind me, commanding a view through the huge front window: our turquoise-tinted, cinemascope view of South Africa.

She's obviously done some homework for this trip. Whenever I draw breath, she's in with a question, and halfway through my reply, ejaculates, 'Oh it *is* so – I thought as much!' And God help me if I don't know the answer. She snaps, 'OK, OK,' as though saying, You're a great disappointment, but I don't want to embarrass you further. At other times, she echoes words I say, or gasps, hums, twitters, tuts.

I'm hardened to all sorts of testing behaviour, but a day or two ago I thought Blanche was going to defeat me. I became obsessed with her voice, unable to concentrate on my own, waiting for her next interjection like a hiccough. But now something else has taken over: the job of befriending her (which I'm paid to do). The brood refuse to be a receptacle for her verbal diarrhoea. If anyone finds themselves alongside her on a walking tour, they flee as she opens her mouth . . . and, unbelievably, she carries on talking, all alone, like she must do at home, addressing thin air, until the story is finished. So I dash in, trying to quieten her, trying to signal, It's alright, I'm here, *someone's* here, I'll fuss you, I'll spoil you; for the next few weeks you won't be alone.

Meanwhile, the rest of the brood are proving quite a handful as well. Old Mrs Gill, our retired librarian from Wickford, Essex, UK, who gently nips the end of her tongue with her fingers as she talks, turning an imaginary page — she needs extra restroom stops, and often gets lost, or overheated, or ill from all the fruit. I'm very patient with her (because of a vague resemblance to my granny), but she really shouldn't be travelling on her own. And then there are the Moonjes. It's not their fault, of course, but I seem to spend all my time protecting them from embarrassment, or worse. The Towers Hotel group tolerates non-white customers now, but there's a flurry of raised eyebrows and pinched nostrils if, say, they head towards the swimming pool. Lord knows what'll happen when we reach the coast — they're still not allowed to swim on the same beaches as the rest of the brood.

Which will suit one of my Ossies just fine: Fred Frawley, a building contractor from Brisbane, Queensland, a lumbering fellow with a great bucket-mouth of teeth, who's very much at home in S.A., sharing our love for barbies, beers, sport, the great outdoors, and one or two other things. However, there is a crucial difference between us and him. It's expressed in his catchphrase, which I've heard other Ossies use, and which must stem, I suppose, from their geographical isolation:

'How are you today, Mr Frawley?'

'No worries.'

'We'll be stopping soon for a rest break.'

'No worries.'

'Mr Frawley, your wife is being necklaced.'

'No worries.'

(In fact, the only worries he's had in this country arise from our plans to change it.)

Perhaps there'll come a day when the entire Australian vocabulary dwindles to those two words: 'No worries.' I can't imagine South Africans ever being so lucky.

I must go to bed. We've got a game drive at dawn.

———

Fri. 22nd. Olifants Camp. Hut 107.

Resuming this letter twenty-four hours into our trip, at my favourite rest-camp. Situated high on a hill above the Olifants River, it's one of the few places in the park where you have to turn your head to see the whole view ... for the rest of the time, you're peering through bushes and trees. Here the winding river and its orange rock banks lead the eye across thickly bushed plains, and forests, and on and on, to mountains dimmed by distance. At sundown, I love to pour myself a colonial-measure of gin, which is rather large I'm afraid, with much ice and little tonic, and then sit outside my hut, overlooking the great, deep landscape. The river continues to hold the light – a drunk, golden road through the greying landscape – and in its gleam, animals appear on the banks: a hippo and calf, waterbuck, families of baboon ...

Today the weather was bad when we arrived, mid-morning, and it continued to rain steadily for most of the afternoon. When it finally cleared at about 4.30, there was an exodus from the camp; fleets of coaches, cars and combis, all going in search of game. The bushland was still stormy, with shafts of sun and rain, the vegetation shining with silver light, a deep blue mist beyond.

Quite soon we had to stop while a group of young male impala crossed the road. Being the only animals which can be seen reliably and in vast numbers, impala are of little interest (the second-class citizens of the park), but I tried: 'Folks, it's fascinating – these bachelors all live apart from the main herd, which consists entirely of females and a single dominant male. But eventually he will be challenged, and succeeded, by one of these young chaps . . .' Our London cabby Lenny Webb called out, 'What happens to the rest – do they turn poofter?' Laughter from some; tuts from Blanche and old Mrs Gill. On we went. Now a sighting of a yellow-billed hornbill. Mainly for Blanche's benefit (she's quite an ornithologist), I launched into: 'Now folks, these are very interesting. They nest inside a tree—'

'Oh that's right!' exclaimed Blanche. 'And the male . . .'

I fought to stay in charge. '. . . The male, yes, seals the female in with mud, and then she has to strip her own feathers to create the nest—'

'That's right!' squealed Blanche.

'. . . And the male feeds her through a small hole, about the size of our fifty cent piece—'

'Fifty cents, fifty cents,' muttered Blanche, fishing in her purse, to picture it clearer.

'. . . And she only breaks free after laying the eggs.' Glancing over my shoulder, I saw that, apart from Blanche, my brood was staring back blank-faced. Several were drunk or hung over, having been cooped up indoors for the day. All were furious about the rain, and, like kids, were blaming daddy: I'd promised them a good time, I'd let them down, and now, to cap it all, I was showing them impala and *birds*!

There's supposed to be a big five which tourists most want to see – lion, leopard, elephant, rhino and buffalo (the ones which the Hemingway-hunters of old regarded as most dangerous) – but actually there's something more important on their shopping list. Blood.

We struck lucky this afternoon, about half an hour into the drive, as we turned onto one of the untarred roads which loop into the bush.

We saw the vultures first. A mixed flock – lappetfaced and whitebacked – already on the ground; more coming to land in that shuffling, crippled way. Drawing closer, we realised they were surrounding a young male zebra, which was sitting alongside the road, head upright, clearly still alive. The vultures stood around, hunched and patient. They looked like nuns; as though they were protecting the animal, or nursing it. We drove closer, dispersing some of the birds, who lifted into the sky, spreading ragged wings, doubling in gruesomeness. The zebra itself remained still, making no effort to flee from our approach. As we stopped alongside, we saw that the hindquarters and tail were dark with blood; his striped pattern blotted out. He'd been savaged by a predator – maybe a single hyena . . . he'd never have escaped one of the big cats. For a while he calmly watched us staring, discussing, photographing, but then, as more vehicles arrived, he struggled to his feet – and we finally saw the injury. As usual the predator had started gorging on the lower belly. Hanging from the zebra was a coil of intestines, and his half-severed penis. I knew I should tell our driver Charlie to move on quickly, I knew I should reassure my brood, explaining that the zebra's suffering wouldn't last long: the smell of his blood would attract a hungry lion, or else one of the bolder vultures would peck out his eyes, encouraging the other nurses to move in. But I couldn't speak. I'm not completely sure what happened then. I think Charlie had to restrain me from climbing out of the coach. I think I wanted to put my jacket round the zebra, bandage it, take it to the camp. I think I managed to turn this into some kind of joke.

On the way back, it suddenly rained again, ferocious rain thumping down and blanking out the light. I led a sing-song; old favourites which every English-speaking tourist knows, wherever they're from; 'I'm forever blowing bubbles', 'Roll out the barrel', and so on; British, Australian and Indian voices all joining together in darkest Africa. Then, as abruptly, the weather cleared, and this tremendous golden-white cloud reared above the plains like a tidal wave, and stayed poised there for five or ten minutes. It was like the dream I sometimes have: a massive body of water is threatening my life, yet seems too beautiful to run from. It's not just a dream . . . it actually happened once or twice in my surfing days . . . I'll tell you about that another time.

Now it's late at night again. Now my instincts are all over the place (and it's not just the wine; it's something to do with *you*). Now the landscape below Olifants Camp looks like the ocean: a giant blackness fringed by beaches of light from the camp. It even sounds like the ocean: the wind washing through fever trees, umbrella thorns, the magic guarri, sickle bush, spear grass, finger grass. It even *smells* like the ocean; the Moçambique coast isn't that far away . . .

So anyway I'm sitting here outside my hut, above this black, roaring African night, and I'm wondering which of the animals we saw earlier are still alive. Certainly not the zebra, but what about those impala? Such crap I wrote before! — the nights out here are exactly like Joburg nights, nights of ambush, terror and death. The only difference is that the curfew is stricter — for humans anyway; we're locked in at 6 p.m., and there's a fine if you're late.

Which we were today. Late. And fined. After seeing the zebra. And it's never happened to me before — being late, being fined. (And I blame *you*, and I don't know why.) And the worst of it is that the flipping warder at the gate announced that we were going to be fined — announced it loudly! — so that the whole flipping brood heard. Oh, I've just written warder, but I meant warden, game warden.

Adrian.

ELEVEN

83143118
Pretoria Maximum Security

Friday I think.

Adrian.

Exercise time is over and there's still not a letter from you. It gives me no heartsore, don't think that. But anyhow. Maybe it's what you said. The letters are going to take longer now you're out the district.

In any case, I've had a big day, and you're going to be the first to know.

I'm glad I've got somebody to tell. Talking time is way over there on the other side of the afternoon. And I'm bursting man I'm bursting.

I've seen HIM.

ME MYSELF AND I. This bloody trinity has seen HIM.

How long have I been here? One year or two? And at last it's happened.

Not just anyone can see HIM. Especially if you're non-white.

But today something changed, and made new things possible. I became one of the chosen few. One of the suckers. The warders' suckers.

Yes I know what I said before. That they're the lowest of the low. Let that be a lesson to you, buddy. Don't rely on me to be standing where I was a second ago. I move with the times, I swim with the tide, I change my spots, I grab that bird in the bush.

STAND UP yells Sergeant Fourie in Afrikaans, just as I've sat down after brushing my teeth, DO YOU WANT BREAKFAST TROLLEY DUTY YES OR NO?

YES SERGEANT I shout back without a second thought.

I'm a bit surprised to be asked, but I think I know what's up.

Sergeant Fourie lost one of his breakfast boys, Lucky Zuko, down the red trap door yesterday.

Why has fat Fourie come to me?

Because I'm not a comrade. I'm not going to be slopping propaganda around with the pap. Plus I'm not interested in escaping the noose. Only the boredom.

Five minutes later I'm in the kitchens.

I've never been in the kitchens before.

Every weapon under the sun.

But you know what my best thing was?

A big fridge was making a small noise that sounded like something else. I put my ear to it. A sort of ticking. A sort of humming. In one of your letters you call it cicadas. I call it a night in the veld.

Man it made me feel sweet for a second.

Only quick, but that's the deal on death row. Here time is like when a person was little. Kid time. I kidded time and now doth time kid me. Fucking numb-dull for hours on end. Then suddenly something happens. New. Nice. A rainbow. You grab for it. It's gone. You're older by a second. You're not sure something so nice will ever happen again.

Next thing I'm wheeling the breakfast trolley up by there in C section where the white prisoners are caged.

Not so different from us.

STAND UP shouts Sergeant Fourie in Afrikaans. Unlocks the door. Click cluck. Breakfast goes in. Door goes click cluck.

On to the next one.

Until we get to one particular cage. The lair of the WHITE WOLF. Alias him who gunned down 8 random kaffirs and maimed 16 others.

I can't believe my eyes.

The light is off in his cage.

Lovely darkness somewhere inside the mesh.

I swear by God this is true.

The WHITE WOLF sleeps in blackness.

Sergeant Fourie knocks on the door.

Mister Strydom are you ready for breakfast?

I can't believe my ears either.

A sleepy murmur replies something like go fuck.

Sergeant Fourie apologises and moves me on quickly and roughly like it's my fault.

I'm thinking, my glory, I hope I get to see this WHITE WOLF one day. This guy's big fry.

Little do I know who I'm about to see round the next corner.

Mind you, round every corner in these parts the world is brand and spanking new. I'm like one of your BROOD. I'm a tourist, I'm a traveller, I'm mister livingstone I presume, I'm the first man on the fucking moon.

We finish in the white suburbs and we turn right. Now we're passing a small chapel. Not like the main one we visit once a week, regular as clockwork, pretending it's for prayers but actually it's just a chance to TALK. In this small chapel here there's no regular visits. There's a one and only visit. On the big day itself. Here a condemned man has his last pray.

Now I'm passing a staircase which goes up from the small chapel.

Jesus, Jesus, it's the ACTUAL 42 steps. The stairway to heaven.

Suddenly Sergeant Fourie shouts WHOA. We've got another stop here.

I'm thinking, what's up? Are we giving breakfast to someone on their way to heaven?

But now I see Sergeant Fourie is unlocking a cage UNDERNEATH the 42 steps.

Then he snaps his fingers at me and says, bring that covered dish there on the trolley.

So I bring it into the special cage.

There in the corner is a fat old man with frizzy white hair. His skin is sort of dead coloured. Sort of white plus black at the same time. And a bit swollen looking. Like skin that's been under water for a month or two.

He's got big dark eyes and a big dead smile.

A funny wet stink is in his cage. Although his own sun in a bottle is burning bright you feel like you're deep in a cellar.

Sergeant Fourie says to me I must put the dish on the floor and take off the lid.

There underneath is a little cake.

A carrot cake, says the sergeant.

I've never heard of such a thing.

He's got bad guts, says the sergeant. Carrot helps.

I'm thinking, oh I see, they're nice to him, like they are to WHITE WOLF.

All this time the old man is smiling at us out of his fat dead face like he doesn't understand a thing.

Now Sergeant Fourie takes a whole carrot out of his pocket and sticks it in the cake. Like a candle.

That's right, the sergeant says to me, it's his birthday, he's 71.

When the old man sees the carrot candle he smiles properly for the first time. You get the feeling he hasn't had a birthday cake for a while. And here's a carrot cake too. For his bad guts.

This is the life.

Now Sergeant Fourie says, we must sing happy birthday to him.

As soon as we start I hear more voices join in.

I see 2 or 3 other warders behind me, looking through the doorway.

I see the old man's smile go dead again.

In Afrikaans we sing HAPPY BIRTHDAY TO YOU. I don't catch the name in the bit where you say it, the HAPPY BIRTHDAY DEAR bit. Sounds a strange name.

When we're finished Sergeant Fourie says to me in Afrikaans, oh loving Jesus he's forgotten to put out his candle, you'd better do it for him.

I'm thinking what's the score? There's no candle. Just one cold carrot.

PUT OUT THE CANDLE bawls the sergeant YOU WANT HIM TO BURN DOWN THE FOKKIN JOINT?

OK fine, no sweat, no arguments.

I turn to get a scoop of coffee from the breakfast trolley.

But the other warders are blocking my way.

Bellowing.

PUT OUT THE FOKKIN CANDLE. THE FOKKIN FLAMES ARE GETTING BIGGER. IT'LL NEED A BIG FOKKIN HOSEPIPE NOW. FOKKIN QUICK.

So the penny drops.

The old man watches me start to sprinkle his birthday cake.

He looks so upset I can't help joining in the jollity.

The more I laugh the more I gush on his cake. I swish it around this way and that. Man the damage I'm holding here in my hand. Feels good. I wash the floor with him and his bloody carrot cake.

Now it's just a lake with floating bits.

Fuck him. We shut him in with the whole stinking mess. Click cluck. Fuck him to hell. Let him fucking rot, let him age in his cage.

As we walk away the warders are still pally with me. I've done good. They even let me talk.

Fat Fourie says, you know who that was?

No my sergeant boss, I says.

Dimitri Tsafendas.

Man.

It's like a fist in the eyes.

That was TSAFENDAS.

The famous one I haven't told you about yet. The one I heard was here, but never had seen.

The one who butchered god himself.

The Boer god.

Butchered in 1966.

Then Tsafendas was a 48-year-old messenger boy in parliament. One day he crossed what they call the floor of the HOUSE. He walked over to the prime minister. Reached into his pocket and drew out a message with a difference. Long and sharp. Poked it in and out. Four times. One-two-three-four. PM-is-no-more.

64

You must remember.

Or weren't you born yet?

I was only 9 but I remember how a whole day stopped in its tracks. Even out in Bonteheuwel where we lived. The news spread. The Boer god was dead. Doctor Verwoerd. Alias the GRAND WIZARD of apartheid. Alias the ARCHITECT of apartheid.

Funny pictures hey? Verwoerd in a tall pointed hat cooking up apartheid with set squares and rulers.

And credit where credit's due, he drew up the perfect plan. A plan to LOBOTOMISE his second-class citizens with second-class schooling.

This plan was mainly aimed at the kaffirs but I got caught in the cross-fire. My schooling was a joke.

I didn't grow bright till I hit prison.

Where god's butcher was also sent for further education.

I say to Sergeant Fourie, but I thought Tsafendas was sick in the skull.

Affirmative, says Fourie. At his summary trial they asked him why he hated Verwoerd. He couldn't say. All he knew was that he hated his own insides. They were inhabited by a tapeworm. A giant and hellish tapeworm. Slowly eating him up.

Does it like carrots, I ask Sergeant Fourie.

Affirmative.

Was today really his birthday?

Maybe, maybe not. Dimitri's not sure of the date himself, so we make sure he has lots of birthdays.

I say, but if he was declared mad why isn't he in the mad house? Why is he on death row?

The warders laugh at me.

I say but.

They say, shut your fokkin trap, SILENCE, d'you want spare diet?

Oh yes they can also change their spots.

Back in my cage I work it out. In 1966 the Boers must've felt a bit fed-up with Tsafendas. He'd butchered the grand wizard, the architect, god himself. They must've felt even more fed-up when they heard they couldn't hang him. Because of a tapeworm. A TAPEWORM. Can you see how fed-up this would make them? So they must've thought the following. If we can't send him to hell we must make hell on earth for him. So they sent him to Beverly Hills. Life on death row. In the cage under the 42 steps. The only cage that can hear the gallows at work. Day in and day out.

Look here Adrian, I'm someone who doesn't mind pain. I've been across the threshold and back. Both ways. Giving and getting. But I've got to hand it to these guys. These guys are past masters.

Just think of him in that special cage. Just think what he hears. Day in, day out. The machinery of the gallows. Men shouting, crying, pissing themselves. The comrades who toyi-toyi their way to heaven. And the laughter of the executioner and his helpers as they strip a body and see how stiff your hanging has made you.

He hears it all. The man who butchered god to death. One-two-three-four, god-is-no-more.

And I met him.

I took hold of my genitals and pointed them at his birthday cake.

What about that hey?

Yours Faith Fully,

Yusuf.

I wonder if it's Sergeant fat Fourie? The guy you've bribed and corrupted. To be our postman. Is that why he was alright with me today?

My bucks are on him.

TWELVE

The Durban Towers
North Beach
Marine Parade
Durban 4000
Room 1616

Sun. 24th Sept.

Dear Yusuf,

Durban always turns me on – sweltering, raucous, lush – a gutter during a carnival, brimming with gorgeous stuff, some of it bright, some of it festering. Everything that pours off the Drakensberg; pours over those icy waterfalls, pours across the rolling green hills and sugar-cane fields, pours down to the sea ... it all collects in Durban; the orchids, ferns and multicoloured lilies overflowing from the markets here, and suffusing the air, along with the aroma of avocados, wild bananas, and paw-paws, heaped in such numbers that half of them are pulp. Animals are everywhere also – crocodiles, spitting cobras, green monkeys – on someone's shoulder, in this cage, in that park, or printed on headscarfs, daubed on rickshaws, carved into the leather wallet an Indian stallholder is trying to sell – 'To keep safe your ID sir, your book of life!' He also sells leather holsters, tassled or plain, Wild West or Secret Service. Next to him a huge Zulu is selling flick-knives that spring out of knuckledusters – 'Phantom knives!' – and here are kids offering township art: windmills made out of coat hangers, or coloured baskets woven from telephone cables. A bearded Afrikaner is cooking boerewors

67

hot-dogs, next to a lady in a sari holding up pineapple pieces on a stick – 'Spicy pines!' – while the counter of her family's bazaar is piled with all sorts of powders and potions; Hot Sour Figs, Birth Marsala, Mother-in-law-Exterminator . . .

'Folks, I notice you looking at those stalls in the Sunday Market on our right . . . well, Durban, or Durbs as we call it, Durbs has a lovely Eastern atmosphere . . . from the descendants of the indentured sugar-cane workers who arrived here in 1860 . . . even Mahatma Gandhi came out in 1893 . . . I'm sure you've all seen that movie! . . . well, what it didn't mention is that he stayed on here for nigh on twenty years . . .!'

Behind me, Blanche Appleton is muttering, 'Indentured workers, 1860, mm-hh, Gandhi, 1893, mh-hh . . .'

'. . . So folks, do try the Curry Carvery at our hotel, which we're now approaching on the left. Today is, as you know, a Leisure Day, and as we say of Durbs, "here the fun never sets!"'

Climbing out of the air-conditioned interior, the wet heat swamps you. Bunny Webb, wife of our London cabby, said loudly, 'Ugh, this is just like New York last August, innit Len? Like a big hound breathing in your face!' But Len didn't hear – he was laughing at a joke which his new mate, Mr Frawley from Brisbane, had just told. Mr F.'s small vocabulary ('No worries') has expanded recently:

'OK, here's another,' drawled Mr F. 'Why do they make some chocolates white?'

'Dunno, dunno!' said Len, already chortling.

'So Abbos don't bite off *all* their fingers.'

'Like it, like it!' guffawed Len, as Bunny hauled him up the steps into the hotel . . . both Len and Mr F. were drinking heavily on the plane from Joburg.

I glanced over to the Moonjes, hoping they hadn't heard – luckily they were submerged in a noisy reunion with their Durban relatives, who'd come to meet the coach. But it is increasingly difficult to protect them from Frawley. Last night, they happened to sit next to him at dinner, and Frawley made a terrible fuss, taking me aside and demanding I rearrange the whole table, which I duly did.

68

'I didn't expect this kind of unhygienic behaviour *here*,' he muttered to me. 'By the bye, d'you know why Abbos stink?' Smiling politely, I raised my eyebrows. '. . . So that the blind can hate them too!'

As a keen collector of jokes, I was tempted to tell him that we used to have similar ones here, but ours are changing; e.g., What d'you call a kaffir with a gun? – 'Sir!'

Sidestepping Frawley now, as well as Blanche, who'd cornered our new driver, an attractive Coloured chap called Gideon ('Did you know that Gideon means "stump for a hand" in the good book? . . . and talking of which, this Samsonite case is mine, don't confuse it with Mrs Thorne's'), I hurried over to old Mrs Gill, and helped her into the foyer. Wet with perspiration, she looked like a little sick bird; hair in threads, yellowy skin showing through a grey frock.

The deputy manager, Deon whatsit, was waiting with complimentary glasses of cooldrink, and the list of room allocations. What a relief to hand over to him, and just stand alongside, smiling and nodding to the brood, telling them I'll see them in the morning.

Exhausted after the last ten days, I felt empty, vaguely sad, when I reached my room on the 16th floor – number 1616 – which I always have here. It has a spectacular view of the promenade with its market, Mini-town, Snake Park, Pirates Life-Saving Club, the beaches of the Golden Mile. A flotilla of yachts were out on the ocean today, the warm Indian Ocean, and long flat tankers were sliding across the long flat horizon. Trying to let in some fresh air, I remembered that the windows here open in an unusual way, just at the top . . . maybe they had some suicides early on.

I glanced at the half bottle of Fleur du Cap Pinotage which Deon whatsit had kindly left for me, and then to my watch . . . 11.30 . . . (was I really going to start this early?) . . . and then to the table where some memos and letters were waiting. Why did I know there wouldn't be one from you? Without confirming this, I unpacked, working out whether, *if* you'd written again, it could've reached Durban by today. Probably not. In the wardrobe I discovered a dozen crisp shirts which our Durban office had sent over (I'll be getting through two or three a day here if I'm to keep up standards), and then finally looked through the mail. As I thought – nothing from you. Pity. It's very important, when living out of suitcases; very important to hear from one's nearest and dearest, or even you.

Don't know why I wrote that. But I'll leave it in. If you don't like it, stop reading, throw away the letter, I don't care.

(I'm puzzled – very puzzled – by some of my feelings since we started writing.)

Lighting a cigarette, I wondered what to do with the day. I most wanted to stroll along Marine Parade and find Magoo's Bar, or what's left of it from McBride's bomb (like the way, on Thursday, I followed White Wolf's trail round Strijdom Square), but decided this was morbid, ridiculous, kinky. Go to the hotel pool then? And risk spending the day with members of the brood . . .? No, best to hire a car, buy a bottle of wine, find a deserted beach, somewhere I could sunbathe nude, prick-tease myself through the day, waiting for some handsome stranger to come along, safe in the knowledge that no-one would. A joint or two could help. Maybe Gideon our Coloured driver had some? Maybe he'd like to come along . . .?

I glanced down: he was still there, still unloading the luggage, and Blanche was just finishing one of her discourses. As she left him and went into the foyer, I turned and headed for the door. If I timed this right, I could be descending in one lift, while she was coming up in another.

I made it along the 16th floor's winding corridors without bumping into any of the brood, and pressed the lift button . . . a pair arrived at the same time . . . I picked the one on the left . . . and, too late, saw a figure huddled in the corner. Old Mrs Gill. Still bedraggled with sweat, she was hunched over our itinerary, her reading specs on her nose, and her other, thicker ones propped on her forehead. I had the impression that she'd been in the lift for some time.

There were mirrors on either side, multiplying our reflections to infinity; two sweeping chorus lines of tour guides and old ladies . . .

'When do we visit the battle sites?' she asked as I pressed the button for reception. 'I can't spot them on your list.'

She waved it at me, copied by her chorus line. Dazzled by all the white papers, I said, 'I'm sorry – battle sites?'

Frowning, Mrs Gill said that, when she booked her holiday at the local travel agent in Wickford, Essex, UK, she *carefully* explained that she needed a tour which included Natal, because her grandfather had fought in the Zulu Wars of 1879, and was felled at the Battle of Isandlwana. All this had been 'carefully explained', she repeated. 'So,' she said now, firmly but wearily, as though still dealing with the Wickford travel agent, '*when* do we visit the battle sites?'

I stared back, speechless.

Battle sites? SATOUR has issued us with strict instructions not to dwell on any massacres, past or present: blacks killing British, British killing Boers, Boers killing blacks, blacks killing blacks . . .

How to explain this? And that we wouldn't dream of taking tourists into KwaZulu (where Isandlwana is situated), one of the most explosive spots on the map of our State of Emergency; home of Inkatha, sworn enemy of the ANC, sworn friend of the ruling government . . . or maybe ex-friend these days . . .?

'Oh golly,' I said. 'I'm afraid Isandlwana isn't really in Natal any more, or indeed in South Africa . . . it's now in what we call the "homelands", y'see . . .' I watched myself in the tiny hall of mirrors, hands flailing around. '. . . And we don't go there. Well, we go into two of the other homelands, but not to uhm . . .' We reached reception. 'So I'm sorry, I can only suggest you take it up with your travel agent in Wick . . .' I hesitated, halfway out of the lift, its nervy doors nudging my knee and foot. Mrs Gill hadn't budged from the corner.

'No, no,' she said quietly, 'we can't miss out on the battle sites. I've saved up for this all my life.'

Behind her, in the endless mirrors, I saw a bald patch in her damp hair, sunburnt pink . . . on and on it went. I had the same feeling as up in the bedroom, a sort of emptiness, and a sort of anger (yes, with *you* – though don't ask me where you come into this). Looking at Mrs Gill, I thought,

No I'm not going to let you get hurt, come on let's bend the rules, cheat the system . . .

An hour later, we were sitting in a hired car, Mrs Gill and I, heading north-west, towards the central piece of KwaZulu (scattered like a jigsaw across Natal), and Isandlwana.

Mrs Gill was wearing a small felt hat, her church hat maybe, and a clip-on sun visor over her thick specs. She said nothing during the journey, but sat with chin raised and hands clasped on her lap, at once both anxious about this momentous pilgrimage and determined to fend off any further attempts by the tourist industry to stop her.

She seemed unaware that I was helping her, that I'd paid for the car myself (well, I'll probably claim it back on expenses), or that I was giving up my free day. I didn't mind . . . I was too excited by this unexpected trip into no-man's land, too alight with the danger of it – a danger I kept sensing (or half-wanting?), despite the beauty surrounding us.

We drove through Pietermaritzburg, New Hanover . . . immense sugar-cane fields . . . over the Karkloof Range, with its forests of pine, wattle, eucalyptus . . . past Greytown, birthplace of Louis Botha, Boer War general and our first prime minister . . . scattered Zulu villages with beehive or prefab huts . . . grasslands changing to thornbush and succulents . . . an aloe tree hung with washing like a windy-drier . . . a goat climbing a tree, seeking moisture near the top . . . across the Tugela River . . . and now the green hills and purple mountains of Zululand . . .

Four hours after leaving Durban, the day had become humid and grey, with electric storms rolling around in the Drakensberg. We drove on across this empty, rumbling landscape, until finally we found a turning to the right: 'Isandlwana – 3 miles'.

It's a curious place. Quite ordinary at first, with a village of thatch and mud homes, a school with a mural of the battle, a church and visitors' centre, where you pay R3 to go further . . . and that's when it changes . . . as your car drives out alone across the plain to the eponymous hill, or mountain. Scarred and patched with dark rock and bright grass, it's an unholy shape – brutish, with an amputated look, as though there are bits missing, rounded bits, bits which would soften its saw-edged corners.

'Both armies were wary of it,' said Mrs Gill, reading my thoughts as I helped her out of the car. 'The Zulus normally kept away . . . something had happened here once, maybe in the Iron Age when it was a smelting site . . . and as for the British, they didn't fancy the way that piece of rock resembled the sphinx on their cap badge, the 24th Regiment . . .'

I stood there, open-mouthed – who was the tourist here, and who the tour guide? – then remembered that she used to be a librarian. She knew a great deal more than me, since my school books, both as pupil and teacher, were of course doctored along with the rest of literature, and certainly didn't devote much space to 'kaffir' victories.

'. . . So it was a place of ill omen,' continued Mrs Gill, gently nipping her tongue with forefinger and thumb. 'And to make matters worse, the Zulu king Cetshwayo had instructed his impis not to fight on the 22nd of January . . . for it was to be a "day of the dead moon". An eclipse. And indeed this occurred during the fighting, at 2.29 in the afternoon . . .'

I glanced at my watch . . . 4.45 . . . puzzled by a sensation in the air . . . a strange dimness, a strange temperature. Either it was because of the story she was telling, or it was something else, something real, something here and now . . .

(A storm? Or ghosts? Or my mixed feelings about being in KwaZulu?)

There are times nowadays when I so want to be with you – locked behind electronic fences and steel doors and thick concrete walls.

She pointed to little pyramids of whitewashed rocks dotted around – she called these 'cairns' – and explained that they were the unmarked graves of the British dead. 'Grandad's here,' she said, choosing one at random, and standing in front, hands folded, a tired, satisfied frown on her face. She told me about him: an army orphan, he was only sixteen when he died, but, being 'a bit of a lad', had sown his wild oats the night before the regiment sailed from Southampton, so bringing into being the Gill family this century.

I nodded, genuinely interested, yet unable to concentrate.

Three horses, which had been grazing on the plains, suddenly set off, slowly but deliberately, towards the buildings back at the visitors' centre, and now I realised that one of the three was a zebra, and I found this very odd indeed . . .

Meanwhile, Mrs Gill was saying, 'Oh, the Zulus were fearsome warriors. One of our officers at the time called them "maddened celibate savages". They weren't allowed to marry y'see until they'd "washed their spears in blood". So, what with their normal needs all thwarted, their natural desires all up in the air, they were horribly suited to warfare, disembowelling every man they killed, and biting on his gall bladder, and boasting "I have eaten!" – in Zulu, naturally.'

A hard wind had sprung up, pushing at me. It wasn't just my imagination . . . the darkness, the temperature . . . it was one of those electric storms, those Zululand storms, heading our way. We couldn't see anything yet, but I'd heard the stories. A massive, single, upright cloud, like a mushroom cloud, or, no, more like an anvil, people say – a dark anvil sparking with lightning, banging with thunder. Hail like fists; the reek of ozone as if the earth itself had gone bad or been burnt; trees splintered, thrown a hundred yards, the stump left smoking; people fried alive . . .

Where would be safe? Inside a car – would that be safe? Its metal shell, its insulation and tyres, would that be good or bad?

I didn't feel frightened for myself; I never feel threatened by physical dangers these days (I mean, I haven't survived you to be hurt by the *weather*), but Mrs Gill was my responsibility, she was in my charge.

I interrupted her. 'I think we'd better get back to the visitors' centre.'

'Yes, bit blowy, isn't it? Let's just get the snapshot done then, and be off.' She produced a little Instamatic, but didn't know how to use it. I showed her. Now she asked me to pose against the cairn, the one she'd chosen to be her grandfather's grave. I protested that it should surely be her in the photo. She said, 'But the family know what *I* look like.'

So, bizarrely, she took a photo of me – me at Isandlwana – me struggling to stand upright in the weird light, the humming, buzzing wind (Mrs Gill said the Zulus made a noise like bees while they killed), and so I'm forever to be linked with the murder of her sixteen-year-old grandfather. I suggested she quickly take a second one (imagine if, after all this, it doesn't come out!), but she wouldn't be persuaded. 'I'm on a bit of an economy drive these days,' she said apologetically, as though I wanted the extra shot for myself.

Now, as we turned to flee, the atmosphere suddenly started to change again . . . lighten, soften. The storm was rolling off in a different direction, which is again typical of these parts apparently. Within moments, as we stood there, amazed, the air became very clear and calm; late afternoon air smelling of grass and dust; and a lazy blue shadow stretched away from Isandlwana Rock across the plains.

Mrs Gill took my hand – hers was like a skeleton's – and said, 'My goodness me, that wasn't an eclipse, was it?'

On the drive back to Durban, she was very quiet again. She kept reaching into her handbag, to touch the Instamatic, which she'd wrapped into a handkerchief, as if it was glass, and tucked into the safest corner. A hundred times she checked it was safe, and then at last broke her silence to say, 'Well, there we are . . . I got back to my roots in the end.'

Now she became quite emotional – I think; there was a brief puffing noise, but I didn't like to look. It's difficult anyway to identify emotion in the English. Take my mother and father. Although born and bred in S.A., they've inherited their parents' ways (Father actually says 'tickety-boo'), and I never know what they're feeling. When my father visited me in hospital a while after our encounter (yours and mine), he sat there chatting about this and that in so casual a manner I began to wonder if the police had told him the whole story. Then, halfway out the door, he stopped, and, facing away, said, still in a chatty way, 'We're awfully thankful you're alright, y'know, no matter what . . .' He couldn't carry on, waited a moment, tried again, still couldn't, and left quickly. Which I regretted. I wish he'd held me.

It was late when Mrs Gill and I got back to the hotel. The night was sweltering; people on the promenade were gleaming like at noon, wearing beachwear, but looking nude in the neon glare. I couldn't face being alone in my room, and she didn't want to go in either, so we strolled down onto the beach, and eventually out of the light from the front, to the dark stretch of shoreline before Battery Beach. Probably dangerous these days, but where isn't? We sat on the sand, Mrs Gill clutching her handbag with its precious contents, me listening to the breadfruit trees and palms above the dunes; their slushing, crackling sounds, soft as water, dry as fire.

I remarked how warm the Indian Ocean looked. She said why not go in? I replied that I didn't have a costume. She said she'd look away.

And so, in keeping with the oddity of the day, I stripped off, smiling at how diligently she held her handbag to one side of her face, and then I strolled into the sea. Its temperature was like the air, but more soothing. Within moments I had swum well away from the shore. Looking back, listening to the solitary sound of my breathing, the beachfront was a distant arrangement of light – strings, blobs and windows of it – across the black water and the black sand, where Mrs Gill sat.

Further and further I swam, wondering what I was doing. There are yellow signs along the promenade: 'Offshore nets are provided, but avoid bathing/surfing at dawn, dusk or at night when shark attack is more likely.'

Yet, like with the storm at Isandlwana, I somehow felt safe. (I mean, I haven't survived you to be hurt by a *fish*.)

As a child in Cape Town, we always heard about shark attacks along the Durban coast, and the news made us (temporarily) grateful for the icy Atlantic currents on our own beaches. When I was a teenager, and began surfing, paddling out in search of bigger waves, bigger swell formations (oh, we loved saying that phrase; it was half-wondrous, half-rude), I would sometimes reach that peculiar distance from the shore where two basic facts of life suddenly changed – the land became insignificant, and I became the only person in existence – and there I discovered that the adults had been lying. There were sharks in our own cold waters! Sharks and sea-lions, and *whales*! Huge shapes and shadows under my surfboard. Some of these things turned out to be the stuff of lies as well (a shark's fin often belonged to a dolphin), but in those teenage years, swopping surfing stories around a braai and a cooler-bag of Castles on a moonlit beach, I believed that my friends and I were a special, invincible tribe, prepared to swim with the monsters of the deep, and climb waves like mountains.

With a vague memory of those days, I began diving tonight – here in the Durban sea – curving down under the surface, kicking hard, going deep, and then floating up again, to just below the air, where I hung, face-down, as though drowned. I don't understand what it means, but it's something I do frequently nowadays, in swimming pools or the sea: dipping and diving, floating and playing dead.

No, I do understand. It's you again . . . (*everything* is you) . . . I always have a sense of you in the moment of surfacing from these dangerous games, as I gasp at the air with relief – or disbelief – before climbing up and out, the water dragging like a cloak, then falling off.

When I got back to the shore, Mrs Gill had fallen asleep. I stood above her, naked, pondering one of the mysteries of heterosexuality . . . some of those men rape old ladies; it's queer. By the time Mrs Gill woke I was dressed again and sitting alongside, elbows on knees, the fingers of one hand combing my wet hair.

We jumped as a figure suddenly slid down the dune behind us. Mr Moonje with an empty bottle of whisky. He was back from feasting with his relations, who apparently persuaded him to settle in the *New* South Africa.

'You know what is out there?' asked Mr Moonje, pointing very precisely across the sea to the north-east.

'Madagascar,' I replied smugly.

'Oh bugger Madagascar!' said Mr Moonje, making Mrs Gill tut, 'I am talking about India, my friend, India, India – the great home!'

'I thought you were from Uganda,' I said.

'I thought it was Leicester,' said Mrs Gill.

'Oh dear,' said Mr Moonje, his eyes beginning to glisten, 'I'm afraid it is all those places yes.' He pointed in different directions with both hands, almost strangling himself. 'I'm a Ugandan Indian from Leicester who's now planning to settle *here*, oh dammit.'

'Never mind love,' said Mrs Gill, 'my roots are in Isandlwana.'

Mr Moonje blinked at her with disbelief, yet respect, like one drunk to another.

Clapping my hands twice, I reminded them that we have a busy day tomorrow: visits to the Vasco da Gama Memorial Clock, the Indian Market, the Zulu gumboot-dance display, the Umnini Craft Centre; and then, in the evening, the Bay Cruise with a Champagne and Curry Banquet.

I hope there's a letter from you in the morning. I've missed you today.

Yours,

Adrian.

THIRTEEN

83143118
Pretoria Maximum Security

Don't know what day.

Adrian.

Now I've got your letters from the Kruger Park and what you call DURBS.

Sometimes you seem a bit cross with me.

I like that.

Before my trial I was under psychiatric observation at Valkenberg. There the doctors said it was alright to get cross. I think you're more than cross. You're looking for a fight.

I like that a lot. Keep it coming, buddy, keep it coming.

Only one thing you said made ME cross. That you haven't got my letter from before. You fucking liar, I DON'T believe you.

There's something a bit funny, a bit snaaks going on.

Leave it with me.

That aside, scrutinising your letters made me think the following.

We've got different landscapes.

Yours are full of dreams. Giant aloes and wild animals and DURBS and battle sites. Mine is just full of me.

So who do we reckon is more honest?

Hey, maybe you're trying to taunt me. With your freedom. With the great outdoors.

Listen pal, I've done that.

I've done the electric storms in the Drakensberg. I've stood in them, not run for a car. I've heard the sound of a thunder that roared out a warning. I've touched the great white in the black sea at midnight. I've ridden a wave that could drown the whole world. I've done it, man. Everything you've done. Everything you'll never do.

And I've definitely done DURBS.

This one time I'm there, they've got a happy-go-lucky funfair along Marine Parade. And there's this tent called the house of horrors. And I find my way in underneath. And there's this one room with a sign. DO NOT ENTER UNLESS YOU'RE OF THE STOUT-HEARTED FOR WHAT LIES WITHIN WILL HAUNT YOU FOREVERMORE. So I enter. And there's this plastic or rubber statue of an Englishman. Called Jack the Ripper. And he's worked by a kind of machine inside him. And you can't see the details but he's opening a whore from tit to cunt. And I think it's more sexy than scary. Then suddenly Jack turns to me and lifts his knife. And my bloody heart stops.

This happened again today.

A new young warder arrived this morning. Name of Knipe. Wears his hair in a crew-cut that could skin you alive. His build is short and thick, specially in his skull. Knipe reminds me of me before I was an intellectual. Knipe can't do joined-up writing. Knipe can't even do joined-up talking. He's a poor white. Lowest of the low, scum on the piss pond. Trouble is he knows it and he's out to prove otherwise. He walks up straight like he's in a steel box.

This morning he follows me and Sergeant Fourie on breakfast trolley duty so he can learn the ropes.

We're in the white suburbs again, C section.

We get to WHITE WOLF's lair. Same as usual. Lovely darkness somewhere inside the mesh. Sleepy murmur tells us to go fuck.

I see Knipe thinking this is bloody damned funny. This isn't how the rule book tells it.

Bad enough he thinks these things but then

The dumb cunt goes and says them out loud.

Fat Fourie doesn't reply. But I see him thinking the following. Right let's teach this kid his A.B.C.

You see, in here the new warders get given a baptism of fire. It puts lead in their pencils, salt on their soles. It gets them in the right mood to hang their fellow beings. By the neck. Till dead.

We get to the special cage under the 42 steps, the stairway to heaven.

I see fat Fourie whisper to Knipe. Telling him who's in there.

I see Knipe's jaw hit the floor.

I'm impressed.

A lot of poor whites are so brain dead they might not know who Dimitri is.

But Knipe does. He's only about 20 but his pa has told him the story. How a messenger boy butchered god right there in god's bloody parliament. How a whole day stopped in its tracks forthwith.

Me and Knipe go into the special cage. Fourie stays by the door.

I'm busy giving Dimitri his breakfast. No carrots this morning. I'm also busy watching Knipe.

Like with me and Jack the Ripper, Knipe is feeling more sexy than scared. He's feeling so sexy, I bet he's going to go out on the town tonight. He's going to plant his seed in some dame. He's going to father a whole line of Knipes, sons of sons, and their begotten. Just so he can say to them this. I met god's butcher.

Then suddenly, like with me and Jack the Ripper.

BANG.

Knipe jumps out of his skin.

Me too actually.

Dimitri doesn't blink.

I'm thinking what the hell was that?

Then I remember.

Dimitri's cage is under the gallows.

But what's the time? This must be well after 6.30. Yet 6.30 is THE hour. On THE big day, 6.30 is THE hour. So it can't be what I think.

81

Maybe they're just practising up there.

Fat Fourie watches from the door. Smiling.

Knipe is shaking a bit. It's not just the fright. He's got something on his mind and it's moving to the tip of his tongue. This takes time. There's a speed-limit inside the skulls of poor whites. Finally he looks Dimitri in the eye and speaks. Just one word.

Why?

He doesn't have to say more. It's the question we all want to ask.

Why did you do it?

Dimitri is the only one who looks like he doesn't understand the question.

BANG.

Out of our bloody skins again we go. Except Dimitri.

BANG.

What the fuck are they doing up there? Repairs?

BANG.

Knipe is sweating in the bright light of the cage.

Why, he asks again.

Dimitri says nothing.

Knipe says, I give you permission to break the rule of silence. You may speak.

Dimitri doesn't.

Knipe repeats it in English.

Nothing.

Suddenly fat Fourie says to Knipe, try your question in Portuguese or Greek. Dimitri speaks 5 tongues in all. It's why he got the job as parliamentary messenger. Go on. Ask him in Greek.

Knipe is blushing. And what's more he doesn't like me witnessing it. He says to fat Fourie.

Sergeant I don't speak Greek.

Fat Fourie laughs and says.

Wouldn't make any fokkin difference if you did. Dimitri SPEAKS 5 tongues but doesn't HEAR any of them. He's stone deaf. Has been for years.

Now fat Fourie comes into the cage. Puts his face nose to nose to Dimitri and shouts ISN'T THAT SO?

Dimitri blinks but it's only from the air blowing in his eyes.

Fat Fourie kisses him on the forehead.

It's a funny small kiss.

You know what? I reckon fat Fourie is also collecting stories for his sons' sons and their seed and their begotten. Stories that'll go like this.

I guarded Tsafendas day in day out. One time I got a coloured prisoner to piss on his birthday cake. Another time I even kissed Tsafendas just to taste if he was real.

Now fat Fourie says to Knipe.

You want to know WHY Dimitri did it?

Knipe says, I've heard about the big tapeworm sergeant.

Fat Fourie says, ag bullshit to the tapeworm. Dimitri also gave another reason at the time. He reckoned that Verwoerd was doing more for the coloureds than Dimitri's own people. The poor whites.

You can see Knipe now really hates these two words. POOR WHITE. Specially in front of me. A coloured.

POOR WHITE, says fat Fourie again with a smile. Rubbing it in. Pretending he doesn't know Knipe is one himself. Giving Knipe a little hiding. For mentioning the rule book at WHITE WOLF's lair. Giving Knipe a little baptism of fire.

Now fat Fourie says to Knipe, you want to know the biggest joke of all?

Yes sergeant, says Knipe in an automatic way, like in the army, what's the biggest joke of all sergeant?

Fat Fourie takes his Bic pen out of his pocket and sticks it through Dimitri's frizzy white hair. It stays there floating like a slim idea. His hair looks like a bubble, like in cartoons, with one lonely pen in it. This cartoon's called A VERWOERD EDUCATION.

Fat Fourie says.

You see? Dimitri is actually coloured himself. The sow who dropped him was black. A Mozambique kaffir who got herself stuffed by a Greek Cypriot. Somehow little Dimitri got classified white. Grew up POOR WHITE. Killed Verwoerd because he reckoned Verwoerd preferred coloureds to POOR WHITES. And maybe Verwoerd did. At least coloureds look like kaffirs and live like kaffirs. POOR WHITES look like us and want to live like us.

Knipe is blushing so much his head is going to take off. He doesn't know where to look. Then he sees me. Now he turns his blushes on me. Like a blow-torch. They've got slow brains these poor whites, but quick feelings.

I think fuck, wrong place, wrong time, here comes major shit for months on end.

If I could just go upstairs now I'd hang myself and get it over with.

Anyhow they bring me back to my own cage.

Here I can't help having a good old chuckle. Years ago they put Dimitri in the only cage which can hear that big bad BANG day in day out. And what happens? The tapeworm gets to Dimitri's eardrums and eats them up. So now he doesn't hear a thing.

Nature always gets the last laugh hey?

But then a new thought wipes the smile off my face.

Dimitri, this worm-eaten mongrel BASTER, he's one of the biggest dudes in South African history.

It's not fucking fair.

I wonder if it makes him happy? Somewhere inside that fat head with no eardrums but 5 tongues. Somewhere in all that mess, is he happy? Does he feel he made his dreams come true?

When he did the big deed in 1966 I was just starting to put together my own dreams and schemes.

This was in Bonteheuwel on the Cape Flats, there where the hot sun rises but never sets. Halfway through the afternoon it goes over the famous table mountain and does its magic on the beaches beyond. You know the kind of thing. The pink and golden postcards your BROODS buy.

My parents grew up in District Six, but Group Areas moved them to Bonteheuwel before I was born.

My daddie worked on a trawler boat. My ma-bitch cleaned fish in Kalk Bay harbour. They met there. My daddie once told me about the time they fucked me. Fish scales glittered on their arms like confetti. So they wed soon after.

That's the nice pretty version of the story. The other one

tells how they HAD to wed because I was on the way now. They HAD to because they were both from religious families. Trouble was, we're talking about different religions. Daddie was muslim malay, ma-bitch was catholic christian. In both households there was much weeping and gnashing of teeth. Daddie gave way and watered down his faith. This brought him a load of terror, he told me later. His religion is very vengeful. He expected to find allah round every corner. Or even just mister Fataar from the mosque there by Jakkalsvlei Laan. Sharpening one of those curved arab swords. Planning to slash off daddie's right hand or foot. Or head. Or to give him a public flogging right down to the bone.

Aborting me would've answered everyone's prayers. But my ma-bitch's pope doesn't like ladies slipping fishing hooks up their wombs. He says a very definite no to that, no-way-José.

Hence I came into being.

Someday you must write and thank the pope personally.

I was born into a house of horror. Full of allah's vengeance and gentle jesus's hell everlasting. Ma-bitch had sinned once. Making me. She didn't plan to sin ever again. Or for any of us to sin. I was the firstling of 9.

She gave me a christian name. John. But daddie called me Yusuf on the sly.

I did some school. School Verwoerd-style. Where you grow dimmer every day.

The only thing I was good at was drawing. Our classes didn't include what you people call ART but I did my scribbles here and there. One teacher was a white lady. She said this.

You've got too many FANTASIES in your little head.

With such a bloody look on her face.

As if this thing, this world, FANTASY, as if it had a whites-only sign above the door.

Anyhow, after I looked up FANTASY in the school library's big grey old dictionary, I got depressed. It told me it was a noun, it gave me a different spelling, PHANTASY, which made me think of ghosts, it gave me a way to pronounce it which made the job harder, fæntəsɪ, it told me it meant imagination, especially when extravagant, and day-dreams.

So if my life couldn't have these things, then this was it. Just life in the herd. Just life as trash. Nothing else.

That day was the end of my childhood, the end of innocence, blah blah.

That day I became ME.

That day I decided to put some FANTASY in my life come hell or high water. Or, at any rate, PHANTASY.

The ghostly word eventually came back to haunt me. After my arrest. When the cops failed to corroborate my confessions and everybody dubbed me the Fantasy Killer.

Meanwhile, aged 15, I left school early and hit the road.

A few years later I was arrested for vagrancy. I think it was only vagrancy. Couldn't have been more serious, because I was given two choices. Jail or coloured corps in the army.

Next thing I'm in South West, what they're now calling Namibia. First the training camp at Walvis Bay. Then to Grootfontein near the Angolan border. I'm suddenly in a war. But the coloured corps is scum, so our war-time tasks are mostly scum disposal. Washing-up in the kitchens, digging sewers and graves. Collecting trash, including some that's alive. Sometimes there's so many prisoners the camp looks like a zoo. Or a picture from the Bible. People tied to thorn trees. In the evenings we sit round the tent where they interrogate the day's catch. The whole camp is in blackout except for this tent. Like a circus. The flaps of the tent are kept raised because of the heat. We sit round watching, behind the white boys. We aren't like nuns, nurses or even vultures. We're like young people with nothing to do. There's no filmshows or TV or anything. Instead we're learning a basic fact of army life. Killing time and killing people can both take forever, but it's what we're here for. So we watch the prisoners being interrogated. They seem surprised to have an audience. Some seem embarrassed. I suppose you would be if your penis is half-severed and you're doing some very dishonourable discharges.

I don't wait for my own d.d. Like with school, I leave early.

I hit the road.

Now listen, life on the road isn't like people tell it. It isn't adventurous like Homer, dead in 700 BC, tells it. It isn't sexy like Kerouac, Jack, dead in 1969, tells it.

There's only one who tells it true. Dylan, Bob, undead. His words of wisdom include the following.

I'LL WALK A HIGHWAY OF DIAMONDS WITH NOBODY ON IT.

The roads of South Africa are long and straight. I don't have to tell you. You're a travelling man too. The land is clean. The dryness keeps things clean. My ma-bitch taught me the importance of hygiene. And you don't stink too bad in the dry. Dead or alive.

I did my first one straight after the army. My first FANTASY. Or PHANTASY. Carried on till I met you.

Then I became an intellectual.

Yours Faith Fully,

Yusuf.

FOURTEEN

The Toorkop
Ladismith
Chalet 3

Fri. 29th Sept.

Dear Yusuf,

After two overnights in Durban, we boarded our coach for the final leg of our itinerary, the section which head office insists on calling the Southbound Tropicana. I've given up fighting this kind of travel-speak – it's easier; you can do it in your sleep. 'In the next five days,' I hear myself say, 'we will be taking in two of the independent homelands – the Transkei and Ciskei – then back into the Republic for the historical town of Grahamstown with the 1820 Settler Monument . . . the Brits among you might have family trees there . . . and talking of which, we then move on into the Tsitsikamma Forest, stopping to snap its most spectacular yellow-wood, "The Big Tree", followed by an afternoon of leisure on the white beaches of Plett . . . continuing along the Garden Route, nipping up to visit Oudtshoorn, with its Cango Caves, its Crocodile and Cheetah Ranch, and its Ostrich Show Farm . . . then an overnight in a charming Karoo hotel . . . and finally Cape Town, and journey's end.'

At present we're at the charming Karoo hotel.

I love the Karoo, more than anywhere else in this country; the baking plains, the small forgotten settlements; tin roofs painted red, peeling like sunburn, creaking through the boiling afternoons; crates of Coca Cola empties stacked against flaking whitewashed walls . . . you can still get Coke in those little greenish bottles here, like in movies of the fifties.

In other respects the Karoo is changing.

Take this little town, where the hotel is – Ladismith ('Not the one you've all heard of,' I tell the brood, 'not the site of the famous Boer War siege . . . that one's spelt with a *y*, and situated in Natal'). Ladismith's giant Dutch Reformed church, circa 1851, resembling an iced cake, a white spaceship, was forced to close down recently because the congregation had dwindled so drastically. At the same time, Ladismith's Coloured population seems to have doubled every time I return. Your people: slim, handsome, loose-limbed, the women often with front teeth missing . . . all very drunk by the time we arrived at 6 p.m. (today, Friday, was pay day), and swarming towards the coach, begging, or selling crudely carved toys and salad spoons. I spotted an old woman shaking hands with Mr Moonje, and quickly shooed her away. She operates with two grandchildren. While she fastens a tourist's hands – 'Welcome, welcome!' – the kids bustle round, patting him affectionately, and removing moonbag, wallet, etc.

But once inside the hotel, the Toorkop ('Named after that 197m cleft-peaked "magic mount" you can see above the town'), everything's tickety-boo again. Margaretta Steyn, a rich Afrikaner lady dressed in the latest Riviera gear, together with her chef and toy-boy, Lourens, have created an environment which seeks to give the visitor a feel of early pioneering life, whilst enjoying every luxury. Furnished with stinkwood four-posters, and cane towel-stands warmed by braziers, the chalets are ranged round a huge courtyard, planted with bluegums and pepper trees, buzzing with heat in the upper branches, cool dark shadows below; also a magnificent old windmill ('a sculpture in rust', says their brochure), and a swimming pool in smoky black. Lourens' menu seeks to cross traditional farm fare – braais and bredies – with nouvelle cuisine.

'Hey, pass the word round – this food stinks!' said Mr Frawley from Brisbane, at supper. There was a tense pause, then the head waiter, Dam, a delightful old chap (he claims to be over 100, and of pure Bushman blood) winked at me, and continued serving, dutifully whispering, 'The food stinks,' to each of the brood. Everyone was in hysterics. I do believe I actually saw Mr F. *blush* as, now, he made a big show of wiping his cutlery, which he does whenever 'Abbo' waiters (like old Dam) serve at table – but no-one was watching. Over the last few days, even our London cabby Lenny Webb has been forbidden (by wife Bunny) from socialising with Frawley, as his jokes became cruder and cruder, and as he started to ignore our on-coach smoking rules (cigarettes only), puffing on dark wet cigars, leaving them everywhere, along with used ear buds and meaty toothpicks, to mark his territory . . . his very isolated territory, I'm afraid. (Well, there's his frightened little wife, but I don't think they've spoken in years.) No, Mr F. has become the new leper of the group.

Our other one, Ms Blanche Appleton, was dining on her own as usual this evening, saying, 'Yum, yum, isn't this good, mmm, delicious,' to no-one in particular. We caught one another looking at Mr F., both interested in his loneliness, for different reasons. Failing to unlock Blanche's gaze, I gave a small smile. She returned it. My smile was polite, professional. Hers was not. My heart sank. I knew what was coming, any day now . . .

Usually, after supper at this hotel, I take my broods on the Milky Way Walk; out into the veld, where, with no man-made lights around, I give them my speciality act, my party turn, which none of the other guides can do: a tour of the night sky. You can see every star in the southern hemisphere here.

But tonight the weather was overcast (perhaps some rain is finally heading this way), so we all retired to our rooms for an early night.

At about 3 a.m. I woke with the usual dream – me among a crowd, your shoulder coming into view – and lay there, heart thudding. But I will *not* let you be a thing of nightmares; I *will* keep you human. So I fetched my TOSHIBA lap-top and sat in bed composing this letter.

(There was, by the way, still no letter from you waiting for me at reception here. Wasn't really expecting correspondence in this isolated spot, but disappointed all the same. Maybe you weren't serious about our agreement – to write as friends.)

I'd finally calmed down when a cat began to cry. Oh, it's a terrible sound. Like from a different arrangement of the universe. Inside that animal skull, just beyond those unfamiliar eyes and teeth, I swear there's a human brain, a human throat, a human soul reborn in a small sleek body, on all fours, and only able to cry, to cry without hope. That's why the sound is so drawn-out, so relaxed in a way; the creature is certain that there's no hope; it's crying out to no-one; it knows that no-one is there.

Even as this thought occurred, the cat stopped crying, and my door began to open. As in a dream, or a Hollywood movie, you threatened to enter. You, somehow escaped. You, having tracked me down.

No breath inside me. No blood running. Ice cold. And then a tingle – of excitement – a tingle that sickens me to mention.

But it was Blanche who came in, dressed, like her namesake, B. du Bois, in a thin nightie, made of faded, silky stuff that doesn't stay on the shoulder.

'The clouds have cleared,' she said. 'I saw your light on. Could we perhaps do the Milky Walk after all?'

I wanted to shout, 'Couldn't you have knocked? I'm not on duty twenty-four hours a day! And you're not interested in the walk. I know what you really want!' But the cat had unsettled me; I didn't want to be alone; so I said, 'Yeah sure, why not?'

As I crossed the room, she didn't clear the doorway; if anything she blocked it more, her gaze on the floor, giving a small hurt smile, with something else in it, something private.

To have stopped in front of her would have been aggressive – intimate somehow, with us both in our flimsy summer nightwear – so I squeezed past, startled by the glow of booze coming off her, and went into the unlit corridor, whispering something like, 'Now let's see which way . . .' She followed silently through the darkness, still smiling I sensed.

Every outer door was locked, with no key or latch in sight; perhaps worked electronically, like the house-protection systems in Joburg. I was appalled. Not just by the thought of what would happen if there was a fire, but because this kind of security wasn't in operation just a month or two ago, when I was here last. I mean, people didn't lock anything in this part of the world; people didn't even *close* their front doors on hot nights . . .

There was no night porter; obviously part of Margaretta Steyn's attempt to create the impression that we're not in a hotel, but a Karoo homestead. Nothing for it but to climb out of a window – a small, rusty window from before the conversion; the only one we found that wasn't locked as well. The manoeuvre was tricky, holding up the sliding insect screen with one hand, the metal frame cutting into your sides, as you climbed – or rather poured yourself – through. I was aware that Blanche was presented with a tangled, but frank view of loins and legs during my exit. When it came to her turn, she couldn't manage it at all, so I hauled her out, and she ended up in my arms. Pressed this close, her nightie and my short pyjamas became irrelevant – like we were wearing nothing at all. The details of her bony female body were curious to feel. Then she slid down, her hips passing mine, our intimacy complete for a moment . . .

Behind the hotel, the gravel route out of town was ringing with insects. Because of a solitary streetlamp and the hotel's art deco neon sign, there was at first no sight of the stars. But within minutes we had left Ladismith behind and reached the veld, where, in a strange unfolding of my vision, the night was suddenly alight; a buoyant landscape, without greens or reds, but all in silver, white and black. It was a flattering light for Blanche; the lines round her mouth and those thin-skinned electric-wire temples were smoothed over, and her beauty became glacial. Garbo was at my side now, descended from the stars; or Dietrich . . .

I began my patter; it's much more heartfelt than when I describe the Voortrekker Monument or Vasco da Gama Clock. Here I throw back my head, basking in the cool light and savouring the marvellous, antique, utterly un-South African words, 'That's Lyra, Cygnus, and Corona, there's Hydras and Centaurus. Oh and look how perfect the Southern Cross is tonight, and the Southern Triangle, and look, just look at the Milky Way – look at the clouds and lakes and long dusty roads of it.'

Blanche wasn't making any of her customary noises: her tuts, squeaks or purrs. She was very peaceful. Then at last she said, 'Indeed, so, there we are – the universe.' I was reminded of Mrs Gill at Isandlwana, saying, 'Well, there we are – my roots.' When one travels abroad, I think one does imagine such things: that you're able to glimpse whole worlds, whole histories.

There were no more stars to talk about. The silence between Blanche and I stretched and stretched. I knew what was coming – I saw her private smile out of the corner of my eye – but I was still surprised by how she put it.

'You've made me so happy these last two weeks. Thank you.'

She described her life as dark and stuffy, and said that I'd brought some clean air to her, some light. 'You shine with light,' she said. 'It's a very decent light.' The particular light in my eyes is, according to her, kind, slightly tired, sad. As though I'd seen things which others hadn't. 'You seem older than your years,' she said. I didn't explain . . . no, I didn't mention you.

'It's with me when I wake and go to sleep, your light,' she said, 'and it's like no-one has seen it before. It makes me dizzy. I'm sick and excited. I'm opening myself to alarming things, but it's a kind of glory too. Here it starts, a voice inside says, here we go, you'll never be the same again, you'll never be well again, never just yourself – but full of his light.'

She took breath and stared at me. I was speechless. Although these declarations have often been made, and always roundabout this stage of a tour, they've never been phrased like hers before. She laughed gently, and said, 'Please don't worry dear. These feelings afflict me often. Five or six times a year, at least. More if I go on holiday.'

I laughed too, then thought about what she'd just said, and was even more astonished. At last I managed to begin a programmed response: 'Well, I'm just sorry that I can't . . .'

She said, 'Please don't. No need. Nothing is expected. It's enough to tell you. I make it my rule. I need to explain to all of you, all my lovers, that although I steal a sense of you, your light, and I take it deep inside me, it is not sordid. We all do it. We steal any light that draws us, from colleagues, or their spouses, or even strangers in the street or a shop — we steal their light, take it into us, and they never know.' She paused, thinking hard, then added, 'Well, I prefer it if they *do*.'

She said again, 'It is not sordid.'

Reassured, I gazed at her beauty in the starlight, and felt happy, privileged in a way, as though it really was Garbo or Dietrich who had decided to spend an hour with me in the veld.

I took her hand. She said, 'No need, but thank you.' She asked if this happened to me often? I confessed it did. She asked if they were always middle-aged women? I confessed this too. 'And I suspect,' she said, 'you'd rather it was their sons.' I laughed, and said she was wrong there. I was celibate. She asked why. I said something had happened; it was difficult to ever trust someone again; to trust sleeping next to another person. She misunderstood, thinking I'd been betrayed in love. I didn't correct her, though I could've told her the story, I think.

Walking back into Ladismith, the darkness suddenly started to vanish, fast. The dawn was gathering like a distant fire behind the hills; the sound of insects gave way to birds, a dog, a rooster, and now a man coughing as he woke . . .

This human sound brought a sense of fear again. I wondered why the hotel needed to lock itself so securely against the local population. I thought about the speed with which that population multiplies, the speed with which Ladismith changes, even the speed of the dawn itself — it rushes at you, takes your breath away, and rushes on. There's a dangerous rhythm in this continent. Like its big game, Africa lies torpid most of the time, heavy, hot, dust-caked, but when it suddenly wakes, suddenly moves . . . God help us.

As Blanche and I climbed back through the window, Mr Moonje was slipping out of one of the rooms (I think he's bonking one of the widows in my brood), and saw us. Last Sunday he found me on a beach with Mrs Gill in the middle of the night – now this. He probably thinks I've got a thing about older women.

Anyway, he smiled approvingly – his religion teaches respect for the elderly.

Yours,

Adrian.

FIFTEEN

83143118
Pretoria Maximum Security

The 6th stinking day in some year of our Lord.

For 6 days now there's been no running water in Beverly Hills.

We can hear plumbing being rattled and banged. And we hear a fire engine come and go. It sounds very close. Like they've driven it right inside. A big fire engine on the loose in death row. Like an elephant. Too big to fit. Only its trunk can reach into the shower room to fill buckets with water.

These buckets is what we wash in now.

But so far the warders have only allowed it twice in 6 days.

Our smells have festered.

They bring round an urn once a day. Round the cages. To flush our shitbowls and fill our sinks. But once a day isn't enough.

I'm sleeping in a lavatory, eating in a lavatory, writing to you in a lavatory.

Sniff the paper, buddy.

At first I tried cleaning myself like on the open road. Like a cat. But the open road always leads over the next horizon, to the sea, a dam, a river. Here there's no horizons. Only more and more of me. And I can't clean ME fast enough. Now my slime is like a skin. Now my shitbrown colour feels like the real thing. Bringing a disease you whities get. Psychosomatic. A sweatiness. A swollenness between the ears. And wild guts.

Causing me to defecate more than once a day. In a bowl I can't flush.

This afternoon, into my stinking cage, comes your letter. Your clean white letter.

Full of your bloody dirty lies.

Still claiming you're not getting my letters, blah blah. Still bowling me that shit. Still messing with my mind. Still busy with some scheme.

I'll sniff it out, you hear? You fucking hear?

Blanche's NAMESAKE, Blanche du Bois. Who the fuck's that? Is she from a classic book of French literature? Is she from a film by Walt Disney? I'm not scared to say I don't know. Education is like burglary. You take what you can. Fast. Some things get left behind.

But I like it when you got Blanche in the veld. Why didn't you pump her? I would have pumped the bitch to hell and gone while the moonlight kept her pretty. Re-reading that bit, I can picture her skin. Smooth, cold and blue.

With this thought in my head and my temper in my hand, I start a five-tackle-one.

Only to be interrupted by Sergeant fat Fourie.

Shoving me onto library duty today.

The books jump around on the trolley. Driven by my damp shivery hands. Down the corridors we go. Long rolls of floor, long white lights, sweaty walls, a stink in the air like a pulse. Man, I'm like my aborigine brothers, or ABBOS as your mister Frawley says, I'm on DREAMTIME today.

As we approach the WHITE WOLF's lair, it looks like, fuck me, his cage door is OPEN.

I'm FINALLY going to see him.

A little scrum of warders are gathered outside. As we squeeze through, I hear the warders saying to him CON-GRATULATIONS, CONGRATULATIONS in Afrikaans. Is this a mockery? Like with Dimitri's birthday cake? No. This is for real. They're bearing little gifts. Smokes, homemade rusks, biltong, blah blah, maybe some frankincense and myrrh too.

Now I remember the news during yesterday's talking time. WHITE WOLF is getting engaged today. To a teacher. Like

McBride before him, WHITE WOLF is using his time on death row to map out his future.

I still can't see the man himself. Too many arms, elbows, butts in the way. But I can see a part of his cage. Religious pictures and symbols on the wall. And, I'm almost sure, a framed portrait of the Boer of Boers, Mister White-earth, Eugene Terre-blanche-du-bois. But now, as we're squeezing through to the other end, now there he is. The WOLF. Sitting on his bed. Still wearing that smile.

He was known as the smiling killer, hey?

It's a smile I've only seen on one other person in my life. That nun who visited me. It's the smile of someone who's a hundred per cent sure about existence. You'd think a person would have to live a long time to earn that smile. Yet WHITE WOLF is young. Early twenties. Slim and fit. Chin so dimpled it's like a pair of balls. Nose so long it's like a Jewman's. Not that he is a Jewman. No siree. Right now he's busy giving the warders a little sermon from the mount. And in the bit I hear, he's telling them how today's Jewmen aren't really white people.

Noticing us pass, he now stops talking for a second.

To smile at me.

A ghost climbs on my back and rides away with me.

I'm not easily scared. But fuck it, that dude is tuned into something else altogether.

The heat in my head is starting to bubble.

Meanwhile me and fat Fourie have turned right. Towards Dimitri's cage. And another surprise.

The door is open here too.

But the man himself has gone.

Prisoners are washing out his cage. With buckets and buckets of disinfectant. Supervised by the coloured warder, brandy Adams.

I think, by gum, they've finally gone and done it.

They've hanged Dimitri.

But then I hear fat Fourie and brandy Adams saying how THE PRISONER, they don't use his name, has been moved to Zonderwater Prison there by Cullinan.

My brain is on the boil now.

McBride getting married, WHITE WOLF getting engaged. Why? If they're sentenced to hang.

Dimitri moved from death row to somewhere nicer. Why? If he's sentenced to hell on earth.

Something IS going on out there. In what your tourist bosses want to call the NEW S.A.

Maybe in this NEW S.A., it isn't Mandela, but Dimitri who'll be released. For butchering the grand wizard and architect of apartheid. Maybe they'll put up a statue of him outside parliament. There in the Gardens where you and me met on THAT fateful day. You remember the fountain? With the statue of a boy hugging a giant fish. Maybe they'll replace it with a statue of Dimitri hugging his giant tapeworm.

Now fat Fourie notices me staring into Dimitri's cage and says what's the matter?

I say, no nothing my sergeant boss, I was just thinking about Tsafendas.

Fat Fourie turns to brandy Adams and says, we never had a prisoner here called Tsafendas did we?

Brandy Adams replies we definitely never did sergeant.

Then fat Fourie looks at me and says, you were called the Fantasy Killer during your trial hey? Are you now aiming to become the Fantasy Prisoner too hey?

He and brandy Adams laugh. Also the other prisoners.

I think, no please don't do this to me. Not today. Not with my brain so sore already.

Fat Fourie tells me to move on. I try to. I try really hard. Fat Fourie helps me try, with a shove. Brandy Adams comes over to help too. MOVE YOU FOKKIN COLOURED BASTARD this coloured man cries in my ear.

As my legs give in I'm half-aware of my face hitting the library trolley. A book called KANE AND ABEL. Is this a new bible? Then my eye slips over its author. Jeffrey Archer. Is he alive or dead?

Now I'm looking up at the ceiling and its endless lights. Adams leans in to shout at me some more. I don't hear what he says. But I get his smell. Brandy and home-rolled smokes.

This smell makes the shape of my daddie.

My daddie. The watered-down muslim who liked a drink. And lived in fear of allah punishing him for it. And for everything else.

My daddie. His face looked stamped on. His eyes looked like it had just happened.

My ma-bitch's face was like one of the fish she spent her life cleaning at Kalk Bay harbour. Flat, cross and old. She looked the same in their wedding photo. With me, their sin, in her belly. Aged 17 there was nothing left of her to fade away. Except the strange fair hair she bestowed on me.

Mind you, she's still got her front teeth in that wedding photo. In your letter, you mention how the coloured women in Ladismith are minus their front teeth. Yes. The passion gap. It makes talking and eating hard. But cocksucking beautifully soft.

So I don't know why ma-bitch had the operation. She would never've done anything dirty with her mouth. She didn't like dirt. We were 11 people in one and a half rooms. Made of corrugated iron, chicken wire, and lino. A small see-through house with all the landscapes of our flesh. But ma-bitch found ways of keeping us decent. We were wrapped up in separate pieces of plastic, or else blue-beaten. In the name of Jesus. And as for daddie, she hammered him most of all.

She could've been a professional boxer, I swear.

In her opinion, daddie's only plus was his singing voice. And this she only allowed on special occasions. Like christmas on boiling December afternoons. Then my daddie was allowed to be like he was in the bars at the harbour. With a home-rolled braai-ing his knuckles and a brandy glass going sweaty.

He did all the klopse songs like Januarie, Februarie, but his all-time favourite was a Bing Crosby number, Danny Boy. Originally an Irish number, according to ma-bitch. She had Irish sailors in her blood. So when daddie crooned this to her, then at last she looked pleased he was her man.

Oh danny boy. The pipes, the pipes are calling. From glen to glen. And down the mountain side. The summer's gone and all the roses falling. It's you it's you must go and I must bide.

What the fuck did he know about pipes and glens? My dull cunt fool of a daddie.

Of course, psychiatrists, criminologists, behavioural geneticists and political scientists try to explain me through my background. Everything must have a reason. A label. Like this.

SOCIO-ECONOMIC FACTORS IMPACTING ON NEURO-CHEMISTRY.

Other scientists talk about my brain wave patterns, my hyper-activity, my high level of the male hormone testosterone, my low turn-over of the brain chemical serotonin. Years ago the scientists would have talked about the size of my forehead or jaw. Or that I only stand 5'5" above sea level.

I do NOT like labels. That's why I meet all my shrinks head on. I will not let them tell me that I removed ALMOST 50 people from god's earth because I don't like kissing.

Remember me not liking kissing?

Mind you, that was reasonable. Kissing a man is like kissing sandpaper.

Once my ma-bitch caught me kissing my darling younger sister Pearl.

I'm 8, Pearl's 6, no harm's done. But my ma-bitch, boxing for Jesus, she took me to 11 rounds.

Does that explain me?

You fool, you fucking fool. Your thinking is as sloppy as a bloody birthing cunt. That sewer.

In any case, many years later I find myself in Beverly Hills.

Coming round from unconsciousness. Back into dream-time.

Now I'm in the shower room, lying in the drains.

The young warder Knipe is throwing a bucket of water over me. Knipe with the razor-sharp crew cut above a very blunt brain.

The prison doctor is here too. Doctor van Zyl. He's the younger brother of the prison priest. Dominee van Zyl. The van Zyl brothers. I don't think either of them get a lot of what's called job satisfaction. I mean, when a person sets out to be a priest or a doctor, he's not planning to work in Beverly Hills, is he? But of the two, Doctor van Zyl is definitely the more pissed off. A priest can still save souls in here, but a doctor is never going to save a single life.

He says to me, now what's the matter with you?

I try to tell him. My swollen headaches, my wild guts.

As I talk, he pulls a funny expression. The bones of his face seem to be ripping open his face. In retrospect I think he was yawning.

I try a different approach. Saying this.

I just need a wash.

This shakes him awake. Hygiene isn't high on his own list of priorities. He looks like a loose sack of trash, his shirt never stays tucked in, bits of things are hanging in his beard. He frowns at me. How can a man be sick just from lack of WASHING? Then he nods at Knipe, who throws another bucket of water over me. And another. Plus another. They smile. They think they're being cruel. But it's so good, man. Lovely clean water. Holy water.

Doctor van Zyl says, better now?

I say, yes thank you doctor sir, bless you sir.

He goes.

I start to rise, expecting to be taken back to my cage. But Knipe isn't budging. He stands looking at me with his small eyes. Poor-white Knipe who didn't like a coloured man witnessing that baptism of fire on his first day. In Dimitri's cage. When Dimitri wasn't just a figment of my imagination.

Knipe lights a van Rijn.

He says, yous want me to clean yous up properly?

I start to reply.

He says SILENCE.

He goes over to the shaving mirrors, unlocks a cupboard and takes out a blade.

As he walks back to me, I reach for it.

He shakes his head. Starts to shave me himself.

Without foam. And the blade is very dull.

I could stop him. My hands are free. In fact I could hurt him. Badly. I've got nothing to lose. He knows this.

We're daring one another.

Meanwhile my arms stay at my side.

Meanwhile he carries on.

Peeling away the sandpaper round my mouth. Hard little strokes. Sometimes the dull blade overshoots. Onto my lips. I taste rust and blood. Knipe leans in close. So close we could kiss. And now he starts whispering sweet nothings. Like the following.

Yous think yous a tough guy hey? We's gonna have a good old laugh when we hang yous.

I try to raise the level of conversation. I say so listen warder Knipe sir, do you feel that socio-economic factors impacted on your neuro-chemistry as a poor white?

I expect him to yell SILENCE. Instead he blinks and says, don't call me that.

I say white?

He says poor. I take home R19,776 per annum.

I say but you were brought up poor white weren't you?

He says DON'T say that.

I say why not? It's only words. Only air inside the face. Speak the words slowly and they just move the mouth around a bit. The first word, POOR, makes a kind of sigh. The second, WHITE, gives the lips a little smile. No, the only problem I can see is that the two words don't belong together.

Still he doesn't shout SILENCE. Just tilts up my chin to work on my throat. The old blade scrapes round my adams apple. Slowly, slowly. Dragging the skin. Till it starts to part. No more. Only enough to put in a sting. Now and then some hot ash from his van Rijn.

I rise away from the pain.

Like I learned going 11 rounds with my ma-bitch.

It gives me power. Rising away from pain. In fact it makes me invincible. Such a good bloody thrill.

It's why I often go looking for a bit of danger.

Like you visiting KwaZulu that time hey?

Something in us likes it hey?

Blood brothers hey?

Hell Adrian, I've just had a brainwave. I know why you're

pretending to not get my letters. I told you I'd sniff it out. Today's fever has helped. Nature can teach wisdom. As can every tree. These are the words of Rasputin, Grigori Efimovich, dead then alive, then dead, then alive, etcetera, in 1916.

The reason you're pretending not to get my letters is because I never answered your first BIG DIFFICULT question. What happened between us in that hotel room? My side of the story. I haven't told you that yet. So you're punishing me.

Hey sorry, buddy. Of course I'll tell you my side of the story.

It was a bad November morning. Late morning. Lunchtime soon. But no bucks, no scoff. A hell of a wind. The hot Berg wind. Grey clouds with messy white edges. Like teeth, old men's beards, spunk in water. I was feeling the weight of my deeds. At that time I didn't have the comfort of the scientific explanations aforementioned in this letter.

All I knew was a kind of hangover. A kind of boredom. Freefall.

I was in such a bad way I'd even stopped washing. A serious build-up of slime.

I think I was quite a dangerous bloke roundabout this time.

The trouble was I couldn't remember my score. Maybe I'd reached the goal. 50. If only I could be clear how many I'd done. If only my deeds had been noticed. If only the cops and newspapers were keeping score. Because IF I was already there I could make the BIG change. Go to the police and become famous. I was fed-up scratching in bins.

What I'm saying is maybe I wanted to be caught.

There has to be a reason why I went for you.

You weren't my kind of thing. Being of the white tribe. Except once before.

Anyhow, I arrived through the Queen Victoria Street entrance of the Gardens. I hate the Gardens so I don't know why I went into them. Unless God wanted us to meet. Or maybe the pope. The reason I hate the Gardens is because I hate trees. They close in on me. They bring darkness. I'm more a veld man. Like you, I like the Karoo. Maybe if we'd met there we would've just been good friends. But don't rely on it pal. I did 34 in the Karoo. Or 33.

So there I am in the Gardens on a windy November morning. The weather is grey and sticky. It rests on you like a spider's web. Not many people around. Working people are working. School parties are being dragged to the Museum. Cocks are crowing. In cages. These look like zoo cages, but there's only cocks, chickens and budgies in them.

How am I going to get through the next few hours?

If I had 30 cents I'd buy a Lexington from that bloke who sells singles on his cardboard box.

I see some coloured kids sniffing a plastic bag. I run into them like a mad dog and steal the bag but the fucking thing is sucked dry.

I'm so fed up, I do the thing I hate most. I sit under a tree. It's the tree in the middle. Near the cages with chickens and budgies. The biggest tree in captivity. Halfway up, like at the waist, five other trees climb out of it. Round the lower part are benches.

On one of the benches is me.

I don't know what kind of tree it is. A rubber tree maybe. The lower part could definitely be rubber. It has melted into a whole floor of tree. Some bits of the floor are rotting away and turning into pulp. Could be the stuff of newspapers soon. Me too, I hope. The bark is like an elephant's skin. Hard wrinkles. Also like a man's skin. Knuckles, abscesses, sores. Also like a plant's skin. Moss, mould, birdshit. The whole thing is so old it makes you ache, man. I sit there staring at the tree's rudeness. Lots of folds and slits. I climb up to the waist and look in. A big dark wet hollow hole is here. People use it as a trash bin. There used to be a wire grate to stop people throwing things in. But now the wire grate is down there as well. I can also see other items. A Fanta tin. Tissues. A piece of tin foil. A woman's soiled broeks. And some light. Deep in this black hole, some light has got in. I kill it with my shadow. Then I climb back down and sit on one of the benches again. Nearby are proper decent trash bins. Blue plastic. With nice writing. KEEP THE CAPE IN SHAPE. Someone has made a fire in one. The blue bottom hangs out all twisted like a baboon's. More rubbish round my feet. Pigeon shit, dusty smoke stubs, used baby preventatives. Rubbers round the rubber tree. The place stinks. People have done their private piss in a public place. People will do anything and everything under this tree. Because of its darkness. And the bushes all round.

In any case, I sit there. In the piss-stinking shadows. Under the big bloody immortal rubber tree. With the wind giving it hell. And a cock in a zoo cage crowing at noon. There I sit, at the bottom of my life.

Then you arrive.

Into the rubber tree circle.

You sat on the bench two away. I was surprised that you would put nice ironed white shorts on a bench where people had done anything and everything. It occurred to me that there must be money in those white shorts. So at that stage, say 10 seconds into our encounter, I was just thinking of begging a few coins. Or taking them off you. But quick, clean. You'd have just gone away with an empty wallet, a red face, and a promise from the police to find the culprit sir.

So.

It's 10 seconds into our encounter.

I think you're cruising for a bruising.

But.

We're both in for a surprise.

Listen here, I'd like to carry on with this story but my throat is still burning a bit from Knipe's shave. Shame hey? And it's bedtime now.

So I'll carry on in the next letter.

That is IF another letter is to be written.

Up to you.

I do NOT believe you're not getting my letters. You are lying.

Meanwhile let's leave our story just as we're about to meet.

The wind is growing. The cock is crowing. You're just about to turn and see me for the first time.

Let's sleep on that.

Yours Faith Fully,

Yusuf.

III. MURDERS

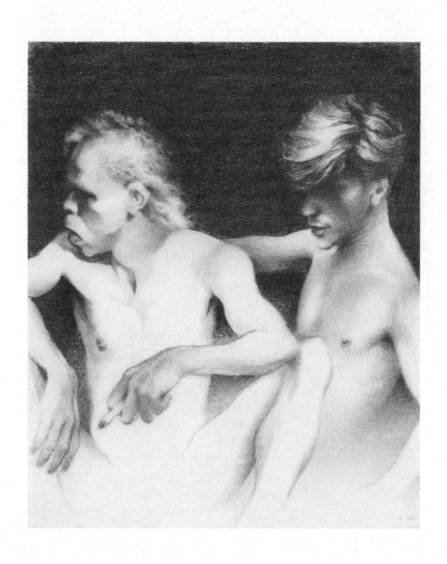

SIXTEEN

'The Nook'
4 Craigrownie Rd
Bantry Bay
Cape Town 8001

Sat. 30th Sept.

Dear Yusuf,

Your letters were waiting for me at home in Bantry Bay
– two of them. I suppose our 'postman' found my itinerary
too complicated, and simply sent them here.

I found the idea of opening the envelopes, of actually
reading the letters, difficult, and haven't done so yet.

From Ladismith we travelled to Swellendam, picked up
the N2, did a long stretch where there's nothing to see;
the brood tried to sleep, but I wouldn't let them, taking
this opportunity to brief them on Cape Town; and then
finally at about 1500 hours this afternoon, looking across a
silvery stretch of False Bay, I spoke the line which always
makes my voice falter: 'And there, folks, is your first view
of the famous Table Mountain, and my hometown . . .'

Your hometown too, of course. As the N2 cut across
the Cape Flats, I departed from my usual script, my
SATOUR-approved script, and mentioned the townships
we were passing, including, on the right, Bonteheuwel . . .
thinking how alien the word sounds.

Unusually, my father wasn't waiting outside the Cape Town
Towers to see the coach draw in. He sets great store by all
partings and reunions (and particularly with me – since my

encounter with you); they're the only occasions I've seen him show emotion, and even then he disguises it with a sort of cough, a sort of gasp. This ritual of waiting for my coach to arrive is sweet but embarrassing: it's absurd for me, at my age, and the tour *guide*, to have daddy waiting there! I never go over to him; I give a half-wave, blushing, hoping none of the brood notice. He seems content with this; it's enough to see me there, returned, well and safe. Then he catches the Sea Point bus, gets off halfway along Main Road, goes down to the beachfront, and strolls home to Bantry Bay, killing a few more hours. He's not enjoying retirement.

When he wasn't outside the hotel this afternoon, I knew something was wrong, but there was no time to phone. I had to check in the brood. Although I was worried and distracted, a different version of me takes over on these occasions — a kind of dance version; head waiters do it too; very deft, it's performed with the tips of your being: on tiptoe, with fingertips touching, and the tip of the tongue going terrif, tremendous, tickety-boo!

An hour later my brood were settled; the rest of the day was theirs, to shop, swim or relax, before the tour's last few days — sightseeing round the peninsula. Young Gideon, our Coloured coach driver, had finished supervising the distribution of luggage to the rooms, and offered to drop me off at home. It was a lovely Cape Town afternoon: bright blue, bright wind. I told Gideon to take the Kloof Nek route, and asked if he had any dope. He did, and we shared a joint, circling Table Mountain, all alone in our luxury coach.

I wonder if my recurring dream of a tidal wave, awesome yet safe, comes from that wall of rock rising out of the centre of my city, rising and rising, with a white crest of cloud curling over the top.

'The cloud is called, guess what folks, the tablecloth,' chanted Gideon, imitating me. I laughed, and joined in: 'An Afrikaner legend tells of an old burgher with a pipe, attempting to outsmoke the devil, while meteorologists offer an equally fascinating explanation . . .'

In Clifton I saw a beautiful youth, a surfer, carrying quite a classy homemade board, about 2m, with rounded pin tail. He was coming up off First Beach, dressed in a small hipster costume and a white shirt, and eating an ice cream. The wind blew the shirt off his shoulders, and he laughed; all by himself he laughed. For a moment he was wearing a small parachute, the white cotton billowing behind his naked shoulders and chest, caught wetly round his tummy and costume, above long naked legs. He looked so beautiful, so troublefree, licking his ice cream, laughing as the wind undressed him. People turned to smile and stare.

'I used to look like that, Gids,' I said. Gideon suddenly went quiet, as though I'd told him I fancied the boy (which in a way I had). Although new to the agency, Gideon's probably been told about me and 'the case'. Ever since they all found out, I'm sure they tell newcomers – and wives, husbands, friends – it's good dinner-party stuff – and I don't blame them, I just wish someone would talk to *me* about it. But I suppose, like with rape victims, there's some suspicion about my involvement. (I need to talk to you about that sometime.) Anyway, here's a joke I heard. What's the difference between involvement and commitment? Think of a plate of bacon and eggs. The chicken is involved, the pig is committed.

Mum was in the front garden, gardening, wearing her battered Panama with elastic chin strap, and little sunglasses, her plump arms shining with sunblock. She waved and buzzed open our flimsy security gate before I could get out my key, saying, 'Hullo there,' as though I'd just been out to the shops, rather than the length and breadth of the Republic.

By now it was just past six o'clock, but Father wasn't on the stoep with his first Scotch and soda. I knew something was wrong, yet Mum looked as jolly as ever.

My mother is irrepressibly jolly, laughing as she speaks; no matter what the topic, little chuckles bubble up among her words like extra vowels. I used to think it was an endearing habit, demonstrating a healthy view of life, but these days I'm not so sure – her constant chuckles sound more and more nervous. Maybe the timbre just changes when she's with me. Because, like the people at work, none of my family have ever talked to me about you. I expect Mum would've been very shocked today to know that you were the author of the letters she directed me to in the hall; in fact, it might have stopped her laughter forevermore.

God, it was strange to see your letters on the hallway table. To touch you again. In my home.

Ours is one of those smallish, single-storeyed houses built in the 20s, with a modest gable and a silver corrugated roof sloping into a beautiful curve, like a breaking wave, over the stoep. During the summer months, this is where we sit, eat, drink, read, sometimes sleep on sweltering nights. It has two squat pillars, their cream paint always peeling, and a red polished floor, worn down to a cement-grey here and there – and pure white where we step most.

We keep all blinds and shutters half-closed against the sun, so this makes the interior rather gloomy, sepia-coloured, dull yet restful, as though frozen one Sunday afternoon a few decades ago. Then in the hallway (where I stood today with your letters, holding them to my nose), here the brownish, still shadows give way to light again, gently at first on the stoep, then blindingly in the garden: a haze of sunshine and sprinklers.

Mum moved about in this bright blur, sometimes visible, sometimes not, laughing all the time, giving me an update on the family tidings: my brother Brian's divorce; my older sister Sheila's progress in the drying-out clinic; my younger sister Maggie in the one for anorexics; rich Uncle Jimbo arrested for shop-lifting again; his wife, Auntie Milly, leaving him for another woman; their children's problems with truancy, drugs and bed-wetting; Auntie Doris's latest 'mystery' illness; her son Graham's refusal to leave home or find work although he's forty this month; and cousin Emma having her face slapped by a beggar.

'No news then?' I said. 'Just the day-to-day life of white Africans.'

We laughed together, and I told Mum the joke I'd heard about this *New* South Africa we're being promised: there's light at the end of the tunnel alright, but it's an oncoming train! Mum laughed again, but she was looking away, and

I knew there was something else, some other news, which she hadn't told me.

'And what about Father?' I said. 'He wasn't at the Towers to see the coach in.'

She said, 'No. He's sitting in the back yard. I'm afraid . . .' but her voice was drowned by the building works alongside the house; they've knocked down the old hotel, the Lion's Head, and are building time-share holiday flats. Where our view used to be of the hotel lawns and the sea, now there's this darkness, this concrete shadow, hanging in the sky. The construction is due to go on for five years, so, like people who live near airports, we've learned not to compete with the noise, but to pause till it passes. Mum carried on gardening and I stood staring at her comfy old Panama, her soft neck, the side of her face, turned away, avoiding my gaze. At last she continued: 'Yes, I'm afraid he was attacked last Friday. Mugged. On the beachfront. In broad daylight. Well, early morning. Taking his constitutional.'

Various urgent questions crowded into my head. For some reason I asked the least important one first: 'I've phoned a dozen times since then – why didn't you tell me?'

'We thought it best not to upset you.'

I imagined the various discussions: with my alcoholic and anorexic sisters, my depressed divorced brother, my cousin who had her face slapped by a beggar, even maybe with my father (how badly was he hurt?); everyone saying, 'Best not to upset Adrian, not after what he's been through himself. Best not to tell him while he's working, best to tell him afterwards.'

My family talking, talking, talking about 'the case', but never with *me*!

I became angry with Mum, but the building works were thundering again, and the giant crane suddenly threw a terrible shadow – like a crashing plane – right into our garden. Mum continued to potter around, as though nothing was happening.

'There you are,' she said when there was a break in the noise. 'That's why we didn't tell you. Knew it would upset you.'

'I'm upset *because* you didn't tell me!'

'The news itself doesn't upset you?'

'Of course. But . . .'

'There you are, y'see,' she chuckled, facing me now, and even taking off her sunglasses, but shutting her eyes in a prolonged blink. 'We couldn't win either way. You get so easily upset these days.'

It's alright to get upset, I wanted to shout, certain things *are* upsetting!

Instead I marched away, through the house.

My family get by on silence and laughter. They're still so very English. Particularly the older generation. You'll have seen them up and down the Sea Point promenade: they speak with gentle South African accents, and are more tanned than any Afrikaner, with huge freckles dappling their foreheads. The ladies wear cotton frocks with faded floral patterns, and the chaps are in long shorts and long socks, in grey, green or mustard, sporting crisp white moustaches, and full, white heads of hair.

Today I found Father with his hair shaved across the back, to make room for fourteen stitches, which looked like a row of black worms. He seemed to be wearing a mask; his features, already caricatured by age, now looked altogether surreal, with swellings and multicoloured bruises.

We greeted one another in the usual way: I begin with, 'How are you old bean?' and he replies almost in song, 'Tickety-boo – you?', then I sing back, 'Tickety-boo too!'

I asked him about the attack, but he wouldn't talk about it.

I said, 'At least tell me who it was.'

He still didn't reply, and it was difficult to repeat the question. You see, by now I was sure it was *you*. You somehow escaped again, as in a dream or a Hollywood movie.

So I sat there numbly, glancing around, fully prepared to find you crouched in a shadow. The security of our back yard is laughable – shards of green glass on top of the walls – it's security, 50s style. I stared at the braai, left over from that Sunday three weeks ago when Lt. General Venter and his driver came to lunch (my parents hadn't yet hauled it back to the lawn), and I thought how ugly and dark and blistered it looked alongside all Mum's plants: pots of geraniums, flowering cacti, a little tree we used to call 'the ice-cream tree', a big, sweet-smelling frangipani, its fat branches tied back with Mum's old stockings, bushes of bougainvillea shedding their red petals, which at first look glorious round the yard, like confetti, before turning to litter in the dusty corners, where there's always a seagull feather or two.

Suddenly the crane from the building works swung its plane-crashing shadow across us, and this brought Father back to life. 'Can you imagine this barbarism being allowed back in the UK?' he asked. 'Smashing down that marvellous old building to make room for more holiday flats!' He produced a magazine clipping about the Lion's Head, our ex-hotel alongside the house. A photo taken in 1904 shows a beautiful colonial hotel, with sunlit walls, long shaded verandahs, and shaggy lawns sloping down to what a commentator called, 'a noble expanse of sea and a coast well calculated for bathing'. Then called the King Edward Hotel, it stood at the border of Sea Point and Bantry Bay – then Botany Bay – and was virtually the only building at the foot of Lion's Head Mountain. Before that it was the Cresswell Hotel, and before that a school, a private house . . . it dates all the way back to 1767, when some rich burghers built themselves a place of recreation, the Societietshuis.

Father peered up at the crane, while the workers on it peered down at us. 'More holiday flats,' he repeated. 'And in the present political climate? The contractors must be totally bloody barmy! Oh, we should never have left the Commonwealth . . .'

(This is his refrain; and has been since 1961.)

Mum came to join us now, with a tray of tea, and fresh scones, which she always bakes for my homecomings. 'Any plans for this evening?' she asked.

I shrugged. 'Probably go down to the Point. The hotels on this tour didn't have gyms, so I'm very out of condition.'

'Gyms!' said Father in mock disgust, his old twinkle returning. 'Beats me what this fashion is about. It's suicidal.

People are dropping dead like flies in gyms everyday. You chaps sit behind your desks or on your coaches all day, and then you think you can go and lift these impossible weights in the evening. *Why?* In this country we've got blacks to lift impossible weights!'

This was an invitation to joust – one of our *political* discussions – but I wasn't playing along. 'Was he black – the guy who attacked you . . . or Coloured?'

Father fell silent again, but now Mum told the story of the mugging: it was two young black guys, the usual petty criminals, non-political, 'the lost generation'. They wanted his money; he was only carrying R10, but refused to hand it over. Afterwards some people who know us found him, and rang Mum. She arrived at the same time as the ambulance, and travelled with him to Groote Schuur. She was so shocked by the amount of blood – his white shirt was dyed red – that they had to change places in the ambulance, allowing her to lie down.

As she told this part of the story she laughed, and he did too, making his face even more like a joke-shop horror mask, or gargoyle; his false teeth were missing – ejected, trampled and broken in the scuffle.

I stared at him. The renowned schoolteacher, the belligerent old warrior, the fearless missionary who'd carried the works of Milton and Keats into the dark jungles of Afrikanerdom; a pillar of society – felled by two streetboys.

And I felt a small, secret pleasure in this.

Maybe Mum was right – maybe it would've been better if I hadn't known at all.

I got up abruptly, and paced through to the lounge, where Venter and I had stood, semi-naked and sweaty, fingers linked over a shabby little Bible. Then I collected your letters and headed for my bedroom.

Before I reached there, I heard Mum in the kitchen, asking Janie, our latest maid (a young, jangly-boned Coloured, a hopeless drunkard, with, yes, missing front teeth), to do something. This was immediately followed by a frantic scurrying noise – 'Janie's noise'. She was brought up in Wuppertal, by ferocious masters I suspect, who must've roared at her, 'When we tell you to do something, you don't walk — you *run*!' However many times we've told her she doesn't have to do the same for us, the habit seems ingrown. Any request sends her scurrying away, frantically and noisily — because of her cheap sandals — slap, slap, slap down the wooden passages.

She came tearing round the corner now carrying an armful of candles. Before I could say, 'Hi Janie, how are you?', she went into another of her routines: desperate not to block one's way, she presses herself against the wall, muttering, 'Sorry master, sorry,' and giving a kind of sighing hiss, like a frail animal, waiting for the danger to pass.

After I walked on, she prised herself off the wall, then began to stack the candles in our *Blitz* cupboard; stockpiled with supplies for when/if the worst happens — canned foods, long-life milk, dozens of toilet rolls, paraffin lamps, gas bottles (filled), packets of cartridges for Father's little revolver . . .

Depressed, I went into my bedroom, and opened a bottle of wine from my fridge. To brace myself for your letters, I drank about a quarter of it, fast, gazing through the glass — its liquid and its light — to the surfing pictures which still cover my walls. These days I look at them with lust — lust not just for those perfect, gleaming boys, but lust for those translucent green waves (for three or four seconds you were inside a *room* of water!), and the way they settled into a mirror of gold at evening time. I long for the tiredness which came then, that pure, clean, beautiful tiredness, a tiredness which stopped us from going home just yet, and made us collapse on the beach — the sand was still warm from the day — our faces blasted red, each eyelash separated and whitened with salt, and half-dozing there, half-murmuring through the adventures of the day, half-touching.

I gave up surfing when I was sixteen, as soon as I realised that I enjoyed those touches more than anything else. This was utterly incompatible with a surfer's life. His eye is trained on curves: waves, boards, and girls.

Now, after a few more slugs of wine, I read your letters very quickly, skimming them, my face almost turned away.

Later I re-read them carefully, several times, and, later still, pored over them obsessively.

So much to say, I don't know where to start. I'm going to leave this for now.

Surprised this morning to receive another letter from you (in which you talk about plumbing problems in the prison), and to realise that we're very out of synch. You continue to fret about my not receiving your letters, so I must finish this quickly, and send it.

I'm sorry you've been so worried about your letters not arriving.

Why did I say that? I'm not sorry at all; I'm surprised and flattered. It gives me a strange, good feeling – upsetting you. Now, of course, you'll deny that I *did* upset you. Never mind. Your word is hardly reliable. As I get drawn into your accounts of life in 'Beverly Hills', I constantly have to remind myself how you were described during your trial – as a fantasist – a view now echoed by your warders. Anyway, as for these letters, we can only expose our own honesty – not one another's.

In reply to your question, Blanche du Bois is a character in a play by Tennessee Williams, an American playwright who . . . well, you'll only want to know one thing about him – he died in 1983.

The real Blanche, *my* Blanche, has been much calmer and quieter since our night in the veld, and we exchange secret smiles which are intimate and innocent at the same time. I suspect she'll give me a handsome tip on Friday when they leave, and, modesty aside, I think I've earned it.

I'm racing through all these points, in order to get to the main one. You've started to tell the story . . . *our* story. Thank you. It's hard to express what that felt like to read . . . but let me tell you what I did as a result.

After today's tours were over, and after seeing the brood back to the Towers, I walked through town to the Gardens.

I went round to the Orange Street entrance, which I used on that November morning when we met. I haven't been back since. Difficult to make my legs walk on between those whitewashed pillars, but I did. Lots of people about, thank goodness; sunny, safe ... I made myself more secure by imagining I was with a brood ... Folks, these are the Botanical or 'Company' Gardens, being the surviving six hectares of the eighteen-hectare vegetable garden, which grew fresh produce for the ships of the Dutch East India Company, and was planted by the man who started the first European settlement here in the Cape of Good Hope in 1652, and indeed in South Africa, and whose name therefore is known to every schoolkid in this land – Jan van Riebeeck!

I walked down the main path, Goewerments Laan, open and brightish, dappled with tree shade, on past the Museum, a stuffed sea turtle in flight through a perspex box, past the 'melting' statue of Smuts, past the war memorial – two naked men restraining a horse – past the fountain, which you mention, with the boy hugging the giant fish; past flower beds and lawns, to where the path darkens and the trees close down on you, and now there's the statue of Cecil Rhodes up ahead, his back to me, pointing northwards – 'Your hinterland is there' – and I turned to the right, into the absolute centre of the Gardens, where there's an old slave bell, and the cages, yes, with chickens, budgies, parakeets. I turned right again, into the clearing with the tree – the huge tree – the tree so huge that five other trees grow out of it.

I don't think it's a rubber tree; I seem to remember that when I used to bring my broods here (I don't any more, obviously), an Australian schoolteacher identified it as a gum myrtle, nicknamed the 'elephant tree'.

I forced myself to sit on the actual bench; the one where we'd sat together on that windy November morning. A Tuesday morning.

Today, a Wednesday, in October, and late afternoon, two Cape turtle doves were sitting on a branch in the tree, looking at me on the bench; one with its head tilted horizontally, and both very still — weirdly still. I longed for them to break the silence with their famous rolling call: how's father, how's father . . .

No air was coming into my body. The shock — the shock of being here again — this shock slowly wound its way through me.

I was remembering the events leading up to our meeting on that Tuesday.

My job, teaching English at Sea Point High, had become increasingly oppressive; my heart wasn't in it — it never had been. I knew I wasn't doing the job properly; my colleagues knew it and kept their distance; the pupils certainly knew it — they can smell bad or weak teaching like hyenas smell a wounded animal, and they react in exactly the same way. The laughter of those kids, and the savagery of their hunt — it still makes me shudder.

I stopped sleeping . . . I drank heavily, smoked a lot of grass . . . I mostly remembered to shave . . .

The headmaster at Sea Point High rang my father to talk things through (which made me *so* angry), and they decided I should take a week's leave, go away, catch my breath.

I went into the Karoo, to right up near the Namaqualand border; an isolated, stoney dorp called Nieuwoudtville, where a varsity chum had dropped out and was playing at being a pedlar, a smous, like his Lithuanian grandfather. I wrote reams of poetry there — but the isolation wasn't helpful to the way I already felt, and so, after four or five days I trailed back into town.

Instead of going home, I went to Rondebosch, to see my lover, Chas; my ex-English prof from varsity, much older than me (yes, I was bedding Father), and a chain-smoking alcoholic, or, as he put it, 'a white man in Africa', which is a cute excuse (and I use it a lot these days). I needed to talk to Chas, and read him some of the poems I'd written in the Karoo. He needed to get into my pants. Our relationship had deteriorated in recent months, focusing more and more on sex . . . his sexual experiments with drugs, mirrors, cameras, the occasional observer. I always had reservations about these experiments, and he always won me over, using another of his cute phrases, 'Oh, just one more gaudy night' (I think it's a quote from something – you'll probably know). Anyway, on this occasion, I refused to have sex. We had a bad row – I called him a dirty old man, he called me a dumb blonde – and we split up there and then . . . it had obviously been on the cards. Over the next few days I became very depressed, but had no-one to talk to; certainly not my parents. I visited our doctor secretly, but couldn't talk to him either, except in unspecific terms, like 'overwork'. He prescribed sleeping pills. I discovered that by crumbling two to four of these, along with some dope, into a tumbler of whisky, I could make a very effective cocktail.

On that Tuesday, I woke late, with a severe hangover. The early summer weather was peculiar – hot yet grey – my pillow was soaked with cooling sweat, and the shutters were rattling in a fierce wind. Mum was out, at her coffee-and-bridge morning, and Father was at school (this was just before his retirement). I could hear the maid stomping around – not Janie, but her predecessor, a fat surly girl who didn't last long. I had no plans for the day, and it struck me that it might be novel to simply ignore it, waste it, stay in bed. I made one of my cocktails. Then another. Soon after, I needed something else . . . it's a particular need . . . something that's a million miles away from our respectable little home with its sepia light and shelves of faded books. You mention it in your last letter, saying it's a characteristic we share; 'looking for a bit of danger'. Well . . . alright. When I was younger, this need was sated by paddling a board out into the sea, and, as I saw it then, 'taking on the gods'. My father had just taught me about the gods, the Greek gods, and I was fascinated by Poseidon, god of earthquakes and water. I recognised his empire. A world that was fluid – yet I could stand on it, dance on it as it moved, climb its strange mountains; liquid slopes which only turned to rock if I lost my footing . . .

A sport. Yet the game was unique. I played with my life.

My sexuality put an end to this strange excitement, but supplied a new one; it replaced the gods with man.

On that Tuesday, I didn't want to go cruising in Sea Point

– too many people know me – so I borrowed Mum's car, and drove into town, to the Gardens.

The wind was even wilder here; I liked it; tugging and threatening – like waves – reaching a strange pitch among the trees, making the whole Gardens roar.

When I saw you, I couldn't believe my eyes. I didn't know what race you were, your skin was so varnished with sun and dirt. Your huge mane of hair, blonde, yet caked with what looked like red clay. Your small, tight body, with weird bare feet, very mobile, like extra hands. In the gap of your shirt, a tattoo on your chest: a green hawk, descending. Heavy brow, no eyes that I could see at first, stubble and redness around a full, twitchy mouth – your most interesting feature. You seemed thrown by the directness of my stare, totally bloody flabbergasted when I got up, joined you on your bench and offered you a Rothmans. (This must be the surprise you refer to in your letter – you were planning to rob me, when I held out a gift.) As you accepted it – 'Thanking you, don't mind if I do' – you sounded like a simpleton, half-singing, in an elastic way, and then I recognised your accent as Coloured. (Your people have always attracted me . . . not sure why . . . the ghost of my race in black bodies.) Now, as I reached into my pocket for my lighter, my fingers brushed the packet of condoms I'd brought along, and also the flat box of sleeping pills – which later, of course, you were to use. When you leaned forward to take the flame from my lighter, your stench hit me. You mention in your letter that you had stopped washing around this time. Yes, you smelled like a drain, a hole in the earth. And I thought, oh no I'm just in the mood for this.

Alright, your turn again.

Adrian.

SEVENTEEN

83143118
Pretoria Maximum Security

My turn?

Is this a game?

You talk about honesty but you don't deal in it. Your words beg borrow and steal.

Hey, you know your story about how I looked when you first saw me in the Gardens? I've heard it before. From two blokes called John. One whom your dad seems to rate. Milton, John, dead in 1674. The other being John the Divine, Saint, dead in the Bible. You've borrowed your description of me from them both. You only left out my tail.

You say you don't want me to be a thing from your nightmares. Then why lie about me? I do NOT sound like a simpleton. I NEVER HAVE.

And I AM NOT A FUCKING FANTASIST.

Oh I see you've sent presents to the devilish simpleton fantasist. A carton of smokes again.

Plus a round blue plastic box, called JOHNSON'S BABY WIPES.

What the fuck d'you think I am?

Listen here to the label.

THESE GENTLE BABY WIPES ARE IDEAL FOR USE AT NAPPY CHANGES.

Adrian. Who the fuck d'you think you're dealing with here?

Your English prof was right. Your grey matter is just soil

where pretty blonde grass grows. Hey pal, enjoy it while you can. One day grey will grow of grey.

OK I'll take my turn now. But we'll change the rules. We'll really deal in some honesty. I know you just want to carry on with the story of our meeting. There's some sick reason why you want that all over again. Tough shit. It'll have to wait.

I told you before that I didn't do my first person until AFTER the army.

That was a lie.

Why did I tell it?

Because I wanted to seem more political.

I wanted you to blame me on the South African Defence Force, or the border war, or SWAPO or MPLA or whatever the fuck. The times they are a'changing in our part of the world. I wanted to be part of it. THE WHITE WOLF, THE GRAND WIZARD, THE RUBICON, THE MAD MAMA OF THE NATION, THE STATE OF EMERGENCY, THE NEW NAZIS. I wanted to be writ large like all this.

I mock the comrades, yet I half want to be one.

But I'm not.

I can't explain my life or what I've done.

My parents were very racist. They hated whites because of Group Areas and blah blah. They hated kaffirs because of them being an inferior form of life. Daddie used to say that allah sent kaffirs from heaven to be flies on earth.

So my parents taught me not to like whites or kaffirs.

But when I grew up I decided I didn't like nobody.

I did my first one when I was 15.

I'd got fed-up at home. Daddie was still hiding from allah, and ma-bitch was still boxing for Jesus. And I'd learned everything there was from that. Pain is a room with no doors or windows. The only way is up. You have to learn to float up and look back. See the sad flesh blushing and bleeding. Pain is a religious experience. One night I wrote a note thanking ma-bitch then I left.

I walked for 5 days north. Inland of where you talk about, the stony place, Nieuwoudtville. I know it well. But this first time, I ended up in Beaufort West.

I took a car there. The owner had left it unlocked, and the keys in the dashboard. Waiting for me.

My parents never had a car. Very few of the people round us in Bonteheuwel had cars. A skinny horse maybe, with a cart to collect scrap. That's how my Uncle Golie made his living. And he decorated his horse's bridle with a medal he'd won fighting in the coloured corps in the world war.

I spent the rest of that day on the outskirts of Beaufort West learning to drive. It wasn't hard. The car was automatic. I think that day was the happiest of my life. I kicked through the windscreen and let the hot air come over my face. If only I'd known Bob Dylan then I would've sang WHEN THE SHIP COMES IN. Over and over. But I did sing it in a way. I sang it in my mind without ever having heard it. The day was as good as that.

Hey light one of your skuifs and come with me, man, I'm flying out of this cage now.

The next thing I learned about cars is that they're dangerous. Even without 15-year-olds at the wheel who've never driven in their life. But it's not cars crashing into one another that's the big danger. Out in the bundu there's no other car to crash into. No, it's cars crashing into living things on the roadside. That first night some animal stepped into my headlights. It showed me two peep-holes into its empty soul.

I missed it but it gave me a fright. The feeling kept coming back. A piece of ice going round with my blood.

The next day I was in De Aar. I went to the edge of town. I stood on the roadside. I leaned forward as cars sped by. I gave the drivers the same fright that animal gave me last night. One man stopped but I ran back to my own car and outdistanced him.

My experiment was complete. Driving was more than dangerous. It was completely fucking mad. And pedestrians were madder. People actually walked along roadsides while these rockets went past. All it would need was one swerve. And think of the kind of people who're driving. Your family for example. Depressed, alcoholic or anorexic, whatever that is. Another white sickness I presume.

At a place called Houtkraal I ran out of gas. I also hadn't eaten for I don't know how many days. I went into this garage and did a take-off of my ma-bitch. Shouting, big eyes, fists up. That's all it needs. People are easily scared. The old fattie behind the counter, he fled. I emptied his till, and filled my engine. Couldn't find no scoff, but he had a family-size Sparletta bottle full of homemade cane spirit to see him through all the days when nobody came through.

An hour or so later in really hot country I saw her.

I later got used to the sight. I later WAS the sight myself. A person walking through the middle of nowhere. How far have they come? How far are they going?

But on that first trip it was new. Strange.

She was about 30 or 40, a basket or bucket on her head, a blanket over it, to keep off the sun.

I saw her start to wave. They're very polite out here. They're pleased to see you. The world isn't empty after all.

I don't know if I meant to do it. I don't know how out of my skull I was with homemade cane spirit. I don't know if I was still upset by that fucking animal last night with eyes that weren't of the decent earth.

Anyhow, when I got out, the car was dented, but she didn't look too bad. Just sort of knocked out. Next thing I notice she's not wearing broeks. Her dress is up and there are these lips smiling at me. Like a pie. So I lick it. My ma-bitch would be cross. The thought of this gives me a temper. I'm the only one in what scientists call my PEER GROUP who's still pure. So now I pump my temper into those lips, that pie, on the hot road.

The male orgasm isn't nice. It isn't a good design. It makes a person feel like he's bursting his banks.

I fell asleep. From drink, hunger, sun in the skull. I slept for about 6 hours. I know because of the light. Think of all the people who might've driven past while I was asleep. They probably thought we were a couple. Probably felt embarrassed and hit the accelerator. Think if one of them had stopped. It would have finished my career then and there. Think. From your point of view.

128

And from mine. I'd have got away with drunken driving then.

Instead I wake to find myself with a temper again. I start pumping it into the woman again. Then I get a shock. This woman, her tits are still warm, but her head's cool as stone. I think of my ma-bitch. What would make her most cross now? That I'm pumping a woman, or that she's been dead for 6 hours? Actually neither. She'd be most cross that the woman is a kaffir. She'd say the following. My forefathers were decent sailors from Ireland. They didn't come all the way across the world for THIS.

I vomited and drove on.

Later I pushed the car into a donga.

Later I threw away all my clothes and walked into the wilderness, forcing my lower parts against the cruel bushes.

Later I washed in a stone dam by a windmill. Witnessed by some goats.

Later I stole clothes from a farmer's washing line and was a new man again.

But I had entered the circle. It goes like this.

I did that.

I can't believe I did that.

I hate myself.

I'll never do that again.

Except maybe once more.

There'd be days, weeks, a month, a year without it. Then suddenly I'd wake up with the feeling. I'd always say no to it. My brain would say no. But my body would find a way round my brain. Through drink. Maybe just coffee. Or anger. Or fear. Somehow my body would find a way to say yes. At some strange time during the day, no would change to yes.

The circle is like one long hangover.

Who doesn't hate the first taste of booze? It burns. It isn't nice. Smokes too. We choke and cough. Later needles and powder, glue and meths. We overcome our instincts. We learn to like things that aren't good for us. Like driving.

So I did a lot more in the next 6 years. Always with cars. People along the roadsides became magnets for my cars. Any driver knows what I'm talking about. Any driver has felt it.

Obviously, I was careful to keep changing my cars. And towns. Also I was careful to aim for the magnetism of people who wouldn't be missed. Poor. Non-white. Female. Trash in the herd.

I was TOO careful.

Later, when I confessed to the cops, wanting to reap the glory of my career, they didn't believe me. They had no records of these people. Some of the cars had been reported missing, but not the people.

My main man Dylan tells it like this. The land that I live in has God on its side.

Hey but wait. You're my main man now.

Thank you for listening. Thank you for releasing these memories. The day has flown by. Which is helpful. You see, they've taken me off trolley duties. I was never completely sure why I was put on, so I don't know why I've been taken off.

Maybe because Sergeant fat Fourie went on a few days' leave. His second-in-command, brandy Adams, hates me for being a disgrace to the colour of his skin. Coloured. And Adams' deputy, the young Knipe, hates me because my skin colour is classier than his. Poor white.

You can't win in this country.

Anyhow, I've had a very nice day, writing down my memoirs. Whilst also having smoke after smoke from your carton. And I can go on through the night. And there'll still be more for tomorrow. Thank you, thank you. Oh and I've read more of the baby wipes label and it says they're also for grown-ups, IDEAL AS FRESHEN-UP WIPES FOR HOLIDAYS, TRAVELLING OR ANY OCCASION. I think I understand. You sent them to me to help freshen up during our water shortage. Actually the water's back on. But thank you all the same.

To be honest for a bit longer, I'm scared. I don't know where you'll be next. My letters could take forever and a day again. Or get lost completely. How will we know? I want your itinerary.

OK I'll say it.

Please.

Yours in friendship,

Yusuf.

EIGHTEEN

4 Craigrownie Rd
Bantry Bay
Cape Town

Mon. 9th Oct.

Yusuf,

I'm not sure what to say. Your letter shocked me a great
deal. I'm not sure why you're doing this; it's as though you're
trying to make me turn away from you, but I mustn't, I won't.
So anyway, please find my itinerary enclosed. As you'll see,
I've got about another three weeks here at my home address,
taking ad-hoc groups on day excursions of Cape Town and
the Peninsula, before I fly back to Joburg and pick up a
new brood.

I saw the old one off last Friday at D.F. Malan Airport;
me standing in the departure hall, waving to each individual
as though they were relatives: Mr Frawley, whom I deplored
(I can say it now that he's gone), Blanche, whom I honoured
(and I was right by the way – she gave me a tip of £50! –
which is R250!!!), old Mrs Gill with whom I shared a trip
to Isandlwana and briefly knew, the Moonjes who decided
not to settle here after all, Bunny and Lenny Webb from
London, whom I've already forgotten (yet they were so vivid
a moment ago), and others.

Of course I've given my card to those who asked. Some
will write to me, and I'll write back, but once only (I make
this a rule); some will send photos of themselves with me,
which I'll glance at, then pop into a cardboard box I keep

under my desk; some will send presents at Xmas ... Mrs Gill has promised to knit a cardigan with the badge of the 24th Regiment ... but most likely I'll never know anything more about these people again.

That's why I was so surprised to get two phone calls yesterday, Sunday.

One was from Blanche, back in Cork, Ireland. Speaking very fast and fluently, as though she'd practised it, she said, 'When I was little, my parents always used to phone the people we had visited, family or friends, to say we got home safely, and we always used to ask people who visited us to do the same thing, and I always liked it – it was a kindly thing for folk to do to one another – because one can get knocked down going round the corner, y'know, so ... just wanted to say, the plane didn't crash, nor did the train or taxi, and nothing knocked me down, and because there's no-one else to tell, I hope you won't mind if I tell you ... I got home safely.'

At last she took breath, and then laughed. 'Please don't worry dear, I'm not going to make a habit of this.'

I said, 'I don't mind if you do. By all means. Make an occasional call ...'

She laughed again, gently, but in a way which made me hear what I'd just said, and the signal it sent. 'No,' she said. 'Thank you, but no. You've been very kind, God bless you. 'Bye.'

The second call was from Queensland, Australia. My heart sank – not Mr Frawley! Well almost, not quite. It was my friend, Leslie, an air steward, and one of the most charming and wickedest fellows I know. He said huskily, 'I'm using the firm's phone darling, so don't flatter yourself too much by this call. Is this Saturday, Sunday or Monday? We've been through so many time zones I'm like that foetus at the end of *2001*. Anyhow, you know you said there was going to be this ogre on my Australian flight ... *well*, I think he finally found his match with mother here. After the overnight from Hong Kong, the cabin lights had just come on for breakfast, when he grabbed me, and said, "Who turned on the fucking lights?" Quick as a flash I retorted, "Shush, these aren't the fucking lights – we've missed those – these are the dining

133

lights!" Oh darling, if you could've seen his face, it would've made all your days of suffering with him worthwhile . . .!'

After Leslie rang off, I laughed till I cried, and then I realised I was crying for real, and I didn't know why, but still couldn't stop for a while.

Then this morning your letter . . .

I won't let you force me away. I'll do the one thing that will confound you.

I will love you.

Adrian.

NINETEEN

83143118
Pretoria Maximum Security

Love ME?

I thought it was South Africa you were writing love letters to.

But I'm glad you're still with me. I love South Africa too. AT THY CALL I SHALL NOT FALTER. So come on buddy, let's travel on. Come with me to somewhere your tours never go. My best place in South Africa. A town in the part we used to call South West Africa. Sorry, not WE. WE cared fuckall what it was called. But YOU people, YOU called it South West, and now YOU call it Namibia. Having surrendered it to the enemy after hundreds of your nice little brothers and schoolfriends died there. AT THY WILL TO LIVE AND PERISH. You people surrendered it all except one little tiny bit. Far away up there. Above the Tropic of Capricorn. Surrounded by the Namib desert. Why just keep one little tiny bit? Simple. From there you people still control the south-west coast of Africa.

Walvis Bay.

If a person doesn't like trees this is the place for him. If he wants to lose himself this is the place. Where better than a place with no edges? The mist and the sea and the desert. Which is which? The dunes are beautiful. Thin orange sand with thin black mica. Orange curves with black shading. But when the east wind blows, things get less beautiful. Now the thin sand is under your eyelids and between your teeth. You've sipped it with your drink. You go to rinse your mouth

135

and the white sink has turned coloured. You reach for the towel and it's got grit sewn into the lining.

It is said that when the good Lord made Walvis Bay He was so ashamed He's been trying to cover it with sand ever since.

Also salt from the sea. Salt and sand. There's a crust on everything.

Walvis Bay is a town of fish factories and churches. And an army camp. Not much else. Choppers Hamburger Place. Maichatz Tea Room. Flamingo Bioscope. Places which aren't really welcoming to those in the coloured corps.

I think I've already told you I was in the coloured corps. But not the full story.

I'd lived rough for 6 years. Taking cars. Doing 11 people. Or 10. But when I was arrested one day in Kimberley it was only for vagrancy. I'm offered a choice. Prison or army. Next thing I'm arriving in Walvis and I'm being trained for kitchen and sewage duty. Later, moved up to Grootfontein for selfsame, except now in the middle of a bloody war.

Actually nothing in the war was rougher than my time in the Walvis camp. The white blokes already there, finishing their basic training, the OUMANNE, they were serious cases. Seriously homesick, seriously desert-mad, seriously shitting themselves about what lay ahead. When we were marched into camp they lined the route and jeered at us. It was a funny noise. Three thousand madmen giving one long howl. For the first time in my life I was scared.

Life in the camp at Walvis was structured according to the following hierarchy.

Afrikaans-speaking Dutch Reformed Christians.

English-speaking Christians.

Jewboys.

Poor whites.

Coloured corps.

The OUMANNE came on hunting trips to our section of the camp. Those caught were taken back to their bungalows in the white suburbs. And a kind of slavery. My master was a dirty little thing called Erasmus, a driver. They were the worst, the drivers. Erasmus was in bungalow Q28. Here is where I'm now forced to report whenever not on official duty. To clean, iron, fetch, skivvy for Erasmus.

I was also useful in alleviating boredom. For Erasmus and the others in the bungalow.

The OUMANNE were training for life on the border. When they'd have to thrash the enemy, LOOI THEM HARD, and question prisoners. For now, they trained on us. One method was with field telephones. The 12 volts from those battery leads can make you feel very sick. Another method was with handkerchiefs. You can drown a man in his own handkerchief. If you keep it over his nose and mouth. If you keep dripping water onto it. If you keep this up long enough.

Adrian, you know I'm a pretty tough cat. But I went under a bit with the OUMANNE. They regarded me as completely dim. I hadn't read anything yet, so I couldn't argue the point. But I sensed they were wrong. I sensed I was actually brilliant. The brilliant me was screaming from inside the ape me. Nobody could hear.

Apart from the aforementioned games, the OUMANNE also sniffed out my own special weak spots.

One was by locking me in a kit cupboard and blowing smoke through the keyhole. They called it the gas chamber. All the lessons I'd learned about pain were useless. I couldn't float up and away from it. The ceiling was already against my head. And all the time the tin box is filling with smoke. People who are suffocating fight with incredible strength. Adrian, you know this. And I'm strong to start with. But I couldn't fight my way out. I couldn't shout. Or even breathe. I found this quite hard to handle.

The other thing they did was pass round a drinking glass and each spit into it until there was a few inches in the bottom. Then they presented it to me. The next bit was even harder for me than the gas chamber. I'd lived on the road and fed like a wild animal. I'd ate grass, dead birds, insects, rats. I've told you I don't care about INNER hygiene. But I couldn't stand the taste of human spit. My ma-bitch had made that taste bad for me. So I found it very hard when they presented me with that glass.

137

Funny how the Jews always survive.

There was this bloke who was also a slave in bungalow Q28. I can't remember his name. He was blonde although he was a Jew. A Jewboy pretty as a girl. Curly blonde hair.

Looked a bit like you.

Except he didn't just resemble an angel, he also sang like one. Had a guitar. And this saved him. Instead of playing their boredom games on him, the OUMANNE made him sing. Day and night. They liked that Tom Jones song. The green green grass of home. Also Sloop John B by the Beach Boys. Oh let me go home, I feel so brokedown I wanna go home.

Also songs by Queen. Man, you should've heard this boy's voice go high on the Bohemian Rhapsody.

MAMA. I just killed a man. Put a gun against his head. Pulled my trigger now he's dead. MAMA. Life had just begun. But now I've gone and thrown it all away. MAMA.

And then all those desert-mad OUMANNE would put their heads back. Jaws wide, eyes blind. Like baby birds.

MAMA.

The Jewboy also sang all Bob Dylan's masterpieces.

Now. At last. I met my main man. Dylan. He and me, we brushed souls.

This bloke, the Jewboy. I wish I could remember his name. He had what is called a sweet disposition. He showed some respect to me. He showed kindness. I think he came from a liberal family. Because he seemed to find nothing untoward in befriending a coloured boy who was going under with the OUMANNE. When he noticed I liked Dylan's songs, he wrote out all the lyrics for me.

I wonder what I've done with those pages? From the back of the Jewboy's diary.

In any case, this Jewboy, he agreed with me that Dylan spoke ultimate wisdom.

Even now after all my reading I've never found anybody wiser. Sartre, Jean-Paul, dead in 1980, maybe comes closest in his Nausea.

On Sunday afternoons I'd go walking by the Lagoon. It looked like open sea but it was called the Lagoon. It was straight out the desert side of the camp. Other guys went on pass into town. But I didn't want the town.

I wasn't bullshitting you earlier when I said Walvis was my best place in the Republic. The Lagoon was why I liked Walvis. The Lagoon is my kind of landscape. Wide water, wide land, wide sky. Nobody can possibly come up behind you. The ground is like grey sponge. Sometimes it oozes up through your toes. It's covered in a thin layer of clear water. From a distance people look like they're doing Jesus Christ's walk. An inch above this clear water are swarms of tiny insects. Higher up there's seagulls, hawks and pelicans. You also find flamingos along the shoreline. A hundred thousand flamingos. Also dead seals.

On one such Sunday afternoon walk I met the Jewboy singer. Like me he was dressed only in army issue black shorts. But he had accoutrements. Beachwear stuff. Sunglasses, a bumbag, a Sony machine attached to the belt.

The Sony machine was a real classy one. He was rich. I wondered why his father hadn't pulled strings to stop him being sent to the army. Liberals, but still patriots I suppose. THOU HAS BORNE US AND WE KNOW THEE.

I asked what he was listening to.

He said your favourite, Dylan.

For the hell of it I said he wasn't actually my favourite. My favourite was a Bing Crosby number. Danny Boy.

There and then he sang it like an angel.

Oh danny boy. The pipes, the pipes are calling. From glen to glen and down the mountain side. The summer's gone and all the roses falling. It's you, it's you must go, and I must bide.

I cried and told him it reminded me of my daddie.

He suddenly asked if I'd like to do anal intercourse in him.

I went along with the idea.

He suggested we go deep into the desert.

I went along.

We walked for about an hour. He sang all my favourites along the way. I was happy. The desert was beautiful. Sometimes I couldn't hear the Jewboy because the wind

139

was so loud against the outside of the dunes. But when you go over the edge, you enter a silent crater. Orange curve, black shading, like a drawing.

The dune he led me to was about a mile deep. He said come on, destination ground floor. He laughed and said even if anyone saw us down there we'd just look like ants reproducing. Then he began to run down. You'd have liked the picture. It looked like he was surfing.

I caught up halfway and said let's do it here. I said I liked the way the sand was like water. I said I wanted it slipping around us. I said I didn't care if people saw. I said sex in the outdoors is my best thing.

He said have you read Lawrence?

I said d'you mean this is like Arabia?

I started to tell how my Uncle Golie fought there with the coloured corps in the world war, but the Jewboy was laughing at my misunderstanding of his reference. I got a bit cross. He apologised immediately. His manners really were polished. Then he showed me what to do. He had vaseline with him. He must've been expecting something like this. He made some jokey reference to the vaseline being in his bumbag and where it should be instead. I found this unnecessarily rude. I think I was a bit nervous. Ahead lay three firsts for me.

Doing it with a bloke.

Doing it with a white.

Doing it with someone who was conscious.

Anyhow, at first I enjoyed it. I liked the way he was on all fours trying to grip the slope. Which was fantastic. Watery orange. And I liked the feel of the flats of my big hands on his back. My own spine was arched up. My face was thrown to the sun. We were like lions.

But then he started saying things and trying to half twist round and kiss. That's the problem if people are conscious. They want to join in. I told him to keep quiet and he did. But it was a bit spoiled now. I was getting sad. It was the back of his head. I'm always saddened by the back of people's heads. On buses or in bioscopes. People must be mad to show you the back of their heads. Don't they realise how easy it is to take advantage of the back of their heads?

Anyhow, I wished him no harm. My BRAIN, it wished him no harm. My BRAIN said no to the next idea. But, like I told you, my BODY always finds a way of turning no to yes. And then I saw the back of his head again. The back of his BRAIN. Sending out these bloody signals. Causing noises. Noises of enjoyment.

If only he'd been a bit surprised by the new power of my pumping. And gone quiet. Or OK, if only he'd been a bit scared. Anything that would've made him go quiet.

Instead I had to use the sand.

He struggled like a madman. People do. They demand to breathe. Something in his face got torn in the struggle. Eardrums or his tongue or a nosebleed, don't ask me, but suddenly the orange sand got richer. Then it was orange again. Sand is running all the time. It's not surprising they use sand for clocks. At the end I got a fright. His voice came over the edge of the dune. Really high like when he sang Bohemian Rhapsody. It was a seagull. It seemed like it was fleeing something. I heard a new noise. I watched the edge of the dune, knowing something huge would come over. The edge of all dunes is razor sharp and blurred at the same time. Always a little wind. I watched that sharp blurred edge. Beyond, the sky was sky blue. Then it bled. I didn't know what was going on. I wondered if some of the guy's blood was in my eyes. It took a few seconds to realise it was flamingos. A hundred thousand flamingos coming over the edge of the dune to see what I had done. Already we were falling, me and the Jewboy. Everything was strange. The earth was watery. The sky was bleeding. We fell.

At the bottom he was already half buried. The rest was easy to do. Climbing back to the edge wasn't. It took half an hour. My lungs burnt at the top.

I was frightened when I got back to camp. Had anybody seen us meet? Had anybody seen us reproducing like ants? Had anybody seen my BODY get the better of my BRAIN?

But I made no attempt to cover up. I didn't wash, which as you know isn't like me at all. But my BRAIN hadn't wished him harm, and I was cross with my BODY. So all that night you could've smelled him on me. His face blood, or the vaseline from his butt.

His absence wasn't noticed till the next day. Must've happened at roll call, I suppose, in the white suburbs. And then more time passed while they wondered if he'd been out on pass. It wasn't unusual for blokes to overstay a pass. It wasn't unusual to go AWOL in the desert. These were guys heading for the border and a serious war.

For two days I didn't wash and he was on me. While everyone wondered where he was.

Everyone was questioned. Even us in the kitchens and sewers. Nobody knew anything. Helicopters searched the dunes. But the sands had run on well and truly by then. Dylan's God was on my side yet again.

The incident passed.

I travelled on. To the camp at Grootfontein. To the sanity and peace of a guerilla war. The OUMANNE now took out their boredom on the day's catch of prisoners. Me and the other kitchen boys sat behind the whities, in what we called the cheap seats, and watched the interrogations. I've told you about that.

Years later, after you had happened, I took the cops back to find the Jewboy singer.

Amazingly we did. Just a skeleton. But definitely him. Being rich, he had dental records.

Thus he became the only one of my score that the law formally acknowledged. I don't count you. The one that got away. No, HE is the main reason why I now sit on death row.

I'm sitting here with eagerness as you know. Eager for the big day to dawn.

Two guys got their notices of execution today. Sipho Mkhondo and Peter 'Godless' Kies. Two. That's unusual these days. From the date on your letter I see that christmas isn't so far away. Maybe a rush is on again. Like in the good old days. Clearing stock before they get short-staffed over the holiday period. Neither Sipho or Godless were comrades. Which I take as a good sign. If they're clearing stock, it'll be all us non-comrades first. The comrades they'll put on hold. In case the NEW S.A. comes true.

So I'm hopeful.

So I suppose you could say that, all in all, things have turned out alright for me.

But at the time I really regretted that guy, the Jewboy singer. I regretted his suffering. Up until then, the others never knew what hit them. A car accident. But HIM. What did it feel like? With sand. Sand takes time.

I thought the following.

I did that.

I hate what I did.

I'll never do it again.

Except maybe once.

So a new kind of hangover began.

I'm feeling a bit fed-up now. I'm going to go lie down now. Excuse me.

I just wish I could remember his damn name.

Yours Faith Fully,

Yusuf.

TWENTY

4 Craigrownie Rd
Bantry Bay

Mon. 16th Oct.

Dear Yusuf,

I suppose you must've heard the news . . . it must've gone round during 'talking time' . . . they released Sisulu yesterday. And seven others. I watched it on TV; Sisulu went back to his small house in Soweto. Everyone's saying Mandela will be next. God, it's happening – what you call your 'cruel dream' – it's happening.

But surely any amnesty won't apply to non-political prisoners, will it? You don't want it to; you say so in your letter . . .

As for the rest of what you wrote . . . you don't seem to understand . . . I don't want to know about the others; the rest of it. I can't bear this. I avoided it before, at the trial and in the papers. I don't want it now. I want you to talk about what happened to me; I *need* you to; I *need* to understand what happened. Please. I can't deal with the rest of it. I'm sorry, but I'm being as honest as I can, as honest as I've been throughout this correspondence. Please. You started telling our story, yours and mine – please just carry on with that, nothing else.

Yours,

Adrian.

Twenty-One

83143118
Pretoria Maximum Security

No. It's YOU who doesn't understand.

The rest of it IS about you.

You dim cunt.

You say you NEED to understand. But you don't understand a thing. You're just like everyone. You just want to look away.

You full-up cunt.

Saying please just talk about me, me. Like blind baby birds. Mommie, please just come to me, me. Like army boys singing. MAMA. I just killed a man.

The Jewboy I told you about. He was blonde. Like an angel. With a sweet nature.

Don't you see a connection?

I spared YOU.

You don't see a connection?

I opened myself to you.

You cunt with teeth.

Fuck you, fuck it, let's just finish.

TWENTY-TWO

4 Craigrownie Rd
Bantry Bay

Sat. 21st. Oct.

Dear Yusuf,

You must forgive my previous letter; it wasn't anything to do with you, or us. I'm on edge these days because of my father. He just sits in the back yard, or paces there like a zoo animal. He won't go through to the front garden; not until we get a new security system there, he says. Admittedly the present one is no more than designer-security; the lightweight gates drift through the air (you'd be through them in a flash), and the railings are only about a metre higher than our old garden wall (no great climb for you). But as Mum and I keep telling him, there are neighbours all around, retired folk like himself, people who are in all day. And all the people on the building site. It may be barbaric to demolish the Lion's Head (née King Edward, née Cresswell) Hotel, but at least there are people watching the house day and night. 'Exactly!' he says, squinting up at the labourers on the crane, as though trying to pick them out at an identity parade.

The mugging has changed him. Now when he says his catchphrase, 'We should never have left the Commonwealth,' we don't mimic him any more. He truly believes that if we were still part of the Commonwealth, everything would somehow be tickety-boo, thoroughly British, fair to all, yet flexible: we could have one man one vote, yet one and one wouldn't have to make two ... the races could still stay

146

apart ... particularly on the beachfront, making it safe to walk there again, and particularly where we live, so that our home could just be protected by a few shards of green glass on the back wall again, and nothing on the front, where we'd view a noble expanse of sea, across the soft lawns of a grand old hotel.

These days Father can get seriously inebriated before lunch (it's been an inspiration to our little dipso maid, Janie, who's been fired and rehired *twice* in the last week), and so, on Thursday, when he was already on the slippery slope at half-twelve, I said, 'Come on dear chap, we're going for a good old constitutional along the front.'

I've never seen him so angry. He came forward in his deck chair, large freckled hands shaking, new false teeth tumbling out, and cried, 'I can't defend myself any more!'

'But I'll be with you,' I said.

He just snorted in reply, as though saying *you*.

If only – at some stage – we had talked about what happened to me! If only I could now say, Father I understand, I know how frightening the world seems suddenly, and everybody in it.

But I can't – I don't seem to have the courage, or honesty, or cheek, or whatever he'd call it – so I drive off on my own, for little trips, playing slushy romantic stuff, from Rachmaninov to Lloyd Webber (not your kind of music at all); like to Hermanus this weekend, to view the whales – the large schools of Southern Rights which gather there at this time of year. Have you ever whale-watched? I hadn't before – it's very addictive. One spends hours scanning the waters of Walker Bay, trying to distinguish white horses from whales. Then, without warning, one of the creatures will lobtail, or breach. Yesterday a black whale crossed the entire bay with a sequence of breaches, like the bouncing bomb in that war movie. And this morning (a beautiful morning, blue and still, reminding me of a day, some day, in childhood), I had another terrific sighting. Clambering down onto a rocky outcrop at the Old Harbour, I found a lone figure staring out to sea. He was a young man, with, I think, a British accent (he only spoke briefly and in whispers); big-eared and skinny, weighed down with binocs, cameras, flasks – a sort of aquatic train-spotter. Pointing to a distinctive ripple of water a short distance away – and now a glimpse of tail as the whale dived! – he muttered that he'd tracked this particular one from the faraway white strips of Grotto Beach, and that it seemed to be heading straight for our rock. Below us lay a deep basin of greenish water, swelling gently in the tide; spacious and light, with sun rays slanting through columns of gold-brown kelp. I felt I was suspended above an ancient forest. 'There!' said the young man suddenly, in such an odd voice that I glanced to him before the whale. He had tears in his eyes. I wondered how far he'd travelled for this, and why. Looking down, I saw the creature rising towards us – unusually, it was pale coloured, a stony-pink – this massive brightness rising through the kelp forest, like a new island being born. Now a sound – its breath – a hollow, almost metallic sound – and then it blew its spray, and a foul mist drifted onto our faces, making us grimace and laugh. And still the monster kept rising and growing, finally breaking the surface, and rolling over – in a stream of wet sunlight – rolling over from its world into ours, and showing the full glory of its ugliness: the closed, pliant orifice of its blowhole, the rough growths of white callosities on its head, the tremendous scowl of its jaws, and one eye, wrinkled and small, which held mine for a long moment.

Then it dived again, and disappeared – for good. Turning back, I was surprised to find a dozen other people crouched around us on the rock; they must've gathered in silence, like people creeping into church.

Feeling better – calmer – than I have for a long time, I started the drive back to Cape Town. Switching on the radio, I heard the news. A bad earthquake in San Francisco, Hungary ditching communism, a demonstration in East Berlin, with thousands forming a human chain; here at home, Sisulu being interviewed again, more conjecture about when Mandela might be let out, some talk of unbanning the ANC, all sorts of reforms . . .

I wanted them to mention the death penalty.

When they didn't, and went onto sport, I thought about

ringing my contact, Father's ex-pupil, Lt. General Venter, and asking him ... what? ... whether he knew when you were going to get your notice of execution? ... *if* you were going to get it? ... but again I didn't have the courage, or cheek, or whatever.

All sense of calm had vanished. I ended up parked in a cul de sac somewhere, I honestly don't know where, with the branch of an oak tree squashed against the windscreen, as though I'd crashed.

Look, neither of us are religious, but surely – whatever happens politically now, throughout the country, and in the jails – surely it's important for you to make your peace. Not with God, or me, but *yourself*. Just to let go of your secret – your version of what happened. In your last letter you say you 'spared' me, in the previous one you say I was 'one who got away'. Which is it? If you spared me that's important – for *you* as well. You must see that – you chose mercy – YOU CHOSE MERCY.

Christ, I'm even writing like you. Like I'm shouting.

Alright, let's go back again. We're sitting there under the tree again, the huge dark tree in the centre of the Gardens, everything roaring in the wind. We've made eye contact. I move over and offer you a cigarette. You accept. When you lean forward to take the light, I smell you. I begin trembling so much, you have to steady the lighter. I'm surprised by your touch. The skin of your hand and your fingernails are baked like an animal's, yet your touch is light.

I can't take you back to the house in Bantry Bay, so I suggest a hotel, the Republic Lodge on Eastern Boulevard. A big, fast-service, American-style joint, sometimes a down-market conference centre, sometimes an up-market brothel, sometimes just a *hotel*, lots of Taiwanese coach parties coming and going. I know the manager there, a real old reprobate, a friend of my ex-lover. He allowed Chas and I to use the rooms there. We could arrive unannounced, we knew where the room rotas and pass keys were kept, we paid a nominal fee afterwards, for laundry and anything from the drinks fridge. He asked only that we tried to be discreet; to let the staff see as little as possible.

There's nothing to stop you and me from using the same facilities.

When I suggest this scenario, you nod, and follow like a lamb.

In retrospect, I realise that for you it was like the Jewish singer in the desert. He proposed going somewhere hidden and quiet, and, in your words, 'I went along.'

Walking to the car, we must've looked bizarre together: me tanned and clean, my fresh white clothes which the maid had washed and ironed; you hunched and dirty, a mane of clay-caked hair, barefooted, and with that odd walk of yours, like the way your people dance, with hips thrust forward and palms splayed outwards – 'Hey, look at me, my ou' chommie, hey ain't I the coolest dude!'

I prayed we wouldn't see anyone I knew.

When you got into the car, Mum's car, I suddenly noticed how much it was *hers*, like a private room – the cushion for her back, the cassette tapes of Flanagan & Allen and other golden oldies, the stick-on reminder that it was time to buy certain seeds for the garden, the can of anti-assailant spray neatly fixed to the dashboard – and I remember thinking I'd have to air the car later. I'd go for a drive along the coast after we'd finished; I'd drive fast with all the windows open; I'd fill the car with sea air.

On the journey to the Republic Lodge, you didn't speak, but you half-sang under your breath. Were those Bob Dylan songs? Were you remembering the Jewish boy taking you into the desert?

We reached the hotel, and I drove into the staff car park, above a grim view of freeways, the industrial side of the Docks, and Robben Island. I wondered how to get you into a room without anyone seeing us?

Throughout the next five minutes, I worked like the devil to stop anyone seeing us. I was with my murderer, yet *I* was covering our tracks; working like the devil at it.

Many weeks later, one of the post-trauma therapists would challenge me about this phrase, 'like the devil', when I recounted what happened.

'It's just a figure of speech,' I said.

'Are you sure?' he asked. 'After all, you were brought up as a Christian.'

'Of course I'm sure,' I said, getting angry. 'I'm an adult, I don't believe in the devil, I don't even believe in evil. I know he was just a man, just flesh and blood, just ill ... mad not bad.'

'Are you sure?' he kept asking. 'I believe that's the case, but I want to be sure you do.'

I became angrier and angrier, because I wasn't at all sure. The sensible side of me knows you're not the devil, yet when you come into my dreams I have one hell of a job exorcising you. And even in these letters ... well, you've already pointed out that I describe you like something from the Book of Revelation.

I don't believe you're the devil.

You can't be. I have proof – it's the Bob Dylan lyric you keep quoting (needless to say, I've now collected and studied all the songs myself) ... 'God's on your side.'

It was certainly true that day. Nobody saw us park, or go in the side entrance, or check the room rota and collect the pass key, or travel in the staff lift to the 6th floor, or go along the corridor to Room 608. Nobody saw us. I worked like the devil, and God was on your side.

At last we were in the room, and the DO NOT DISTURB sign was hanging outside, swinging madly from the urgency with which I'd slammed the door.

We both laughed nervously – because of the adventure we'd been through, and the one ahead.

To break the ice, I brought out my dope. You looked happy about that; even happier when I opened the drinks fridge ... and just very intrigued when I produced the pack of Mogodon. I remember worrying about you seeing the pills; not because I had any inkling of what was going to happen, but because I didn't want you to think that I was someone who *needed* sleeping pills. I quickly said, 'I make a cocktail with these.' Then I laughed in a half-jolly, half-nervous way (like Mum) and said, 'Oh I might as well empty all my pockets,' and I put the condoms on the bedside table – to reassure you I was into safe sex – and also my money, about R15. This was to show you that I didn't have much cash on me, but that I was happy for you to take it as a gift; you wouldn't have to rob me. (In fact, the rest was hidden in my shoe, with my credit cards.) Then I made us each a cocktail: two pills and some dope crumbled into a glass of bourbon.

As we downed our first one, you spoke: 'Smoking and drink doesn't cause sickness, but if a person gets caught in the rain, then he must get his clothes off pretty damn fast, 'cause that's the only thing that can kill a person. That's anyhow what my daddie always reckons.'

This was the most you'd said so far. It made me think, *What?!* Then I thought, Yes they talk gibberish like that, the coloureds – he's probably illiterate, possibly a simpleton. (I know it angers you when I say that, but it's what I thought.)

I said, 'I don't know about rain, but there's a shower next door. D'you think that's safe?'

We both found this very funny. Then you immediately went into the bathroom, and I heard the shower. I was relieved. I'd been trying to find a diplomatic way of suggesting that you wash.

You reappeared a couple of minutes later: clean, and sopping wet. As you dripped onto the carpet, I said, 'Uhm, wouldn't your father want you to dry off?'

You said, 'Only if a person's wearing clothes. I'm not wearing clothes.'

I said, 'Yes, I can see that.'

You weren't even wearing a towel. But you didn't flaunt your nakedness; you were as unselfconscious as an animal. Your body was like an animal's too: built to run, feed, and rest; nothing spare on it. And it had markings like an animal's, with a striking, inexplicable design – for camouflage, or mating display? – the red-black sunburn on your face, neck and hands, the light brown smoothness of your limbs and torso, the two green tattoos (I couldn't see the third yet), the bluish dark of your nipples and privates. And your walk, which had been a bit ludicrous in clothes, was now a very natural thing, like an animal's: an easy prowl, stopping now and then to shake off the water from the shower.

I thought, I'm with a wild animal in this room.

You suggested I take a shower too. I remember being slightly offended; I had of course showered, applying talc and scent afterwards, before leaving Bantry Bay; but I didn't protest.

When I returned to the room, a towel round my waist, you had made us another two cocktails.

If I had looked in the Mogodon box then, I'd have been stunned by how many were missing; the sheet of silver sealing was dotted with punctures like little bullet holes. But I didn't look in the box – why should I? – my attention was elsewhere.

You had an erection. More surprising, you seemed embarrassed by it; your previous unselfconsciousness had vanished. I was puzzled and moved by your unease – such a tough guy being embarrassed by his erection. (I understand it differently now; your 'temper' was up.)

We drank from our separate glasses – I remember thinking you'd made them very strong, but this excited me. I was already quite stoned. You remarked on this, smiling, and rolled us a big joint ... you called it a 'three-blade slowboat'.

The condoms ... you called these 'raincoats'.

At last I had finished my drink, and at last you let me cuddle you. Again I felt I was with an animal, but a tame animal now; leaning into my arms with trust. I started to kiss you. You said, 'That's the only thing I won't do.' I thought this was odd, but assumed it was something to do with safe sex. Now you told me that you'd never been screwed before, but wanted me to do it to you. I said I, in turn, had never screwed anyone; it was always the other way round. We said it was going to be a first for us both, and we laughed. When I picked up the packet of 'raincoats', you said I needn't bother. I was puzzled, but assumed it was because you were uneducated: you thought kissing was more dangerous than screwing. Anyway, I didn't wear one; I knew you were safe from me.

What you said in one of your letters is right: the back of someone's head is a very tender place. On the back of yours, the mane of hair was wet and flat, smelling of the hotel shampoo. It touched me to think of you, the animal, in the shower, trying to open one of those slippery little sachets, so that you could smell nice for me. As I reached orgasm, I was kissing your neck; it was sunburnt as a piece of earth; it should've tasted salty and sour, but it was sweet.

Now, as we changed over, I realised how far gone I was. I wondered if, back in Bantry Bay, I'd had more cocktails than I realised before leaving the house. I remember thinking it was a shame I was going to miss the next bit. I remember smiling to myself, thinking I'm going to sleep through it, like a bored wife. I remember thinking I must keep it together long enough to make sure he puts on a 'raincoat'. I remember achieving that. Then I remember the open window – the wind had dropped, and afternoon sunlight, strong and hot, was resting there – I heard the sound of cars on the freeway, and, from this angle on the bed, could see a corner of my beautiful Table Mountain. I remember thinking that this hotel wasn't such a dump after all.

My memory of what followed is in separate pieces. It's impossible to know how long the gaps in between lasted – I was far too drugged – sometimes they seemed to last only seconds, sometimes hours.

First, I remember a struggle with an almighty force – a tidal wave breaking, a mountain falling, a whale attacking – incredible to think it was only you.

Then I remember dying. The doctors later confirmed that this was feasible for a few seconds; the heart, lung and brain functions pausing briefly. Something in me remembers the sensation. It was like you describe pain: lifting away, looking back . . .

Then I remember surfacing; this was exactly like coming up from too long a time underwater: frantic gasping, throat raw. The impression of water was so vivid, I was surprised to find myself still on a bed; surprised also that you were still there. I didn't yet realise that you'd been involved, but now, as I became aware that the bed really *was* soaking –

and reeking with it – I couldn't understand why you would stay somewhere so unpleasant. I thought this wetness was blood, but later they explained there was none . . . it was caused by vomiting, and a loss of control over my bladder and bowels.

I have other, vaguer memories of surfacing a few more times – each time the atmosphere was different: light, then dark, then light again . . .

Now I remember the door opening. A bellboy showed in some guests. (Was it the next day?) I remember the look on their faces: such shock it looked like fury. I noticed you were *still* there, despite all the mess on the bed.

I remember being in the ambulance, and becoming upset because I was in the wrong vehicle. I should've been in Mum's car. How would she know where it was now? And I hadn't had a chance to clean it, to air it of your smell – so even if she found it, she'd be very disgusted by that. No, not disgusted . . . I remember the word 'disappointed' . . . she'll be very disappointed.

My last memory is in the hospital . . . coming to, and needing the toilet. There I looked in the mirror and was amazed by how the whites of my eyes had turned blood-red, and how there were strange little red marks on the eyelids and round the sockets – like a rash. (From small blood vessels which had burst during the struggle.) Just before they sedated me again, my parents were allowed to see me. When I spoke, I was surprised how hoarse I sounded. I apologised to Mum about the car. She didn't know what I was talking about – the police hadn't told them the story yet – so she assumed I'd been involved in a motor accident. She did a version of her jolly laugh, and said, 'Never mind dear, it's only a car. You're in one piece, and that's the main thing.'

Later, when they were told everything, Mum found it impossible to face me, and never visited again (Father managed once, which I've told you about), although she kept sending those cartoon Get Well cards, and rang me on my birthday, chatting cheerfully about this and that. I didn't see her face to face again until I returned to the house in Bantry Bay months later, and there she was, gardening as usual, and she turned and waved, and sang out 'Hullo there' as though I'd only popped out to the shops. At first the *Britishness* of it all was such a relief: nobody talking about what had happened; everything normal again.

This homecoming was two and a half months after our meeting. It took that long to repair the damage. Some of it was physical. In the fight, I'd broken my wrist and four fingers, trapped by a section of the bed-head; and my head had struck the bedside table very badly, leaving me with severe headaches and slight deafness on one side. But most of it was mental, the 'psychosomatic' sicknesses you say we white Africans get. Like the breakdown I now had. And like the fear of sleep. That was the hardest thing: learning to sleep again.

You bastard, you bastard . . .

(I should take that out, but I won't.)

I've made a fairly good recovery, but I know I've still got further to go. Yet I can't without you . . . I have to know what happened from the bastard's side. Why he stopped, the bastard, and why he didn't flee. You bastard – tell me! I don't care if you're sick of me asking. I don't care if I've made you angry. You *must* tell me! Neither of us knows how much time you've got left. Please, you *must* fill in the gaps – your side – of our story.

Adrian.

TWENTY-THREE

83143118
Pretoria Maximum Security

The date is when I got your last letter.

Adrian.

I feel nothing.
That's what everyone said in the army.
One person asks what d'you feel?
The other answers I feel nothing.
Again and again. Men sing it to one another.
What d'you feel?
I feel nothing.
It wasn't nice to read your letter. To read what I was like
before. A simpleton. Now I'm an intellectual. Has anyone
noticed the difference? God maybe. Or Verwoerd turning in
his grave.
In any case, you have two questions for me.
One. Have I ever WHALE-WATCHED at Hermanus?
No I haven't. In general, your South Africa is not a place
I've been to.
Two. Can I please fill in the gaps, my side of the story?
OK.
My side of the story is still in Walvis Bay.
I'm in the army camp. Outside the camp lies the Jewboy
singer in a dune of sand.
Later the cops told me something. Because it happened in
winter and because the lower layer of sand is like a fridge,

157

he would've kept his good looks for a couple of months. I was glad to hear this. Because the Jewboy singer was my masterpiece.

I wish at the present juncture to bring to your attention the following subject. Anger as art. Or vice versa. This subject is demonstrated variously by the work of two painters. Bosch, Hieronymus, dead in 1516, and Hitler, Adolf, dead in 1945. We can also refer to the work of Mishima, Yukio, most especially his masterpiece, i.e. his death, in 1970.

In my own case I should've been a sculptor. I see life in chunks. I have strong hands. I have feet that grip. But I was brought up in the lower echelons of society. At school an uncaring teacher described my artistic efforts as FANTASIES. Meantime, my career opportunities pointed me towards scrap collection or trawler boats. Oh shame, poor deprived cunt. Yes. I was thus forced to sculpt with life. This surely explains me as VALIDLY as the other stuff. Genetic disorder, neuro-biological behaviour and moral dereliction. Me as modern artist.

With the Jewboy singer as my masterpiece.

There's no spring season at Walvis. In October the summer comes. A desert summer. Roasting sand full of tiny insects. The Jewboy singer would've lost his looks very quickly.

But I was gone. Up to the border war. Our Vietnam. The world came forward to meet me. I became normal.

During the war I did a lot of people. All from my own side. I settled scores with my former OUMANNE. Erasmus and the rest. For the gas chamber and the glass of spit. I picked them out from the flap of my kitchen tent. They thought it was an enemy sniper.

Hence I sendeth my rain on the unjust. St Yusuf, after St Matthew 5:45.

I don't count the ones I did in the war. I can't. It was too easy. But if I did, my score would be WELL OVER 50.

Anyhow, the war wasn't interesting. It was political.

Then I got sacked from it.

Or did I get bored and slip away?

Choose whichever fits your picture of me.

I stayed up in those parts. I lived for a time in the Etosha

Pan Game Reserve. I teamed up with a mad German. Can't remember his name. He claimed to have been a big game hunter. I think he was just a big bullshitter. I think maybe before the war he was a tour guide. The lowest of the low. He sometimes fucked me. Yes sorry you weren't the first. Don't believe anything I tell you. I love you by the way. Anyhow, Etosha was nice during the war. No tourists. Mind you, life ceased to be a bowl of cherries for the animals. God didn't put animals on this earth to be photographed by tourists. He put them there to be eaten. Which the enemy side did. Or to be used as target practice. Which our side did. Mainly when high on dagga or a dop too many. Elephant herds were mortared. Cute little lion cubs were taught to fly with a lobbed grenade. Giraffes were decapitated with machine gun fire.

Meantime me and the German had some lovely times. We walked through lion grass unarmed. We swam with a half-dead baby hippo. We lived in a tree. Once a zebra tried to climb our tree. It was being chased by a pack of wild dogs. We watched the dogs eat the zebra alive. It was like sex. Them getting stuck in down below, and him with his head back, mouth open. Hey you saw the aftermath, didn't you? The zebra with the chewed-off dick. Me and the German were watching from less than a foot above. As tourists say we were THIS CLOSE.

Then the German got sick. He was delirious. One day he was sleeping and I was guarding him from the animals. Then I thought fuck it and walked away.

I went back to the Republic proper.

For a while I had a legit job. In Cape Town, our city. I worked as a busker. On a corner of Greenmarket Square, there by the flea market. I did my Dylan songs. Hey, you probably walked past me long before we met. HEY THAT WAS ME BUDDY. That was me in the bright satin waistcoat gashed big round the armpits. That was me with my old harmonica. That was me, head down, eyes closed, in love.

Hey mister tambourine man. Play a song for me. I'm not sleepy. And there is no place I'm going to.

Then I started travelling again. Doing cars again.

But my masterpiece in the dune of sand had left me with a new hangover. A new appetite.

It wasn't enough any more for the cars to do all the work. Hit and run. This didn't feel like my style any more.

So I began using the cars to pick up people and take them somewhere else. People who were hitch-hiking. Or showing you where to park in an empty car park. Or begging at robots. Adrian, you lock your car door at robots. Me, I open it wide. So long as the person is from the herd, poor and non-white. Male or female now immaterial.

But I must make it clear that I'm not one of your kind. What the kaffirs call SITABANE, meaning somebody with a cunt and a cock between the same pair of legs. What the Boers call MOFFIE. What you English boys call GAY. This is not me. No male never got nothing from me above the waist. Nothing from my heart, soul, brain, or even lips. None of my sweet nothings at all.

Anyhow, over the next 8 years or so I did another 37 people.

Nobody noticed.

A hundred eyes saw them and me together, but nobody noticed.

I wish I could be sure it was 37.

One girl stands out.

Aged about 15. Or 12. Or 9. Hard to tell when kids have lived on the street. Their faces grow thick. Exhaust fumes and so on. Her body wasn't thick. She was begging. I offered a lift. She had a home. I was surprised. None of them had a home before. She said, come back, my mom will make you fly.

Her mom was a dealer. I thought why are you begging if your mom is a dealer? But I was keen to fly so I just did my usual thing.

I went along.

It was a bad day I remember. So hot. White sky sagging in the middle. An animal's belly. Now and then it sweated on you. Then went dry again. Weather for pumping. Weather for bombs to go off.

I think this was in Port Elizabeth.

In any case, there was lots of rust and seagull shit.

We went back to her place. The street was like where I was born. Houses made of tin, chicken wire, plus lino. But I think she was poor white, not coloured. Not sure. Even when I saw her mom I wasn't sure. The woman had one of those skin diseases where patches of dark show through light. Or vice versa.

Anyhow, although they had a tin, wire, plus lino house, the front door was from Fort Knox. Because her mom's a dealer.

The girl's brother took 5 minutes to open the door. Mind you, he was only a toddler. Very stoned.

Her mom was serving customers in a back room. I just caught a quick look. The customers were white, in summer shorts and flip-flops, like off the beach. But definitely poor white. I can tell them at fifty paces. If you got close to their summer shorts you'd be sick.

The whole house was so dirty it smelled of nothing. The smell of real dirt dries to nothing. My ma-bitch would have been very revolted. She worshipped things that were clean. I've always thought she might secretly worship my work. Cleansing the streets of society's waste matter. But I've never had the chance to ask her. Like your mother she steered clear after our meeting, and during the trial.

Anyhow, the girl's mom was under a bulb hanging from the ceiling. She was smoking a bottleneck. The white pipe. She sucked from the broken bottle's mouth. Then she held the thing up to the lightbulb like she was the statue of liberty.

The girl took me to her room. She didn't have anything there. Except glue. One torn tin of grey glue. The girl's eyes were like this glue. She had dribbles of dried blood under her nose.

I said is this all you're offering?

Glue.

Your mom's a fucking dealer and you're offering me GLUE?

She said take it or leave it.

Later, during her struggle, I heard myself sounding bored. Like a doctor. I heard myself say, now come on, relax.

She did eventually.

Later I heard myself ask the following. Ready?

She was.

Later I felt like allah. I did to her right hand what daddie always feared happening to his. It wasn't easy. Without a curved arab sword. I had to make do with things in the room. The torn tin. Glass from the window. But it was something I wanted to try. To see if it would alleviate the boredom.

Later I was too bored to run.

Later her mom came in.

She saw her daughter and just gave a sigh. In retrospect I think she may have been an intellectual. I think she may have known that moms give birth astride a grave.

Anyhow, then I ran.

I was thinking this is it. Someone has SEEN. They've got to get me now.

But nothing.

Later, after you had happened, I took the cops back to that girl's house.

Still nothing.

The woman said she never had a daughter.

Maybe she was confused. Maybe she thought SHE was being accused of something. And maybe she was. She was a mom after all.

So once again I got away. As you and Bob keep saying, God is on my side.

Until we get to your bit of the story.

And once again you beg me to tell it.

You fool, you dumb cunt. You keep asking and you keep expecting an answer. You keep thinking you'll find a way of making me tell you. But you won't.

Because why?

Because I'm a BASTARD?

No.

Because I'm a FANTASIST whose word isn't worth 2 cents anyway?

No.

What then?

Because I don't remember.

It's not that I don't want to tell you. It's that I can't. There's nothing in the memory box.

I remember us in the Gardens. Vaguely. I've told you that

bit. I remember you were different from my usual sitters or models. You were definitely white for a start.

Hey you like jokes. You know the one about the bloke who'll fuck anything that moves. Well I'm the one who'll fuck anything that doesn't.

You took me to a hotel. It was boring. The rest is history. In other words, a blank.

This must be disappointing for you. To you, the event was a big deal. To me, boring.

I honestly can't remember the details.

Except this.

As an artist I'd lost my touch.

Yours Faith Fully,

Yusuf.

TWENTY-FOUR

4 Craigrownie Rd
Bantry Bay

Thurs. 26th. Oct.

Dear Yusuf,

I wonder if we might meet?

I'm due to come up to Joburg next week to take charge of a new brood, and begin another South African odyssey, another 'World in One Country' tour; the great journey all over again. Well . . . our slightly condensed, two-week version. No overnights in Pretoria, but I could easily pop across.

However, is this of interest to you? Indeed, is it *possible* at such short notice? How complicated is it to arrange a visit? What are the visiting times exactly? Don't feel you need to answer these questions – I can easily find out through the prison.

But I thought I should check with you first; in principle, that is; I mean, check what you think. That's all I need to know really: what you think.

I'm terribly nervous as I write this.

Look, my letter is all in separate paragraphs, like yours.

It's in gasps of breath.

So what do you think?

Yours,

Adrian.

Twenty-Five

83143118
Pretoria Maximum Security

Sure. If you dare.

TWENTY-SIX

D.F. Malan Airport
Cape Town

Tues. 31st Oct.

Dear Yusuf,

It's all fixed then. You've requested me as your visitor
for tomorrow, Wednesday, the 1st of November. Since the
request has to come from your side, I wish you'd just checked
first, and allowed *me* to choose the day – tomorrow is when I
pick up the new brood. Anyway, now that the visit is arranged,
I'll just have to make some excuse, and abandon the brood at
the hotel during lunchtime ... for I have to be at the prison
between twelve and two, and mustn't be late apparently. Gosh,
I feel very nervous again ...

Before I left home this afternoon, I went to say goodbye
to Father. He was in the back yard, drunk and asleep in the
deckchair. What writer was it – and you'll probably know
– who said of their father, 'I disappear alongside him'? I've
often felt this (Father was the famous teacher, I the failed
one), but not today. He looked half his normal size, with
one bony hand lodged above his head ... like his skeleton
was waving goodbye. I leaned forward to kiss his forehead.
It smelled of his body oil. He suddenly woke and stared at me
with thick, almost dusty eyes. He said, 'Whaaat?', as waking
people do; but also as though he'd caught me out. I almost
laughed. I felt like saying, It's alright Father, I wasn't doing
anything perverted, I just wanted to kiss you goodbye. Dear
God, heterosexuals are so queer.

166

Mum appeared, to say her farewells, and to get Father sobered up – some of their crowd were coming round for afternoon tea. I had an odd sense of exclusion, vague jealousy ... the sense of their lives going on without me, behind my back as it were ... then realised that actually none of their crowd had come round *during* my stay. (Still embarrassing for everyone, I guess.) Anyway, Father had no recollection of the teatime arrangement.

'I think that mugging has given you Alzheimer's,' said Mum, chuckling.

'Wouldn't mind,' he replied. 'Sounds like quite a pleasant disease. You make new friends every day.'

Mum and I laughed, shaking our heads at what a character he is!, then I said, 'Well, I'm off.' The same thing I've said a hundred times since I became a tourist guide. But these days I pay attention to each parting in a different way; going over it afterwards, memorising it, or writing every detail into my diary. I'm not sure what frightens me most. The thought of something happening to my parents (murdered in their beds? – by drunk little Janie, setting light to our *Blitz* cupboard, with its gas bottles, bullets and candles?), or something happening to me: a coach accident, a plane crash, or a piece of masonry landing on the taxi as it drives me to the airport – some of the young 'comrades' have started doing this on the N2, from the motorway bridges.

Anyway, the taxi made it in one piece. I've checked in my baggage, and now I'm sitting in the Business Class lounge, with my second free Scotch. Nothing more to report. I'll post this at the other end, but of course we'll have met by the time you receive it. God.

Looking forward to seeing you.

Yours,

Adrian.

IV. PUNISHMENTS

TWENTY-SEVEN

83143118
Pretoria Maximum Security

Adrian.

They've just put me back in my cage after your visit.
I feel a bit mixed-up.
Nothing was like I expected.
Starting with my first sight of you. Which was
Just a shadow.
As they brought me into the visiting room.
Why do they call it that? It's more a passageway than
a room. Divided into cubicles, with that thick, thick glass
cutting it down the middle.
You were late. By the time I was brought in, there was only
one other person on the visitors' side, finishing off a visit.
Since this person was seated and you were standing in the
doorway, I straightaway knew which was you. But all I could
actually see was a sort of shadow. The word is silhouette.
Against the light from that little lawn outside. I remember
that lawn from when the nun visited.
I'm not sure if you recognised me at first. You looked
unsure. Nervy. Maybe because you were late.
The warder Knipe said to me SIT. I obeyed. Choosing the
cubicle opposite the door. So I could keep seeing the lawn.
You sat opposite me. On your side of the glass.
You leaned forward.
Now your head came out of shadow. Into the electric light
of the room.

Your head. Fancy haircut. Face sweating a bit. Maybe because of being late. But clean and very brown in that way you whities think is cool. Features smooth and pretty as a girl, but not sly, moffie-style.

Now you also got a good look at me.

And my face definitely rang a bell.

Because one of your arms shot up. Gut instinct. To near your face. Palm of the hand towards me. I couldn't figure it out. I thought, is he waving? Maybe he doesn't realise we can talk to one another through the big old microphones on each side of the glass. Then I realised it wasn't a wave. It was self defence. Like when a person thinks he's going to be smacked.

I couldn't believe it.

There was Knipe and another warder on my side of the partition. There was this thick, thick glass between us. So thick we couldn't even hear one another without the microphones. I mean, this place was built for one hundred per cent NON-CONTACT visits. Even on the eve of execution. Even then, a man can only reach out and touch the thick, thick glass, and not his stupid sad relatives. Both sides could bang and scratch at the glass till kingdom comes, and they still won't get to touch one another goodbye. So how in hell could I have hurt you today?

Yet you stayed with your arm half up for most of our time together.

We made conversation. Loud, fuzzy and hollow through the big microphones.

How are you?

Yes OK thanks.

Sorry I'm late.

Yes. Thought maybe you had a change of mind.

No, no. Long story but made it in the end.

Yes.

So. This is strange isn't it?

Yes.

And on and on it went like this. The smallest of small talk. I had expected you to come along with all sorts of tricksy questions. To grill me on the subject of the case. Knipe would

172

probably have stopped us, due to rules and regulations, but you didn't even try. I tried to introduce some erudite topics. But it was no good. You just sat there all nervy. Mouth all dry and tongue-tied. One arm lifted to stop me hurting you.

The half hour dragged by. Who would've thought it?

I was relieved when Knipe said TIME UP.

As I started to go, you suddenly said, I've brought some things. Presents.

Knipe went still. On his guard.

You looked worried. Like you shouldn't have said it aloud.

I was confused. You weren't carrying presents. Even if you were, you couldn't have passed them to me.

Anyhow, I said thanks.

I was away from my microphone by then, so you probably didn't hear.

You said goodbye in a funny way. Half standing, bent over, sort of cringing with fear. Face all squeezed up. Like tears were on the way.

I just wanted to get the hell out of there. Knipe obliged.

What a let-down.

Until I got back here to my cage.

On the bed, your presents.

Inside me, some feelings they're bringing.

I'm not sure what to do.

Three items.

One is a box. It says SONY WALKMAN STEREO CASSETTE PLAYER. AUTO-REVERSE. DOLBY B NOISE REDUCTION SYSTEM. 5 BAND GRAPHIC EQUALISER.

I open the box. The Sony thing itself is lying in a compartment of that stuff, I don't know what it's called. Snow-white cardboard or plastic stuff that doesn't weigh anything. In other compartments are the ear things and other knick-knacks. I lift it all to my nose. I don't think I've ever smelled anything so brand new before.

I look round my cage. Like I'm expecting a hand to reach out of the walls and grab this thing back.

The other two items are cassette tapes.

One a sort of plain one, no picture, no cellophane. Homemade handwriting on it. I'll read it in a moment.

The other one all nice and smart from a shop. Still packaged in its cellophane.

BOB DYLAN. GREATEST HITS.

I'm on my bed as I read this. I sit back. My shoulders bump the wall. My jaw is hanging open wide like a fool's.

I don't trust what I'm seeing.

So I lift it to my nose.

Cellophane. No real smell.

But inside the cellophane. Which I haven't taken off yet. Inside there's going to be a smell that's going to do me some damage. A smell that's also a sound that's also a feeling.

You see, I don't care how many copies of this tape have been made. And I don't care how many people tell me the following can't be true. But I know that somewhere in this tape, there's a bit of the man himself.

Dylan is in here.

Dylan's breath.

I can't unwrap the cellophane. I can't man I can't.

I put the tape down and pick up the other one. The plain one.

The handwriting on it is yours. It says.

Dear Yusuf. It took a while but I tracked down your father. In a bar called the Captain in Kalk Bay. He recorded a message for you. Love, Adrian.

Again I have to sit back against the wall.

Why do I feel like this? It's only going to be his voice. Daddie's dumb voice. It can't hurt me. Even if he swears at me. But I suppose you wouldn't have brought it if he swears at me.

The Captain Bar. I know the joint. Near the harbour. Drinking round the clock. Men only. From the boats. Poor white and coloured. Some Chinese. The glasses are heavy and greasy. The men are too. They can hardly move. They were safer out at sea. Here they're drowning on their feet.

But I'm impressed daddie was there. It's up-market for him.

I've only used a Sony machine once before in my life. Out on the Walvis lagoon. When the Jewboy singer let me hear what he was listening to. But I vaguely remember the drill.

And here's a book of instructions in English, French, German and Japanese, but not Afrikaans.

I put the little black sponges in my ears.

All the time I'm still looking round me, eyes going like a lunatic. There's all these windows in my cage. On either side and above. Any minute now I'm expecting a voice to shout in Afrikaans STOP, PUT THAT DOWN, STAND UP, HAND IT OVER.

But no.

Sergeant Fourie goes by on the mesh walkway above. Glances down between his fat boots. Gives me a squiz. Strolls on. Warder Adams goes by in the corridor. Glances in with his brandy eyes. Gives me a squiz. Strolls on.

Hell.

It's like you've bribed and corrupted the whole world.

Mind you, the beauty of these Sony machines is they don't break the rule of silence.

As I press the button called PLAY a small hiss starts in my skull. It turns into everyday sound. The Captain Bar. Men, glasses, jukebox. And daddie.

Now it's a bit later.

Now I've heard daddie and I don't know what to do with what I've heard.

OK I must write it all down. Carefully. He sounds like he's got a dop in him, well over the limit. He talks and waits. As though he expects me to answer. Maybe he thinks your tape recorder is a kind of phone.

Anyhow, this is what he says.

Hullo there Yusuf, my son, my sunshine, long time no see, long time no hear. How's things wit' you? Uh. You OK? We OK here. Uh. Your ma went an' died of course. Foeitog, shame. The ou girl never liked our life. But ag, she was sommer jus' a ou fokkin TEEF. I don't visit your broers an' sisters no more. I'm banned. They don't mos' like the kids to be around me. Who the fok do they think they are hey? Haai no, wag 'n bietjie, hou my bek, I lie. Pearl, jou baby sister. Pearl still lets me come call. She's nogal still a good girl. Jaa. Uh. Dunno, wat nog? Uh. Hope yous fit as a fiddle. Look after yourself, hoor? Don't get wet in the rain, don't do what I

175

wouldn't do, salaam alaikon, an' fingers crossed. Alright hey I must fly. Here's to bygone times.

And then he starts to sing. An old dronkie crooning in a bar. The other men join in, or cheer like they're farting. It's the Bing Crosby hit. Which daddie used to croon to my ma-bitch. She's dead now. Nobody told me. I'll see her soon. And all my dumb cunt of a daddie can say is fingers crossed. And this.

Oh danny boy. The pipes, the pipes are calling. From glen to glen. And down the mountain side. The summer's gone and all the roses falling. It's you, it's you must go and I must bide. But come ye back. When summer's in the meadow. Or when the valley's hushed and white with snow.

What does he know about snow? The fucking old fool. He's never seen snow.

Listen Adrian, I won't bestow pardon on you. You meant good, but it was the wrong thing to do. Bringing me these things. Giving me these feelings.

Dylan's tape is lying there now.

I must not open the cellophane, I must not.

Joy will start, and when joy starts so does a journey. It's a journey that's always going to end less well than it began.

I must not open the cellophane.

Now. As I'm thinking this. Now. Suddenly it happens.

The light goes out.

The light, the eternal sun, my sun in a bottle, it goes out. For the first time ever. And not just in my cage. Also in the walkway above. Also in the corridor. Also through the window above my bed. Everywhere.

Complete darkness.

I lift my face into it.

I lift my arms like it's something to hug.

I touch it with my fingers. I touch this invisible thing. Like it's sweet smoke. Or Dylan's breath.

The most beautiful thing.

Darkness.

And already it's over.

BANG.

Lights back on.

Sound of feet running and warders shouting. The POWER, the GENERATOR.

That's all it was. A power cut. Followed by the emergency generator springing into action.

An ordinary thing. Like the plumbing problem a few weeks ago. Can happen in any home any day of the week.

Completely ordinary.

Yet I bet if you looked in every cage up and down these corridors now, you'd see men like me. On their feet. Arms up, face lifted, mouth open, eyes blinking.

Like we saw a miracle.

And we did.

We saw darkness.

For me it was more than a miracle. It was a sign.

I sit back on my bed, to catch my breath.

Next to me is the Dylan tape.

In one second from now I'll unwrap the cellophane.

Yusuf.

Twenty-Eight

Satara Rest Camp
Kruger Game Park
Hut 3

Sat. 4th Nov.

Dear Yusuf,

You must picture me in a new way.

Picture me here in the Kruger, at 4 p.m., trying to round up my new brood for the dusk game drive. They'd been up since 4 a.m., for the dawn game drive, when we saw nothing of interest ... just some impala, and a distant elephant-shaped blob a mile from the road. During the day, there was thin grey rain, and the group retreated into their huts to indulge half-remembered Hemingway fantasies of drinking and screwing in the African bush; or they settled into the ubiquitous carvery to eat-as-much-as-you-can, or into the cinema – to watch *films* on Africa's wildlife.

Picture me at mid-afternoon, trailing through the drizzle, from place to place, trying to rouse them, a feeling of being unwelcome, unliked, of having lost my grip with this bunch ...

And picture me not giving a damn.

We got off to a bad start when they arrived on Wednesday. First of all, the airport was evacuated because of a bomb scare, which meant my UK group having to proceed to the hotel *without* their luggage (very traumatic for them, this); BA promising to send it on. When I returned at mid-morning to meet my Australian contingent, I learned that their flight was delayed. I waited and prayed, but eventually there was nothing for it – unless I was to miss visiting hours at your prison, all the way over in Pretoria, I would have to leave Charlie, the driver, at the airport to meet the Ossies ... silent Charlie, lurking behind his pitch-black shades, sizing up the females in the new brood; new prey for the overnights ahead.

By the time I got back from visiting you in Pretoria, the full brood was assembled at the Joburg Towers; the Ossies reeling about, horribly jet-lagged, fuming because Charlie couldn't answer any of their queries; and the Brits twittering through the last stages of luggage-withdrawal (it still hadn't arrived!); and, to cap it all, head office had, at the last minute, added three extra *pax* to my brood – three Israelis.

But because of what had happened at the prison (I'll come to that in a moment), I didn't care, I didn't care remotely.

Things got worse over the next two days.

Some black commuters were machine-gunned at a taxi rank in one of the townships, elsewhere a bomb went off, killing and maiming white passers-by; and while the TV and newspapers gorged themselves on these things, and while I began to relax into the experience of civil war (I mean, I haven't survived you to be hurt by *flying glass*); at the same time, more and more of the brood started bunking off from the tours, preferring the hotel's sealed-off, in-house pleasures: the bars, shops, and bedroom movie channels.

I thought things would improve once we put Joburg and civilisation behind us. However, halfway on the run here to the Kruger, the good-looking but ferocious Brigadier General Hazor (from the Israeli police force), interrupted my 'This is the Africa of Rider Haggard' speech, to ask whether the video screen above my head was functional, and whether we had any decent tapes on board.

I was dumbfounded, but Charlie, who's got his sunglassy eyes trained on her short and beefy body (I'm convinced she's gay), slotted in a Schwarzenegger video; and I didn't say another word for the rest of the ride.

This afternoon, when I tracked down half of the brood in the Satara cinema, watching a David Attenborough documentary, this Brigadier General Hazor was on the aisle seat.

'Time for the dusk game drive,' I whispered, trying not to disturb the rest of the audience.

Some of the brood leaned forward, or half-rose, grudgingly, reluctant to take their eyes off the screen where a hippo was giving birth.

'Ach no, sit down,' Brigadier General Hazor said to them in that brusque tone of hers, 'at least *here* we are seing some wildlife game.' Then she waved her knuckles at me, as though dismissing a servant.

I paused, stunned – as if those knuckles had made contact – then heard myself say, 'You know what . . . you'll all go back to Tel Aviv, London, Sydney, and people will ask you what you saw in South Africa. And you'll answer, Well we saw *Batman* on the movie channel in the hotel, and a video of *Terminator* on the coach ride to the game reserve, and then finally the real thing – David Attenborough in the cinema there!'

I'm not sure how much my anger registered – this brood know me so little, they may have thought it was my sense of humour – but it shook *me*. I've never spoken to a brood like that before; I don't know why I did today.

I went back to my hut. Stood in the middle of it, listening to the rain, heavier now, big drops knocking on the roof. I don't normally travel with alcohol or dope, but I have a supply of both on this trip, I don't know why.

(Why do I keep saying, 'I don't know'? Of course I do – it's because I've met you, I've actually met you again!)

Anyway, a little later, my mind dreamy with dope, my tummy sloshy with whisky, I walked singing in the rain to the hangar where the game wardens (or warders?) keep their helicopters, and thornbush-proof jeeps. The pilots and drivers were all sitting round playing cards, getting blotto as well, work finished for the day, silhouetted against the massive open doors and a streaming African afternoon.

I headed for a warden I know, called van Rensburg, fingering a small roll of rands in my pocket.

Now picture me alone in one of the jeeps, driving it fast. I've left the tarred roads far behind, even turned off the gravel ones; I'm heading straight across open grassy land. This is scarred with rocky outcrops and small dongas, but

I'm ignoring all caution, and so is my jeep, which heaves, twists and crashes along like a living thing – I could be riding a rhino! I grin into the blast of rain and blue light . . . the wind would be streaming through my hair if it was long enough!

As the jeep rushes to the crest of a hill, I imagine I'm back in my surfing days: that moment when you're paddling onto the shoulder of some gigantic swell. You see only the muscular curve of water against the sky, every sinew of it – exactly like wind-whipped savannas – and then, getting to your feet, you're suddenly balanced on the edge of a liquid cliff, riding a volcano as it spills, looking at an unbelievable, scooping, falling view beneath you . . .

. . . And so my jeep crests the hill, and there below lies Africa. Africa as it was long before the Rider Haggards, etcetera, ever saw it: Africa, with its slightly scuffed, slightly raised skin – that layer of heat, flies, dust – and its valleys of immeasurable distance, with any number of different skies; over there one is indigo, streaming with rain like waterfalls, over here a rainbow glows above oceans of grass, further still, huge light burns on the plains, then lowers, soggily, into black-green jungle; and then, just at the edge of your sight, there are more dry-lands, more cloud shadows, more vast sad green landscapes, and other weather, far worlds, more horizons . . .

Picture me like this please. Because all the time, I was picturing you. At our meeting on Wednesday.

I reached the prison so late, the guard at the reception block said visiting hours were probably over. At the edge of my tether, I snapped back, telling him to phone Major Steenkamp and mention my name. Within minutes of him replacing the receiver, a combi arrived to take me to your section. Now began a dream-like journey: inexplicable routes, doors opening and closing, exteriors leading to interiors and out again.

The combi driver took me up a hill to Maximum Security, dropped me off in front of its big black steel gates, shouted something towards a mirrored window, and left. After a while a door to the right was unlocked. As I went through, so did a delivery of meat. You've said you can't always identify the food you get; I had the same problem with these carcasses. Now I was in a cool and gloomy corridor, now being led across a hot, bright courtyard, now waiting at a massive, medieval-type wooden portal, listening as keys unlocked a door-sized hole in this wall-sized door. When I stepped through, at last into death row itself, and when the lock fastened behind me, I had a sense that, although this visit had been my suggestion, it was a trick, a trap. The crime in that hotel room four years ago had somehow been mine, not yours, and they'd caught me at last. When a fat warder (Sergeant Fourie?) summoned me into an office to the right, I wouldn't have been surprised if he'd photographed and stripped me – but I was only required to show my ID. On his desk lay a stack of prisoners' letters, opened . . . he was busy censoring them . . . his waste basket was full. (How lucky we've been.) I was allowed to proceed. A gate was opened, letting me into a large pen, its iron bars white, except for around the locks, which were blackened, as though burnt, with use. Keys hung from each warder's belt, at the end of a long dark strap, like barbers use to sharpen their blades. Another gate was unlocked, and locked behind me, I went up some stairs, and suddenly was outside again, in a rectangular yard with lawn and flowers (beautiful orange canna lilies), and no warder to guide me. I stood, nonplussed, wondering if you would be released from another doorway, and we'd be free to meet properly – shake hands, embrace, or fight? But now, when someone stepped from one of the doorways, it was a nun (perhaps the same nun who once visited you?). I said, 'Is that the visiting room?' She said, 'White or non-white?' When I answered, she gestured to the right-hand door, then said, in a peculiarly hushed way, 'God be with you,' and departed, vanishing into the maze through which I'd just come.

I stood in the doorway, the weird journey over, my normal senses returning. There was one other person on my side of the glass, a black woman in the corner, coming to the end of her visit. I was sweating and angry; angry with the airlines for making me so late, angry with myself for abandoning a brood to black-eyed Charlie, angry with you for anything you care to mention . . .

And then they brought you in – wearing your green fatigues,

182

clutching a floppy hat (like a beach hat) in the same green material. Why a hat — had they given up on me arriving, and taken you to exercise? The awkward way your hands held this hat, as though wringing it dry, and your shuffling walk (what's happened to the swagger, styled 'to dance or pump pussy'?) . . . these things made you look so humble, so timid. The warder you call Knipe told you to sit, so you sat. I sat opposite, on a worn red vinyl stool, like the kind in passport photo booths. The sunlight from the doorway behind me, from the lawn and flower beds, this light blazed on the glass partition. I couldn't see a thing, so I held up one hand, throwing a patch of shade into the glare. You thought this was me flinching from an imaginary blow . . . I roared with laughter when I read this in your letter; I'm laughing still.

At last, through this hole of shade, I saw you. How small you looked, how pale your skin was, how old you seemed — shorn close to the bone, your hair was almost invisible.

This was you — this small, bald-looking, twitchy man — this was *you*. I couldn't think what to say. Again you interpreted this as fear. It wasn't; it was someone waking up from a nightmare, or from love-sickness, contemplating the loved one with a terrible sense of shame: shame for one's own weaknesses, and shame for the other person, for their ordinariness, their ugliness.

Then you spoke. You — you who've lectured me on literature and philosophy — you spoke. So awkwardly that the consonants grated and the vowels dragged, squeaking, along your tongue. I got a fit of the giggles . . . graveside giggles . . . painful as hiccoughs. Fighting to hide them, I had to limit myself to brief comments, or staying silent altogether. You, meanwhile, thinking I was speechless with fear, continued to make conversation, inching your way through long words, syllable by syllable, making great writers seem like characters from Toyland. You sounded like a talking clock, a budgie, a computer toy. Really you just sounded like what you are: a half-educated half-breed.

Again and again, I tried to speak back. But my breath wouldn't hold, my words dissolved into giggles, dry hurting giggles. By now I had the tightest hard-on I've ever known.

I don't think this had much to do with you. It was me: me restored, me well again, me feeling very strong indeed. It wasn't just the present situation – you trapped behind unbreakable glass; brutal, dumb Knipe behind you, propped against the wall like a sports trophy – it was something else, something I knew about, and you didn't. During our meeting, our 'postman' was delivering my presents to your cell. What effect, I wondered, would these have on you . . .?

The idea turned me on so much, I became totally indiscreet: as we parted, I blurted out, 'I've brought some things!', by now in agony from swallowing my vicious giggles (you note, 'Tears were on the way'), and from my hard-on, which I tried to hide by stooping over (you note, 'Cringing with fear').

As I walked out of the prison complex, gulping the beautiful, pure, hot air of a Highveld summer afternoon, again and again I was hit by the sensation of waking from nightmarish sleep, or surfacing from dark water, or returning to life from a brief death.

My joy hasn't subsided since then . . . it gets sidetracked by the new brood, the mutinous Brig. Gen. Hazor, and so on . . . but it's still there, this most tremendous new feeling. This afternoon, in the game park, I gave it full rein . . .

After I stopped the jeep, I took off my soaking clothes, all of them, and walked out of the rain to where there was sunlight. The grass was drying here. Red grass, already starting to roast again. I lay down in it, stretching out my arms and legs, flattening the whole area within my reach.

I was, of course, aware what I was doing. In this part of the world, I'm forever warning my broods to spray insect repellent on any area of bare skin . . . there are creepy-crawlies here that don't just bite you, they lay eggs in your flesh. Also, just to the left of my head was a small, oval-shaped hole in the ground, and I recognised that . . . the burrow of a scorpion, the Transvaal thick-tailed scorpion. And in the branches of the tree above me, a golden orbweb spider was evidently in residence; one of the most poisonous species in Africa. *And* this was big cat country, big snake country. Smiling, I lit a long, strong joint. As I breathed deeply, I caught the wonderful aroma of wild aniseed growing nearby me. I smoked and breathed some more, then rolled over, and found myself eye-to-eye with the scorpion's burrow. Lifting my face, I slid in my tongue, moving it gently back and forward, sampling the moist dirt. Now I realised that a crumbling stone nearby was actually elephant dung, and I rubbed some in my fingers, and tried to light it – there are tribes who inhale the smoke to cure headaches (which I still get from that *bang* on our bedside table) – but the stuff was too wet from the rain. Talking of elephants, what a pity this wasn't the right season for marula fruit, which makes them drunk, and me too ... what a pity, because there was a marula tree right above me. Rolling onto my back again, I remembered it was also the tree with the deadly spider – which I could see now – look there! – suspended among the raindrops in its beautiful web, which doesn't just look like gold thread, but is as tough ... there are tribes who use it to sew up wounds. (Don't ask me *which* tribes – I'm a white man in Africa, what do I know?) Then I just lay there, and smoked and listened to the rustle of things in the grass around me, and felt, or imagined, them touching my nakedness, sniffing it, tasting it. I was completely at ease. I knew that I would come to no harm. I couldn't have survived you, and come to harm now, like this, on the floor of Africa, under a brilliant, clearing sky. It simply couldn't be. It wasn't written in my story; I felt sure of that.

I began this letter by asking you to picture me in a new way. Now do you understand? Picture me in a world without nightmares. Picture me in a world where *you* don't feature any more. Picture me as free again.

With my thanks,

Adrian.

TWENTY-NINE

83143118
Pretoria Maximum Security

Adrian.

If you ARE still Adrian.

You sounded so funny, so snaaks in your letter. So cross
with me again. And you're lying. You WERE on your nerves
when we met. Not laughing at me. I don't know what I
must think. Maybe you're lying because I've done ditto in
the past. Maybe things will never come right between us till
I stop lying.

And maybe now's the time.

Now while I feel so good.

Dylan is playing in my skull. Did you know that the Sony
machine you gave me has something called CONTINUOUS
REVERSE MODE. You can just leave Dylan playing. Or
swimming. He swims in my skull. Morning noon and night.
Eternally there. Like god. Don't laugh please. People worship
worse things.

My ma-bitch's god for example. Who told her to hammer
us. The good shepherd was a wolf in sheep's clothing. And
daddie's god was no better. Waiting round every corner to
slash pieces off a person.

But now I've got Dylan. Dylan and his hymns.

I'd never heard him before you see. I possessed his words
and tunes. From the Jewboy singer. But I never possessed
the man himself. His voice. His voice in my skull. You've
given me that and I'll bless you until the end of time. Even

when you're lying about me, like in your letter. Even then I'll pardon you and bestow a blessing.

But hey, my news. I haven't told you my news.

Yesterday. I think it was Monday. The headman of Beverly Hills, Major Steenkamp, he came to my cage with a sheet of paper. He called this a WRIT and said it had been delivered to him by the SHERIFF. I was confused, thinking about cowboys, so it took a moment to sink in. This thing he was holding. It was my notice of execution.

Major Steenkamp asked me my name. I felt like saying, I've been your guest for several years and you still don't know who I am? But I just answered properly, using my christian not muslim first name. Then he read out that sentence would be carried out in exactly 7 days time, and that I would be hung by the neck UNTIL DEAD. I thought, what other kind is there? Then he asked if I wanted him to send a rail warrant to my family? I said no. He said it was FREE. I still said no. He looked so bored. I was surprised. I know he's only doing a job and I know he's done it hundreds of times before. Particularly 3 or 4 years ago. But there's been less and less executions recently because of political developments. So I expected him to show some interest.

He didn't.

When he left I felt flat. The big moment I'd been waiting for had come and gone. Without living up to its reputation. I wanted this more than anything in the world. Why did I feel so flat? It was like I'd caught the governor's boredom.

Next Dominee van Zyl came in to see me. This must be part of the routine. Sheriff gallops in with writ. Head of B. Hills delivers writ to condemned man. Priest pops in to offer man succour.

I think that's what Dominee van Zyl was doing. Older, thinner, chain-smoking brother of Doctor van Zyl. Both men lacking in hygiene and job satisfaction. So now Dominee van Zyl looked at me sorrowfully with his nicotine-stained specs and talked to me about god in his bad breath.

This made me more bored.

A boredom stretching and stretching like the line that architects draw into the distance.

Perspective.

Which is the concept of Brunelleschi, Filippo di Ser, who died in 1446, at last finding out what lay at the end of the line.

Now things hotted up a bit.

The warders came to move me to the Pot. The corridor with 7 cages where you spend your last 7 days.

Still all part of the routine I suppose. Sheriff gallops in with writ, head of B. Hills delivers selfsame, priest pops in with succour, warders put prisoner in Pot.

I was holding onto my Sony machine and my 2 tapes when they came for me. Holding on really tight. I expected them to tell me to leave the stuff behind. And due to the rule of silence, I couldn't have argued back. But my eyes were doing it for me. Sending this message. If you try taking Dylan off me I'll butcher one of you, I've fuckall to lose now.

But they said nothing about leaving Dylan behind. They just said MOVE.

As they were chasing me doubletime to the Pot, we passed Robert McBride's cage.

I almost shouted out this.

Tell your people outside, quick, I've been given my notice of execution.

It's a system he's got going in here. As soon as a person is served with the notice, big baby-faced McBride gets the word out. He writes the prisoner's name or number on his arm. Then, during visiting time, he casually shows it to his Paula lady as they sit talking through the glass. She casually memorises it, then goes away and tells the newspapers plus whoever. A campaign starts, and these days they're quite successful. Particularly for comrades. Quite a few stays of execution these days.

I was really shocked I almost asked him for it.

For help.

The warders chased me into the Pot and into my new cage.

It didn't take long to settle in.

My Pot cage is like my old one. Upright coffin with windows. Eternal sun in a bottle. But there's a difference. It's completely bare.

They have to guard against suicidal despair here where the end is nigh, so everything is removed. No mattress, blankets or pillow. No towel, toothbrush or even soap. Nothing that you could smother over your face or stick down your throat. No vest or underpants. Just fatigues. You're not even allowed to keep your shoes inside the cage. These wait outside your door, like I noticed in that hotel where you took me on our day together.

Yet they let me keep Dylan.

Couldn't I swallow him?

What a way to go.

Why have they let me keep him? I don't think it's just that you've bribed and corrupted them. I think there's another reason. A better reason. A deeper reason.

I sat on my bare bed, trying to work it out, shaking my head.

Still in shock over almost asking McBride for help.

I put Dylan into my ears to soothe me.

And immediately I heard him say to me the following.

DON'T THINK TWICE IT'S ALRIGHT.

So then I knew what I must do.

And quick. Without thinking twice.

I banged on the cage door and Sergeant fat Fourie came to the window.

I said, permission to speak please sergeant.

He said, you don't need permission here in the Pot. You can speak as much as you want, 24 hours a day. To us, to yourself, to god, to other prisoners. Well, there's only one other in here at the moment, and he only speaks Shangaan, but you two can gibber at one another if that's what you want. Because what WE want is for you to be as relaxed as possible for the next 7 days. You give us no serious trouble, and we'll make your last week with us as pleasant as possible, sir.

He said this last word with a laugh, but I think he was serious about the rest.

Jesus, think of the SERIOUS TROUBLE some men must've given them in the past. At this stage of proceedings.

Meanwhile I had to absorb this news. No more rule of silence. My mouth hung open in shock.

Fat Fourie said, now you've got the freedom to talk, you don't know how to use it, hey? Typical of you people. And then you want us to give you the vote.

While he laughed loudly at this, I remembered why I'd called him over.

I said, can someone get my advocate over here please sergeant, I want to see him.

He said, who is your advocate?

I made a noise like stupid people do in cartoon films. Like duhh. Because I was remembering that I didn't know my advocate's name. We only met a few times. Before my trial in Cape Town. How many years ago was that now? Anyhow, he was just a new young advocate they found for the trial because I had no bucks. They let these new young advocates practise on people like me.

Now I had to think fast.

I said, it's not just one advocate. It's that whole klomp of them. The human rights klomp. Them who help the comrades.

Fat Fourie said in a scoffing way, you mean the HRA?

I said, that's them.

He laughed and said, OK.

And went away to phone.

I stood there, panting like I'd been punched. Was it really that easy? Was someone really going to come from that organisation? Does one only have to ASK? Then why does McBride go to all the trouble of writing on his arm? Maybe prisoners don't know they can ask. Then again, why did fat Fourie keep laughing?

Waiting to see if anything would happen was very hard. Fat Fourie never came back. He'd gone off duty, Knipe told me. And Knipe knew nothing about no phone call to any human rights advocates. Knipe didn't laugh when he said these words. He spat them. Being poor white he probably didn't know what the words meant. But they tasted dirty. Anyhow, I waited for 3 hours. 3 hours round and round the cage. 3 hours of saying don't think twice, don't think twice, it's alright, it's alright.

Then, next thing, Knipe strolls back to my cage, unlocks it, and says like to a dog, c'mon.

I pull on my shoes that are outside the door. Then I trot after him.

We go in the direction of the visiting cubicles. Past them into a small room. Here a woman is waiting. Much younger than I expected. Maybe they're letting her practise on me too. Indian, smartly dressed, plump, pretty, but works too hard. Dark eyes all in rings, brown skin looking grey.

I can't believe it. Although Knipe stays in the room, near the door, this woman and me, we can touch if we want. There's no glass partition. This is a CONTACT visit.

It scares me.

It's years since I've had CONTACT with someone who isn't a prisoner or a warder.

And this is a WOMAN.

I feel very, very scared.

In case I harm her.

She doesn't look scared at all. Just a bit bored, like everybody today. Now she makes CONTACT. She shakes my hand. Jesus, just SMELL her. Indian perfume, sugar and spice and all things nice. She introduces herself as Mrs Malik. MRS? So young and already married? Mind you, they do that, the coolies. Now she starts talking very fast.

Sorry I took so long getting here, the HRA offices are only down the road in Pretoria, but it's been like a madhouse today, anyway what can I do for you?

I say, I've been served my notice of execution.

She says, OK, what d'you want to do about it?

I frown at her. She makes it sound like I've got a choice. Now I glance over to Knipe. Mrs Malik and me are talking in English, and Knipe can hardly even understand his own tongue, but all the same I don't like him there.

Raising her voice, so Knipe can definitely hear, she says the following.

The rule is that a warder is within sight but out of hearing.

I notice Knipe shuffle back a few steps.

I think, fuck me, this bitch has got both class and clout.

Now I say the following. Which I've practised a bit over the past 3 hours.

I didn't think either when I committed my felonies, nor when these selfsame felonies were brought to trial, that there was any political motivation contained therewithin. However, I have, over the 4 long years of my incarceration, been arduous in educating myself, and during the course of this education have found myself exposed to opinions like, say, the following from Aristotle, dead in 322 BC. MAN IS BY NATURE A POLITICAL ANIMAL. More recently, I have also been exposed to something even richer than education, i.e. the milk of human kindness, this having been supplied by two gentlemen, one by the name of Adrian, and the other, a Yank, well let's just call him Bob. Through their endeavours I have begun to consider a new and challenging concept, viz., that life may be worth living after all. Therefore, taking into consideration that I never appealed against my sentence when it was originally passed, and given that there is perhaps, after all, a political context to both my life and my misdemeanours, which you might help me please to clarify, I now feel both inclined and entitled to request a stay of execution.

Mrs Malik is staring back in utter fucking amazement.

Unlike you, you CUNT, she doesn't think of me as a budgie or a talking clock.

She is impressed that someone of my deprived upbringing can have turned into such an articulate and sophisticated intellectual.

However, she is quick to point out that HRA is not a political organisation. As she speaks now, she keeps making these two funny marks in the air, like little devil's horns.

Although we were formed by a number of so-called LIBERAL lawyers, and as a so-called LOBBYING group, we are not specifically a so-called POLITICAL body. We passionately oppose the death penalty whatever the nature of the so-called CRIME.

Then she adds, quite loudly, and with regret.

And that even extends to Barend Strydom, the so-called WHITE WOLF, here on death row at the moment.

I glance at Knipe. Nothing shows in those small eyes.

As I look back at Mrs Malik I see she's smiling. I think she enjoys talking in front of warders like Knipe. After all, it's only like having a dumb animal in the room.

I smile back.

It's a long time since I smiled at a lady.

I feel my temper rising.

She gets up to go. Which is probably just as well.

She promises to track down my advocate from the Cape Town trial. Called a PRO-DEO advocate she says. And she promises to get him to send up all the transcripts and his notes. And she promises to come back tomorrow with it all.

I say, how will he be able to send them up that fast?

She says, by fax.

I ask what that is and she explains.

Sounds good.

I think to myself, pity me and Adrian never used that scheme. He should've bribed and corrupted our postman to put one of those machines in my cage. Then we could've been in touch round the clock.

Mrs Malik smiles again and, before she goes, we do another CONTACT handshake.

My fingers are trembling like a dronkie's.

Back in my cage, I sleep pretty well. Despite the other Pot prisoner, the Shangaan man, who howls and pines through the night like a fucking dog. When I'm not sleeping, I lie there thinking about Mrs Malik. Thinking and feeling. Look, the Valkenberg shrinks explained to me that my emotions aren't always as grown-up as my intellect, but all the same I'm wondering the following. Is this love at first sight? And maybe she feels the same. Who's to say she's not one of those people who find murderers sexy? You know what I mean. More than anyone, you know what I mean. So, in any case, I think I'd like Mrs Malik to become my Paula McBride. I'm sure she could get her present husband to go fuck. And if she can't, I will.

This morning, true to her word, Mrs Malik was back with all the notes from this pro-deo advocate.

She began by saying this.

The only way we'll get a stay of execution is by offering fresh evidence. Now, you confessed to and were convicted of one count of murder and one of attempted murder. You

193

also confessed to a number of other murders, a number which you couldn't specify, but thought was not less than 45, not more than 48. You were not convicted of these murders, due to lack of evidence. However, the prosecution made a big deal of these other confessions, as did the newspapers, and this factor may have influenced the outcome of the trial. Do you have anything to tell me about these other murders?

Complete fantasy, I replied. Looking her straight in the eye.

Good, she said. So why did you confess to them?

It was my upbringing, I told her. Deprivation and brutalisation. The bigshots round where we lived were all gangsters. So I thought I could become famous as a criminal. I'd heard about people becoming very famous overseas as mass-murderers. So when I was arrested in that hotel room for attempted murder, I thought I might as well go for the jackpot. That way I would achieve some standing in society. It was my fantasy.

So, she said, we could offer as fresh evidence your retraction of those 45, 6, 7, or 8 other confessions?

We most definitely could, I replied.

She said, good, very good.

Now we dealt with the case of the Jewboy singer.

With Mrs Malik's help I realised I'd been remembering it all wrong. We did meet on the shores of the lagoon at Walvis. We did go into the desert together. We did have sexual congress in the dune. All that is true. What I've remembered wrong is that I forced his head into the sand.

This ISN'T true.

What happened is the following. During the sexual congress, he had a sort of fit underneath me. He must have swallowed some sand and then vomited and choked on it. The forensic evidence when his bones were recovered years later could only prove that he died with a weight on top of him. This may be true. But I didn't do nothing. When I realised he had choked I panicked. I ran. I feared I'd be blamed. A klonkie with a rich white Jewboy. Also I was

194

ashamed of what we'd been doing. Even though it was his idea and his fault. White people's perversion, European decadence. An act of gross indecency. My parents' strict religions, both of them, were dead against this kind of thing. Yes it was wrong to run, but others might have done the selfsame. You can't hang a person just for running.

So, said Mrs Malik, we could offer as fresh evidence your retraction of the confession to that murder?

We could, I said.

Now we turned our attention to the other charge.

Attempted murder.

You.

Adrian, during the course of these letters I've messed about with you a lot. I've given you a whole load of rap about this plus that, such and such, different stories and all sorts. Including that I can't remember what happened in the hotel room.

This ISN'T true.

We were there yes. The shower yes. Cocktails of drink and dope and sleeping pills yes. You having sexual intercourse in me yes. Me starting to have sexual intercourse in you yes.

All this is true.

What you don't know about is my state of mind. Mrs Malik helped me understand it today.

She was very interested in my life as a tramp.

She said, have you ever lived in a squatter camp?

I said, well I've crashed out in a few along the way.

For more than a night or two?

Ja, maybe a week or so, maybe a month.

You've LIVED in squatter camps, she said, like this was good news. You've been part of the vast, homeless, unemployed black population, she said.

Coloured, I said, correcting her.

BLACK, she said strongly. You might be coloured, I might be Indian, but in the eyes of the law of this country we're BLACK.

By now, it was dawning on me that these human rights

advocates were maybe a bit more political than Mrs Malik said yesterday.

On and on she went, her pen wagging around in her grip like something else I wished she was holding. She asked me about life on the open road. Years of cheap drink. And worse. Meths. Buttons. Glue. By the time of meeting you, I couldn't tell fantasy from reality. Right from wrong.

And to make matters worse

You FORCED more chemical substances upon me.

And then

You FORCED me to commit another act of gross indecency.

And that's when it happened.

Me and Mrs Malik are very precise about the moment.

The moment when assorted politico-socio-economic factors impacted on my neuro-chemistry.

Yes I've laughed at these things in the past.

But Mrs Malik has helped me to stop laughing.

The moment of impact was this.

Seeing the back of your head. Your neat richboy's haircut.

Imagine spending money on a HAIRCUT.

If you had that much money to waste, shouldn't I have some?

As Mrs Malik said, my poverty had reached DESPERATION LEVEL. This was a clear-cut case of SURVIVAL ROBBERY.

I knew you had more than the few rands you put on the table with your packet of raincoats and other stuff.

In order to find it, I had to knock you out. I didn't want to do it, so the first blow sort of missed. You just felt a little slap on the head and half smiled. You thought I was playing. This made me cross. Where I was brought up, pain hurts and kills. But you whities use it for FUN.

It was easy holding your face in the pillow. At first. For a long time. A long long time. It's a miracle you're still with us buddy. A beautiful miracle for us both.

Suddenly you came back to life. Your struggle was super-human. But I could have subdued you. I don't want to brag but I could have.

I CHOSE not to.

Because why?

Because I remembered the Jewboy singer. In that case, although I was blameless, I ran. I didn't help him.

But I helped YOU. I turned you over. I helped you breathe. I didn't run away this time. I lay alongside you to make sure you were alright. Even though I knew I'd land in deep and everlasting shit.

So.

I don't deserve your anger.

Maybe I even deserve some thanks.

So.

At last I've told it to you. The TRUTH. And nothing but. So help me god.

Mrs Malik was very pleased we'd got our facts straight at last.

In fact, she was very pleased with me altogether.

She smiled till I hurt.

She said, one last question Yusuf?

I said, anything you like.

She said, when you were arrested how did the police treat you?

I replied like this. By gum Mrs Malik, you're a woman of the world and an advocate to boot, so pardon me for saying so, but that's a darn stupid question. I was a pigshit coloured, sorry BLACK, tramp accused of trying to murder a respectable white citizen. How do you think they treated me?

Was actual physical violence used, she asked, her pen wagging all stiff with excitement.

Excessive physical violence.

And during your confessions?

Even more excessive.

So we could perhaps say that these confessions were the result of coercion?

We most definitely could.

197

She said, Yusuf I don't want to raise your hopes, but I think we might be in with a chance.

So then, she and me, we leaned closer and wrote out an affidavit. She was impressed that I could write it myself, the pen now wagging in my own hand. Usually she has to do it for the prisoner. Then she went away and I went back to my cage. Then she came back, having drawn it up all nice and formal, and we had another visit. Then no less a personage than Major Steenkamp himself was summoned to witness me signing it.

By the time I got back to my cage for good, my head was bloody spinning. Because why? Because of a new fact of life staring me in the face.

I might go free.

No, I think it's more certain than that.

I WILL go free.

Hell I never thought I'd write those words.

And hell, I never thought I'd WANT to.

When I get out, I'm planning to marry Mrs Malik, as I've told you. I know this sounds like madness, but I think it's OK to talk about one's good dreams. I've spent a lot of time with my bad ones. Anyhow, what I also want to do when I get out is devote my life to you. In whatever way you want. I'll be your friend. Or more. Or a servant. Or anything you want. You won't have to pay me. You can use or abuse me. I will be yours.

My soul feels so light.

Everyone has noticed the change in me since Mrs Malik left this morning. Even the warders. Fat Fourie came into my cage to play cards. I cheated a bit. My life makes me. I can't help it. I think he knew when I was cheating but he let me. That's because he thought he was playing cards with a man who's only got one more Wednesday Thursday Friday Saturday Sunday to live.

It makes me smile. Him letting me cheat. I've misjudged the warders I think. They're only doing their job. Doing their best. We all try and do our best. In our own eyes. And in god's eyes. Whoever your god is.

Ring them bells ye heathen from the city that dreams.

Ring them bells for the time that flies.
For the child that cries when innocence dies.
Ring them from the fortress for the lilies that bloom.

With my deepest love.

Yusuf.

THIRTY

The Durban Towers
Room 1616

Thurs. 9th Nov.

Dear Yusuf,

Today I said goodbye to some of the brood; seven of them, catching flights back to the UK and Australia. They decided to cut short their trip because of the worsening political situation.

This brood have been more upset than most by the horror stories in our papers every day (I barely notice them any more), but it was when they finally witnessed an incident themselves that some decided to leave. It happened on Tuesday, our first day here in Durban. The coach got caught in a traffic jam, behind a school bus. Something happened – I'm not entirely sure what – but some Zulu road-workers started arguing with the school bus driver. Next thing, we saw two men inside the bus produce guns (a lot of school buses have armed escorts these days), and then one of the road-workers drew a gun as well, and then all chaos broke out. The kids started shrieking, the escorts were yelling at them, 'Get down, get down!', the road-workers began wielding their spades and pick-axes, bellowing and banging the windows, people were jumping out of other cars, some holding guns as well. The traffic jam made everything worse. The school bus started to shudder, almost buckle, like a trapped animal, as the driver tried to mount the pavement, or find some way of getting the hell out of there. And all the time we were stuck behind them, watching as though it was a piece of street theatre, laid on specially for us.

Not a shot was fired, and the whole incident lasted less than a minute – then the police arrived, the Zulus were arrested, the traffic was cleared, and we were able to move on – but my lot were very shaken. One lady had peed her pants; another asked me to stop the coach, scrambled off and threw up in the gutter. The Israeli policewoman, Brigadier General Hazor, was storming up and down the aisle, saying how *she* would've handled the situation.

I sat there listlessly, vaguely disappointed . . . I would've liked to see the shoot-out . . .

I've had feelings like that recently . . . ever since those few hours of ecstasy in the Kruger Park on . . . when was that? . . . the weekend, anyway. It wasn't as clean or easy as I thought – freeing myself from you. I haven't slept at all for several nights now . . . it's giving me quite a good high, the slight daze, the blur . . . when it fades, I drink, I smoke . . . I remember to shave, mostly . . . I shower a lot, I get through bottles of mouth-wash and scent . . .

(I mean, I presume it *is* the political situation, and not me, that caused some of the brood to leave today. Difficult to tell.)

Here in Durban our driver is that Coloured chap again, young Gideon; he wasn't prepared to risk the airport run – past Umlazi township – so I had to drive the deserters out there myself. En route, I held the coach mike in one hand, and composed a farewell speech: 'Oh come on, why are you leaving? This is a once-in-a-lifetime experience . . . being present while history actually happens! How many of your friends will be able to compete with your slide evenings? They'll have pictures of one another at the Parthenon, trying not to look bored, with soaking armpits and nasty sunburn. You'll have pictures of tanks, riot police, tear-gassed crowds, toyi-toyi-ing gangs armed with pangas and assegais (for tra-ditional purposes only), necklacings, taxi massacres, people thrown off trains, gang rapes. Come on, your slide evenings will be the talk of the town!'

But I never switched on the coach mike . . . I've already

been reprimanded by head office for my remarks in the Satara Camp cinema. (I suppose it was that Israeli policewoman who reported me.)

So I was mainly silent on the drive, politely answering, or, at any rate, deflecting, their questions about refunds, insurance, etc. (They're in for a surprise – there's no holiday insurance in the world that covers revolutionary unrest!)

The fifteen-kilometre run to Louis Botha Airport normally takes about twenty-five minutes; today it lasted almost three hours ... army diversions because of car-stonings, car-burnings, car-hijackings, etc.

Watching the London group board their BA flight, I suddenly became terribly upset. I was imagining my grandparents arriving in the 20s, and their optimism, and how handsomely it was rewarded in this beautiful, sunny British colony.

On the drive back, the diversions were even worse; army chaps in bullet-proof armour waved me from road to road, until I was completely lost. I ended up on one of those bridges that span the highway; the sort one usually drives *under*, glancing up at the graffiti (wondering how the artist worked upside-down), or keeping a look-out for young 'comrades' dropping masonry.

The bridge was manned by a lone soldier; I couldn't see much of his face for the armour, but I suspected he wasn't more than eighteen. When I asked him for directions, he laughed, in a non-mocking, boyish way, saying he wasn't from these parts, he was from the Free State: he had less idea than I did where we were. A patrol vehicle had raced along this route hours ago, dropping off soldiers every few miles like traffic cones, and he had simply stood guard here, bewildered and apprehensive. He asked me what I did, and when I said, 'I take tourists round South Africa,' he began laughing hysterically. I wasn't surprised when it turned to sobbing. He climbed onto the coach, fell to his knees, and hugged one of my arms, begging me to stay with him until the relief patrol arrived. I said, 'Yes of course I will.' He said, 'But you won't tell anyone, hey?' I said, 'No, no, don't worry, rest, cry, do whatever you need to do.' His helmet fell off; he was even younger than I thought, spotty, plain, unsexy.

I stroked his hair, his short army haircut, thinking of you and the Jewish singer. I tried to make conversation. I said, 'Do you surf?' He reminded me he was from the Free State, and we both laughed. Then we went silent, and I just hugged and rocked him, I suppose for about twenty minutes until I spotted the relief patrol arriving. I tipped him off, and he got himself together smartish, putting on his helmet, wiping away his tears and snot. I suggested he pretend to be searching my coach for bombs, weapons, or whatever, which he did, and this seemed to go down very well with the sergeant who arrived. The boy'll probably get a medal for initiative.

Finally back at the hotel, I was desperate to get to my room – and a drink – when I bumped into the fearsome Brigadier General Hazor buying cuddly Zulu toys at the souvenir shop. (Needless to say, none of the Israelis have fled – our political situation is just like normal life for them.) She said, 'Somebody was telling me you were involved in a murder case here a few years ago.'

I went cold. (*Who* told her?) My left hand clawed through my trouser pocket, but your letter was there – where it's been all day – it hadn't fallen out somehow – it hadn't been read by her. I recovered and laughed. 'I was the *victim* in the case, Brigadier General . . . you make me sound like the perpetrator.'

She laughed back. 'Do I? Well, after years of experience,' she said in that husky way, rolling her 'r's like a leopard warning you to back off; 'After many, many years of police work, and especially murder investigation, I find that the victim and the perpetrator are often like blood brothers.'

'Is that so? Our societies are less similar than I thought then.'

We stared at one another coldly. I can't remember ever being so reluctant to disguise my feelings about a client.

(I honestly don't care if she reports me again, I don't care if head office fires me . . .)

I turned my back on her and walked out of the foyer, onto the promenade, hands deep in my pockets, one fingernail scratching the surface of your letter.

But – more trouble – other members of the brood were

heading towards me. Darting to the right, I saw the Snake Park, and bought a ticket.

It was about 4 p.m.: feeding time. A young attendant, dim blue eyes, thick neck, not unlike your warder Knipe, was carrying around a plastic bucket full of live rats and mice, feeding the occupants of the glass cages. Holding the mice by the tail, he dangled them in front of the smaller reptiles, like mole snakes, inviting them to strike – a small cry and spasm from the mouse – and *hey presto* it vanished into a spiral of snake. The larger creatures, like the carpet pythons, were presented with puppy-sized, brown and white rats struggling at the end of a long tweezer-stick, and, once they'd taken possession of their prey, their massive coils were rearranged by the attendant, like a head waiter making a diner comfortable. Schoolkids squealed and laughed, adults gawped and tutted – someone said, 'I need a Rennies' – and the attendant showed off, grinning with big skew teeth, now sending the mice on spiralling flips through the air, into the open tree-snake pit. In one large glass cage, containing the most venomous snakes – green mambas, puff adders, Egyptian cobras – there was also a man. He sat under a hand-written sign: '*World Record Snake Sit-in Attempt – 9 days to go – already done 111 days – gained 15 kgs in weight.*' I lit a cigarette, leaned on the glass and we gazed solemnly at one another. The skin of his face was yellow from lack of daylight and fresh air.

Meanwhile, my finger was scratching at your letter, tracing its shape, dipping into its torn slit, feeling inside.

What to say about it?

You've been honest, or tried to be . . . I don't believe that you didn't 'do' all the people you originally claimed to have 'done', but I don't blame you for changing your story. I guess I'd do the same with next Monday looming up.

The good thing is that you've finally told me what happened in the hotel room, and that's extremely important to me. Yet . . . now that I know the truth, why don't I feel that everything makes sense?

I mean, it *is* the truth . . . is it?

Anyway, let me repay your honesty.

After our encounter in that hotel, and after I was released

from hospital, I joined a group therapy session at the Victims of Violence Clinic, which is situated, coincidentally, in the former District Six, where your people are from.

In one early session, I confessed to the group that what I most wanted was to hurt you. Before your execution. I wanted you to suffer terribly.

The therapist said that this was a very common reaction in victims of violence, but that while we could explore my need for revenge, discuss and even express it (in drama therapy), this was not something that should ever involve *you* personally. He gave three reasons. Firstly: as in ordinary therapy, once you've discovered that your parents have inflicted a certain amount of damage while rearing you, it's better to assault a cushion in the therapist's office rather than the old folk themselves. Secondly: the Law *was* going to punish you, and, whatever our opinion of the death penalty, we could just leave it at that. Thirdly: this therapist had studied your case history during the trial (who hadn't, with the coverage it got? . . . 'The Fantasy Killer', etc.), and he thought you were so seriously psychopathic, so separated from your real feelings – he described them as having been 'amputated' long ago – and so used to feigning emotions, that there was actually no means of influencing you one way or the other.

I found this idea horrifying – a human being without emotions – and in a way satisfying . . . it was enough revenge for me. I was about to abandon the subject, when one of the other patients in the group, a woman, a rape victim (from a specially vicious attack), spoke up.

'I disagree,' she said. 'I believe there *is* a way you could revenge yourself on your attacker. Use love.'

The room went silent, shocked by her combination of words: revenge and love.

The woman continued. 'Open him to feelings he doesn't know – kindness, sensitivity, charity, *love* – open him to these things in a situation where he's vulnerable, frightened, powerless, like in prison, and you'll open him up wide.'

'And then do what?' I asked.

'Whatever you want,' said the woman.

The therapist intervened. 'I'm sorry, I don't think it's

205

helping any of us to talk in these terms. Revenge is never an answer, never a solution. Not in the long term.'

So the subject was changed. But it stuck with me. The idea that I could hurt you, really badly, *before* your execution, by showing you love. I kept putting it out of my head, and it kept coming back. Meanwhile I expected to hear of your execution – surely, any day now – yet never did. I thought, time is passing, I must be getting better now. But no, I couldn't, nothing had changed, nothing had gone away . . .

This phrase haunted me: 'nothing's gone away'.

And then, one day, my father's ex-pupil, Lt. Gen. Venter of the Dept. of Prison Services, came to lunch. And then, of course, a few days later, I began to write to you . . .

It's said that revenge is a dish best eaten cold. That's fine to start with. I certainly set out coldly. If you were to look back over our early correspondence, you would see what I was doing. Despite flashes of anger, without which the letters wouldn't have been convincing, I showered you with tenderness, care and patience. Love. The trouble was remaining cold. As you walked further and further into my trap, I experienced different feelings – relish at first, then pity, then a kind of concern, almost protectiveness – and all of these feelings, even the initial sadism, all have some *temperature* in them. It was like a childhood game. You were blindfolded, I was hiding, a voice was saying, 'Warm . . . getting warmer . . . getting hot . . . hotter . . .' Then suddenly you touched me. And it *was* hot, your touch. And suddenly I had a fever, and it was exactly like the real thing. Love. I thought about you all the time, I counted the hours till your next letter. That woman in the therapy group was wrong. We can't use friendship as a weapon. When we open our arms to someone, when we embrace them, we experience an irresistible human sensation: the warmth of their blood, of their hearts. And then it's difficult to hurt them . . .

Maybe it's a good thing . . . maybe there *is* something redemptive going on . . . at least I'm proving to myself that I'm not capable of your kind of violence . . . maybe it's all part of a healing curve . . . this strange, half-circular shape in my life since I met you, like a tunnel wall, which I'm still fumbling along . . .

Maybe . . .

Or else, I'm the one who's been trapped, not you.

You see, I don't know what I want from this any more. The one thing I never thought you'd relinquish was your own death wish. But now, from what you say in your latest letter, your sentence will probably be commuted, you'll probably spend a few more token years inside, as some flipping model prisoner, and then you'll probably be released, and I'm going to wake up one morning to find this short, freakish, blonde-and-dark monkey-man on my doorstep, who's programmed to talk very slowly on Sartre or Freud, and who's offering to be my eternal friend, lover, or slave.

No. I don't need that. I don't need you. In a letter maybe, but not in the flesh – not that again. *I just want to get better again.* I must back off from this whole evil business, your evil and mine . . . we're quits now.

So good luck to you.

I suddenly know what to do: I won't post this letter. In fact, you'll never hear from me again.

Adrian.

THIRTY-ONE

83143118
Pretoria Maximum Security

It's Friday morning.

Nine bells.

These days I know the day of the week and the time of the day.

I only have to ask.

There's just me and a new silent man here in the Pot now. They hanged the Shangaan man yesterday morning. The new silent man never seems to want anything. He's too busy being born again. So the warders have time on their hands. You could almost say that they cater to my every wish and whim.

They give me smokes, bubble gum. Fat Fourie even got me new batteries for my Sony machine. He popped out and fetched them from his cottage in the prison complex. From his older son's bedroom. From a special drawer where his son keeps different sized batteries. Fat Fourie stole 2 from this drawer and brought them to me. Laughing about how naughty he was being.

So yes they're very nice to me. Even old brandy Adams.

The only thorn in my side is Knipe.

Who came on duty about a minute ago.

Never mind. I'm feeling on top of the world. I switch on my Sony machine and god starts to sing to me the hymn called IT AIN'T ME BABE.

Then I think, better just find out the time so I can smarten up for Mrs Malik.

I got a message from her late yesterday. Saying she'd be here between 9 and 9.15. Don't know what it's about but it sounded important.

I think today's the day I find out about the rest of my life.

So now I call out to Knipe, pardon me what's the time?

He says, too late for you my friend.

I say, what d'you mean by that?

He says, yous expecting some news today.

I say, so what?

He says, start reading your Bible, making your peace.

A small ghost climbs on my back. But I don't let Knipe see. I say to him, you wouldn't hear my news before me.

He shrugs and starts to stroll away.

I shout after him in a calm way, you're lying. You've got a dirty heart. And you've always been the hell-in with me. Ever since your first day. There in Tsafendas' cell. When I witnessed Sergeant Fourie giving you a baptism of fire.

Knipe says, in whose cell?

I say, Tsafendas'.

He says, who's that?

I say, hey don't you people start with that business again. Messing with my mind again. You and me, we were in his cell together, with Sergeant Fourie.

Knipe says, ag yous dreaming it.

I say, less calmly now, WE WERE IN DIMITRI'S CELL TOGETHER. THE CELL UNDER THE GALLOWS.

He says, but there is NO cell under the gallows.

I stare at him.

He says, yous want to come look? I'll show yous now. There is NO cell there. C'mon.

He unlocks my door. I don't move.

I'm thinking. What if the cell IS gone? Bricked up say. Or what if they can prove it was never there? With forensic evidence and suchlike cheating. That might not be good for my state of mind.

I don't want to become the Fantasy Prisoner at this stage of the game.

Knipe locks my door again.

He says, that's better. Now just calm down man.

All of yous talk gibberish in the Pot. But try not to, hey? Just read your Bible, make your peace.

I start to argue again but Knipe is looking at me with such a funny expression. A kind of boredom. Like I'm not there. Like he's just examining the mesh on my window. For insects maybe. Like the cage itself is empty.

He walks away.

I sit on my bed. Feel a bit on my nerves. There's no rule of silence in the Pot, yet I've never heard a silence like this one now. More like a vacuum.

Into this vacuum walks Dominee van Zyl.

I jump up. I say, why are you here?

He says, but I visit you every day.

I say, oh that's right you do.

I sit down again feeling better. But not for long. The dominee's expression is funny too. Normally his specs are full of sorrow, nicotine-stained. But today there's something else, I swear there is. As if, like Knipe, he knows something.

I keep stock still. So does he.

The silence lasts for several minutes.

Then I say, do you mind if I put god back on?

He doesn't know what I mean but looks pleased.

I press the play button.

I sit listening to god. Who's singing about WHEN I PAINT MY MASTERPIECE. The dominee offers me a smoke and lights one himself. We puff away as I listen. The dominee looks more and more bored.

Eventually I say, excuse me but what do you want?

He shrugs and replies that he's at my service.

I suggest he go fuck then.

He obeys, leaving me the pack of smokes.

Which he's never done before.

I'll carry on with this letter after Mrs Malik has been.

It was 11 o'clock before she arrived.

I was feeling pretty damn cross by then. Cold cross. When they took me to the consultation room.

Mrs Malik said, sorry it was the traffic.

I said, oh it must be hell this time of morning.

She didn't seem to notice my tone. She took a deep breath and said, I'm afraid I've got bad news.

I said, it's OK I know.

She looked surprised.

I stopped myself from remarking that the whole fucking prison seemed to know. Instead, I asked her to tell me what happened. She did. It was difficult to follow. Lots of legal jingo and jargon. But this is what I understand from it

She explained that it's always best to request a stay of execution directly from the judge who presided at the original trial. Also she was pleased it was THIS particular judge. Can't say I can bring his face to mind myself, but I didn't pay much attention at the trial. Anyhow, Mrs Malik reckoned he was one of the decent ones, quite fair, quite liberal, not a member of the Broederbond. They had the hearing in the supreme court late yesterday afternoon. Mrs Malik. And the advocate for the state. And the judge, who had a bad cold. There was a box of tissues on his desk. He said my affidavit didn't contain sufficient fresh evidence. Mrs Malik said what about the retraction of confessions? He said he wasn't convinced by these retractions. He'd sat through the original trial and listened to my confessions being read out by the prosecution. They contained the kind of details which nobody could make up. Particularly the ones relating to the other 45 to 48 murders. The judge regretted that the police failed to find any evidence of these. He thought it a sad indictment of our society that 45 to 48 people could vanish without trace, simply because they were poor and non-white. He added that the psychiatric reports from when I was under observation at Valkenberg substantiated his view of the case. The doctors were sure I had been involved in far more than just one murder and one attempted murder. In fact, those doctors were VERY convinced by my confessions to the other 45 to 48 cases.

Mrs Malik said the judge kept sniffing and blowing his nose

as he spoke. And wiping his eyes. Almost like he was weeping. Meantime the other advocate, the one for the state, he hardly needed to open his trap. The judge was so set against me. Dead set, as they say. In the end Mrs Malik left empty-handed.

As Mrs Malik came to the end of her story, I felt calm. I reached into my pocket for one of the dominee's smokes. The pack was empty. I realised that in the 2 hours between the dominee and Mrs Malik I'd finished them all.

That's not like me.

I said to Mrs Malik, OK so what now?

She said, well there are still several avenues to explore.

I said, good I've always liked avenues. The avenues of Cape Town. There by the white suburbs. Pointing up to the mountain. Tall trees and smart houses. I like those roads pointing up, up, up. Tell me which ones we'll explore.

She said, well we can try LOBBYING. Which means via MPs. Or we can try PRESSURE. Which means via the media. Or we could go INTERNATIONAL. Which means via Amnesty.

I said, alright which d'you want to try first?

Mrs Malik stared at her hands. I suddenly realised she wasn't looking me in the eyes today. On her last visit, she really bloody met my gaze, no fear. But today her eyes were tired again and downcast. I don't think it was just shame. Over her failure with the judge. Her failure to make him change his mind. In fact, I think maybe he changed HER mind. Him with his box of tissues.

Sniffing away at the tragedy of all those poor non-whites being wiped off the face of the earth with nobody to mourn the end of their days.

Well, I'm a poor non-white too, so people had better watch out, or the same tragedy is about to befall them once more.

I said to Mrs Malik again, louder, the following.

Tell me which avenue we're going to explore first.

She sat forward and rubbed her forehead. Hiding her eyes from me.

She said, of course there's the problem of the weekend coming up. It's a pity our last day is Sunday.

I said OUR? Will you be joining me?

At last she looked me in the eye. But it was a bad look.

Like everyone today. Straight through. Like I've already gone.

I said, why are you letting me down? When we meant so much to each other.

She frowned. Then she said, what on earth are you talking about?

Over at the door, old brandy Adams, on duty, he made a little noise. Like a chuckle.

I went still.

I realised I had done it again.

Spoken a dream out loud. Put it into life. Which is a dangerous business. Reserved for what they call the ELITE. Artists can do it. But not criminals.

In retrospect, I don't think Mrs Malik was as much in love with me as I thought.

And from my point of view, I don't know how I could've ever found such a fat coolie cunt-bitch worthy of my hand in marriage.

I quickly covered my tracks and said this.

I'm sorry, I'm getting mixed up, it's the situation, I'm sure you can appreciate the shocking nature thereof, but I thought this case, this CASE, not ME, I thought this meant something to you.

She said, with respect, it isn't just this case, it is the death penalty. I am PASSIONATELY opposed to it.

I said, then why don't you save me?

She looked at her hands again. I had a look too. They were the only bits of her which could still get my temper up. Nice rubbery fingers. Nice glittery jewellery. Her wedding ring plus a few baubles and beads in the Indian style. I wondered if she was muslim? I fancied taking one of her hands back to my cage. One hand on its own.

In a whisper, making sure brandy Adams couldn't hear, she said the following.

Look, this is an outside chance, but they keep talking about releasing Mandela at any moment, and we've heard rumours on the quiet, that, coinciding with his release, several organisations will be unbanned and the death penalty suspended. Now, if they released him today, or tomorrow, or even as late as Sunday, and let's not forget they released Sisulu on a Sunday, then they'd HAVE to stay all executions.

I said this.

Pardon me Mrs Malik, but can I tell you something? I care fuckall for mister Mandela. The feeling is probably mutual. But it really pisses me off that our fates are intertwined as it were. I don't want to be intertwined with a kaffir terrorist. My crimes are as naught compared to his. And if mister Mandela is expecting any thanks for getting the death penalty suspended, then he can go fuck. Like you can.

She stood and said.

I can see that you're feeling negative. Which is only natural in the circumstances. But I'm not feeling that way. I'm going to investigate which of our avenues is still worth exploring.

Her waist was level with my eyes. I sang a song of my daddie's.

Lady of Spain. I implore you. Drop down your broeks. I'll explore you.

She said in a fed-up voice, is there anything else I can do?

I said, like what?

She said, would you like me to make out your will?

There was a bad silence between us.

Then I said, why do I need a will if there are all these avenues we can still go exploring? All these avenues with tall trees, all leading up to the pretty mountain. Why are you treating me like a fool? Is it because of the way I sound? My tongue might sound dim, but a bright brain burns behind it, lady.

Old brandy Adams had to pull me off her.

Shame. I didn't mean to hurt her. I'm very sorry about that. She tried to be helpful. But unfortunately she thought she was dealing with a fool. I could hear it in the way she talked to me. Slowly. Spelling it out. I'm afraid, all things considered, she's a bit of a cunt. Now she's a cunt with a black eye and a cut lip. Beware of cunts with cut lips. You can catch things off them. And beware of the black eye in a cunt. The wet black eye.

Anyhow, she's gone now and I'm writing this letter. I know you'll want to know about these developments as soon as possible. If anyone can help you can.

Jesus. It's just hit me like a thunderbolt.

The way out.

It's something you once told me to do. If I was ever in deep shit.

I'm carrying on this letter later.

This is what happened after the last bit.

I banged on my door and asked to see Major Steenkamp.

Fat Fourie was on duty and very helpful as usual.

In less than 15 minutes the major was in my cage. But with fat Fourie as well.

I said, sorry Major but I must speak to you alone.

Fat Fourie interrupted and said, I wouldn't advise that, sir, the prisoner attacked his own lawyer this morning.

I interrupted and said, Major it is in your own interests that I speak to you alone.

For the first time ever, Major Steenkamp didn't look bored.

He said to me, it's OK you can say whatever you want in front of Sergeant Fourie.

I said, well don't say I didn't warn you.

The major and the sergeant exchanged a smile.

I thought, I'm going to wipe that off their faces.

I said, Major I have proof of bribery and corruption in this prison, including your good self, in exchange for some bottles of whisky. And going right up to one of the highest officers in the Department of Prison Services. A lieutenant general whose name escapes me just at the moment. But what I'm saying sir is this. Unless we can come to some deal, I plan to give this proof to the newspapers, blah blah.

This DID wipe the smile off the major's face. Trouble was, he just looked bored again. So bored he didn't even reply. He left this to Sergeant Fourie, who said

What is this proof?

I said, these letters here.

I started to reach for them. Then several things hit me all at once. This Pot cage is so similar to my last one, I'd forgotten

215

that I've moved. And on the day of the move, I was so worried about them taking Dylan away, I forgot about everything else. Like all your letters. Which must still be there. Back in the other one.

I said, oh.

Then I said, can I just go back to my old cell? I've left some things there.

Fat Fourie said, your old cell? What do you mean? It's somebody else's new cell. Bloke by the name of Karstens. But after you vacated it, and before he occupied it, we hosed it down. And we found none of your belongings there. Not a thing.

Major Steenkamp waited a bit. Then he said to me, is there anything else?

I shook my head.

He left.

Fat Fourie left.

I had a feeling that I left too.

Like Tsafendas. Who was never here.

Like the letters. Which never existed.

I am the Fantasy Prisoner hey?

I don't know what to do. I must think think think. I must just go into the corner there and sit down very low like a ball in the corner and just calm down and just think. OK you mustn't go away OK? Don't go away. Just wait for me.

———————

It's still Friday. I'm finishing this letter before exercise time. So I can leave it here for our postman. I presume he's still on the job here in the Pot. But I must say I'm surprised not to have heard from you for a few days.

In my present state of mind, I'm more than surprised.

Your silence gives me a funny feeling.

Like even YOU know I'm gone.

But I won't lose trust.

Not in you.

A while ago they took me to a room where they weighed and measured me. I asked why. They said you know why.

Don't make it hard for us. Of course I know why. But why are they so shy talking about it? They prefer to go about their business in a silent way. And looking bored. It's Major Steenkamp's doing. He must make it one of the rules if you work here. BE BORED.

The man doing the measuring. I'd never seen him before. Young, with big hairy freckled hands. I watched these hands move the measuring tape round different parts of me. When it came to my top half, he held one end of the tape against my neck. Except the fingers on my neck weren't just holding the tape there. They were sort of feeling my neck. The amount of muscle there. How close the little neck bones are to the surface.

I said, are you the one who'll actually do it on Monday?

He said nothing.

At the same moment I became aware that there was a door at the back of the room. The door was half open. I think someone was standing there. I'm sure they were. Now I remembered stories from talking time in the old corridor. Stories about how the state executioner operates. How he stands just out of view during the weighing and the measuring. Because he likes to get the MEASURE of the prisoner in his own way. To hear anything the man says, to observe his behaviour.

I'd given away too much already. I shut up for the rest of the time. As they took their weights and measurements.

Dylan writes about these things. He writes about all things. Yes. But he even writes about THIS.

Here. Listen. I'll find it for you.

AND THE HOME IN THE VALLEY MEETS THE DIRTY DARK PRISON. AND THE EXECUTIONER'S FACE IS ALWAYS WELL HIDDEN. WHERE BLACK IS THE COLOUR AND NONE IS THE NUMBER.

Something is starting to happen. Something is going wrong. The song is stretching. The sounds are going funny. Like when the batteries run out. But these batteries are new. What then? I didn't hit it earlier. No I didn't I promise I didn't. Have I just played the tape too much? It's pulling apart. Don't let this happen please. Maybe if I just let it rest for a while. But I can't sit in silence. But I can't listen to this. It's like a joke version stretching stretching. Like Dylan is yawning as he sings. Like he's bored with me too.

Adrian my friend, I'm waiting for them to take me to exercise now. I'm going to leave this letter on my bed. I pray I haven't fucked our system by talking about it to the major. I pray also that you've made plans for my letters to reach you fast. Wherever you are. Even though there's the PROBLEM of the WEEKEND coming up. Please hurry to my side. I know this will be difficult for you. To leave your BROOD. But you must come. I've still got an important piece of our story to tell you.

Sworn in love and honesty,

Yusuf.

I waited several hours before I remembered there's no exercise time here in the Pot. Jesus. I must've thought I was back in the old cage. Jesus. This letter won't go till the morning now. During my shower. Saturday morning. That's getting quite late. But it'll reach you. I'm sure. You must've made plans.

THIRTY-TWO

I still think of this as 'correspondence' although these pages will just be slipped into my diary, a big solid book which nobody's posting or faxing anywhere.

So . . . where are we? Your last day. Sunday. Today.

Today we were travelling to Ladismith across a weird landscape – blank plains, bold cloud shapes. Things felt upside-down, back to front. I mean, usually it's the brood half-drunk, and me going through the motions; but there I was, slumped in my seat, mike in hand, telling one of those anecdotes, one of those time-fillers, rambling and inconsequential . . . while the brood made a pretence of listening, or not . . . it hardly mattered . . . their brains are like sieves by this stage in a tour . . .

'. . . Two-thirds up the 2126m Elansberg mountain, a tiny light shines at night . . . you'll see it when I take you on the Milky Way Walk after supper . . . but what people don't realise is that it's actually operational twenty-four hours a day! It was placed there by Ladismith resident, Stanley de Wit, in 1962, to mark the first anniversary of South Africa becoming a republic. In successive, perilous climbs, he hauled up various hydro-electric equipment, including a bicycle lamp. Now this is the really interesting part . . .! Did you know that the bulb of a bicycle lamp will burn continuously for only three months? Therefore, to date, our doughty republican has been forced to repeat that arduous climb for a total of . . .'

I hesitated. The only figure that came to mind was forty-five

. . . or forty-eight? . . . and I knew that wasn't right . . . that was something to do with you . . .

(Our 'postman' had faxed your letter to last night's hotel, and I held it, rolled into a ball. Such a strange modern substance . . . some of the surface feels like crushed paper, but mostly it's smooth and clammy – more like a facsimile of skin.)

Meanwhile my mouth was open, halfway through my story, trying to remember the figure, the total score of something. It was hopeless – nothing else would come to mind, so I heard myself say:

'. . . Forty-five or forty-eight. Which doesn't include the one and a half murders that he was convicted of. So the actual total was either forty-six and a half, or forty-nine and a half, agonisingly close to his goal of fifty. If only the half-murder, which was mine, had been a whole, then . . .'

The driver, Gideon, reached over and grabbed the mike. I snatched it back.

'. . . Yes, sorry, you don't want to hear about this, you want to continue with your holiday, and then go home. You all keep going home. It must be great there – *home* – can I come too? Month after month, year after year, you stream through my hands, we have such intense times, I look after you, body and soul, you either ignore me or want to screw me . . . but then you go home again. Well . . . *don't*. Stay this time! See it through! Israelis, some of you . . . you'll be good to have around . . . when the shit hits the fan . . . your people will send in planes, daredevil raids, bravery beyond the call of. So, come on, hands up, who's staying to help? Brigadier General Hazor . . .?'

She was fast asleep when I swung round now. Elsewhere, down the vast, bluish corridor of the coach, dappled with cooled and tinted sunlight, the rest of my depleted brood were either also sleeping or gazing listlessly out at the Karoo.

No-one looked shocked.

Puzzled, I turned to the front again, then realised that Gideon had turned off the volume – five minutes ago.

He keeps doing this – saving me. I wish he wouldn't. It's very difficult taking the plunge, the deep dive, the big wipe-out

... and *very* boring if someone saves you, and you have to summon the energy all over again ...

By now we were in Ladismith, pulling in at the Toorkop. Being Sunday afternoon, the crowd of Coloured beggars was thinnish, not too threatening; though I spotted the old crone, who fastens tourists' hands – 'Welcome, welcome!' – while her grandchildren pick their pockets. I decided the brood could fend for themselves, and hurried indoors for a drink.

Locked in my room, I had to make a decision. I unrolled the ball of fax, and examined the second last paragraph. Your request – 'please hurry to my side'; your hook – 'I've still got an important piece of our story.' What was I to do? There was still time. By now it was about 3 p.m., and I know executions are scheduled for 6.30 in the morning. I could drive through the night; I'd probably get to Pretoria in time ... just. But would they let me see you, so close to the end?

On the other hand ...

I stood in front of the phone, one hand resting on it, the other tapping into the Directory-mode of my TOSHIBA lap-top, searching for, and finding: 'Venter, Kobus, Lt. Gen. (Prison Dept.; ex-pupil/F's; religious; seems unmarried/gay?; v. helpful); (w.) 012 342135, x.212 (h.) 012 349238.'

Over the last few days, I'd often thought about phoning him. I felt certain he had the power to arrange a stay of execution, officially or not – but how would he react to being asked? Probably wouldn't be that surprised or horrified; amused maybe ...? As I've said before, everything in his life, from his Calvinist upbringing to his career in the police force, leads him to expect the worst in human nature, and sort of celebrate it. I'm remembering his twinkling eyes, his whisky-rose cheeks ...

I picked up the phone, and started to dial, when I suddenly remembered the phrase: 'nothing's gone away'.

It's why I never got better ... it's why I never would ... not until *something* went away ...

I thought, no, it's time ... time to let it go away ...

And put down the phone.

Then sank onto the polished wooden floor, and wound

myself round and round, limbs splayed, like an infant or animal or lunatic.

I got more drunk during supper . . . I no longer care if people notice. Afterwards, I was about to round up the brood for the Milky Way Walk, when Margaretta Steyn, the proprietress, called me over. She whispered that there had been 'incidents' in Ladismith since my last visit, and that it really wasn't advisable to take the brood out into the veld in the dark. Instead, she asked me to announce that none of them should leave the hotel perimeter until daylight. I decided *not* to broadcast it; knowing that this particular brood would just naturally retire to their rooms and watch the inhouse movie, or the M-NET documentary on Thursday's events in Berlin, when the Wall came down. I was right.

After they'd gone, I asked old Dam, the head waiter, if he'd join me for a Milky Way Walk. He's the delightful old party, you'll remember, who claims to be over a hundred, and of pure Bushman blood.

Out in the veld, it was the most beautiful night. The stars had never been brighter, or nearer . . . I felt I only had to reach up.

I asked old Dam to tell me a story, any story, as long as it was uplifting and wondrous. I was thinking of you, you see, so I didn't want anything sad.

I was expecting some quaint Bushman tale about the stars and the moon; their version of how these things came to be, you know the kind of thing. So I was surprised by what he told me.

He began by saying, 'Yes, I'll tell you a wondrous story. It's a true story, and it happened to me, myself and I, when this old body was young. Nothing in my long life has ever been as wondrous again.'

The story concerned the massive springbuck migrations which occurred across the Karoo at the end of the nineteenth century; migrations which naturalists have never been able to explain.

At the time, Dam was working on a farm in the North West Cape. One morning he felt what he describes as 'a sound in the ground'. Yes, that's how he put it . . . he *felt*, not heard, the sound. It was very particular, like a heartbeat, yet absolutely of the earth. He recognised it, because his father had once experienced the same thing, and often described the miracle of it.

Dam couldn't see anything on the horizon yet, but knew that there was little time to make the necessary preparations.

The farmer could neither see, hear, nor *feel*, the approaching herd. So at first he rejected Dam's advice to move his family onto a nearby hill and to surround the base with a makeshift barrier of planks, fencing, heaped thorn bushes, and anything else they could find. It was only about an hour later, when there was already a faint dust cloud in the distance, that the farmer acquiesced.

By the time the farmer, his family and dogs were safely on the hill, and the barrier hastily constructed by Dam and the other Coloured farm labourers, the heartbeat in the ground had grown clearer, into a kind of drumming, and the dust cloud had grown hugely, right across the horizon, as far as they could see in both directions. Dam now emptied oil lamps over the barrier, and stood alongside, to ignite them when the buck got nearer.

At that stage, Dam said he was more frightened than ever in his life. The herd itself was still invisible within the dust cloud, but other animals started appearing, fleeing the stampede: hares and jackals, veld mice, whole meerkat families, racing past the hill, racing for their lives; snakes as well, moving faster than Dam would have thought possible – several of them sliding under the barrier, right past Dam's legs, to hide themselves under the rocks on the hill. The farmer and his family threw rocks at the snakes, and the dogs barked, but they kept coming, driven by a greater fear.

By now the front rank of springbuck, running faster than galloping horses, could be seen, but the enormous cloud they were trailing was so dense it was impossible to gauge the depth of the herd. Dam and the other labourers lit the barrier and then ran up the hill to join the whites. Like with the snakes, the farmer's dogs tried, and failed, to drive them off – it was unprecedented for Coloured workers to be so close to the woman and children.

The first buck swept past on both sides of the hill. Then the pressure intensified, the animals became more crowded, and it was no longer possible for them to swerve aside when they reached the flaming barrier. Within moments the barrier was flattened by burning creatures, and these were quickly trampled by the mass coming from behind. The base of the hill became a graveyard of dead and injured buck, the jammed heaps growing before Dam's amazed eyes . . . a new barrier being built out of a tangle of jerking limbs, horns, hooves, splitting bellies, gasping jaws – beige buck faces turning black. This living, dying wall grew higher and higher, with some of the oncoming buck vaulting it, either crashing into the hill or clearing it on either side, so that the air was filled with flying animals, flashing light, yellow dust – thick as smoke. The people could no longer speak, and the dogs were arched over, choking. At the height of the rush, the noise was deafening. Dam says there was a moment in the middle of it when he could neither hear, see, nor breathe, and that it was like a brief death. 'But I felt no fear,' he added. 'It was *nature*.'

I started to speak, when, without warning, a sob came out of me. I tried to disguise it, but not quite in time. Dam touched my arm. I quickly said, 'So, how many buck . . . how many d'you think there were?'

Dam pointed to the stars. 'That many.'

He frowned at me, wondering what he'd just glimpsed, then let it go, and continued his story.

It took about an hour for the main stampede to pass, but hundreds upon hundreds of stragglers continued to appear during the rest of the day; some of these were exhausted, some crippled and bleeding.

Finally at sunset it was over. The air was clear, but every time someone moved, dust rose again. It coated every inch of ground – pale yellow dust. The people were covered in it too (the farmer and his labourers all the same colour now); the dogs too; also the snakes which had sheltered on the hill, and now rippled away through the thick powder; the earth and every living thing on it had turned yellow. 'The sunset lay on us,' said Dam, 'long after the sun had set.'

The next day they discovered everything devastated around

them. Every tree, all vegetation, the farm buildings, the poultry and animal pens full of corpses, the veld littered with small game that hadn't reached cover in time: tortoises crushed like eggshells, fragments of fur that had been hares. And every donga, and the dry river-bed itself, was filled with dead springbuck; the first few must have hesitated on the brink, considering whether to jump across – but before they could decide the mass was upon them.

His livelihood destroyed, the farmer and his family trekked away that same day, on foot – all their horses were missing, probably borne away by the stampede of buck. Dam and some of the labourers remained in the ruins of the farm, and lived there for several years.

Dam had come to the end of his story. I paused, shaking my head, then said, 'At the beginning you promised me a wondrous, uplifting story. I half understand. It must have been an incredible thing to see and experience . . . but it ended in so much death, and the farmer's life was destroyed.'

'He wasn't a good man,' replied Dam impatiently. 'He had been a cruel master, he didn't deserve good luck. We, his labourers, we'd worked hard, and now at last we were rewarded.'

'In what way?'

Dam looked at me in astonishment, unable to believe I didn't know the answer. 'We ate well,' he said. 'We, who the farmer had never fed properly, we feasted on the buck for days. We ate until we were sick, and then we started eating all over again. And those buck that we couldn't eat, we dried into biltong, and ate later. You ask how we were rewarded? You ask why this is a wondrous story. For a year we *ate well*!'

We walked back to the hotel in silence. I was hushed, smiling sheepishly. Look, see! There he goes again, the white man in Africa . . .

But back in my room, unable, as usual, to sleep, I began leafing through some of the books that Margaretta Steyn had stacked in the mock-antique stinkwood case. One was an old volume on the Karoo, written earlier this century. In it, I found Dam's story, almost verbatim. It did mention a young, unnamed Bushman who participated in the incident, so I suppose it could've been Dam. On the other hand, he might just have read the story, liked it, and made it his own, the old charlatan.

And now, of course, I've made it mine. Copying every detail from the book. And when I put all our stories together, yours and mine, it'll be there among them: just another African tale of death and slaughter.

So who's story is it now? The man who wrote it down, the man who retold it, or the man who's just stolen it? And if nobody knows, how can we be sure the story is true? I mean, you and I have both lived through the same story (two men meet, one tries to kill the other, is sent to prison, and his victim starts writing to him), but what happened – during our original meeting, and during our correspondence – what actually *happened*?

I've just picked myself up from the floor, where my chair unexpectedly tipped me, lightened by laughter, Paarl Riesling and best Cape grass. And, in this whirling mixture of chemicals, feelings and planes – horizontal and vertical, earthly and spiritual – I'm trying to work out if truth is any better than I am, at staying still.

And now, suddenly unable to keep smiling, I'm thinking about you, and what you're doing on this particular Sunday evening. In the end – it's incredible – my revenge plot worked out better than I could've hoped. As that woman in my therapy group promised, you've been 'opened up wide', and there you are now, craving some ordinary human love, trapped in your *cage*, with tomorrow morning coming up. I got what I wanted, and I hate it, I fear it . . .

So why don't I do something? I could still phone Venter, maybe stop the whole thing. Why am I sitting here?

Must stop writing. Don't know what I'll do instead. Won't sleep. Probably just hide in that corner there, thinking about you, trying not to, watching the red numbers change on my travel alarm clock.

THIRTY-THREE

83143118
Pretoria Maximum Security

Adrian.

I've just asked the time again. 9 o'clock. Sunday night. Earlier today they checked with me about last visits. I said don't worry I'll be getting one. One at least. Actually when you come I think you'll bring my daddie along as well, my dadda, like we used to call him when we were little. I think that's a surprise you've got in store for me. You're leaving it late but I'm sure of it. This afternoon I had a visit from Mrs Malik. I was a bit damned surprised to see her again, black eye and all, but she's sticking to her guns. She is against the death penalty. Even for the WHITE WOLF or the FANTASY KILLER. She still talks about last-minute reprieves. Shame, she sounds like a kid. Talking like from films. The good guys arriving at the last moment. Dylan makes jokes about these things. THE CAVALRY CHARGED. THE INDIANS FELL. THE CAVALRY CHARGED. THE INDIANS DIED. OH THE COUNTRY WAS YOUNG WITH GOD ON ITS SIDE. He's quite political I think. I've never been political. Which is why it's a laugh that the only thing that can save me now is Mandela getting released. Mandela would probably hit it off with Dylan. As for me, I can't listen to Dylan any more. The tape stretched and stretched and never came back. I can't stand to hear it. It mocks me. Dylan yawning. So now there's silence. I'm scared to play my other tape. Dadda. Him singing oh danny boy. What if he stretches also? I'll have nothing left.

227

Mrs Malik asked again if I wanted her to make out my will. Everyone has to leave a will. They have to leave something. Otherwise they were never here. I said to her no and then she went away. I haven't got anything to leave in a will. Only a Sony machine and 2 tapes. One is fucked. And they all belong to you anyhow. I'll give them back when you come tonight. I suppose the other thing I've got is my feelings. I have all these new feelings. I don't know what to do with them. I leave them to you too.

But I have to say one thing. I don't understand why I haven't got any letters from you for days and days. I DO NOT UNDERSTAND. Thou hast not forsaken me, I'm praying this is the truth. Because if you have, god I'll fucking MOER you. I'll come back from hell, you hear? A hard rain will fall on you. No listen no sorry no I don't mean that. It's just that I DO NOT UNDERSTAND why your letters have stopped. Is it our postman's fault? Who IS our postman?

Did I tell you they weighed me AGAIN today. I said what the fuck. What is all this fucking thing about weighing? WHY? Do you honestly think it's hard to stop a man breathing? Have you been doing this job all this time and you still think it matters to get the WEIGHT right? They let me get cross. They let me do or say anything. That's the worst thing in the last 24 hours. People letting you do or say anything. It isn't like life. I think it's another of Major Steenkamp's rules. Like his boredom. DON'T BOTHER ARGUING WITH POT PRISONERS, IT DOESN'T MATTER. Their patience torments me. But when I shout about it they just get more patient. I'm in a circle I fear.

11 o'clock. Or no it must be about 5 past 11. Because at 11 the warders changed shifts. I said to brandy Adams and fat Fourie hold on what's up? They said we're going off duty. I said hold on hold on you can't leave me with these guys. Wasn't Knipe or anybody I know. Must be the ones who are normally on at night. When I'm normally asleep. I won't be asleep tonight. I can't spend tonight with strangers. Can you believe it? I didn't want brandy Adams and fat Fourie to go away. Two of the biggest cunts in captivity and I didn't want to be without them. But they've been nice recently. Letting

me cheat at cards, plus telling me the time whenever I ask, plus giving me smokes, sweeties, even a dop from Adams' brandy flask. So I didn't want them to go. They said sorry but there are rules and regulations, times and shifts, work and rest. They said but don't worry we come back on duty at 5. So don't worry we'll be with you WHEN. Here they stopped speaking. Everyone is scared to say IT. Earlier I forgot what time IT happens. I asked and everyone went red. Finally but only after I shouted a lot they told me. 6.30. This IT that no-one can say out loud happens at 6.30. I'm afraid I got a bit upset about that. 6.30 seems a bad time. I mean the new day has started by 6.30 hasn't it? Early worms are going to work and a golden morn is born. I think 3 or even 4 would be more humanitarian. Or right now would be fine by me.

It's 2 minutes to midnight. I keep asking what's the time what's the time what's the time? It must torment the new warders but like everybody they don't show anything except patience which torments me to FUCKING hell. Anyhow it's 2 minutes or probably only 1 minute now to Monday.

It's Monday now. I've just asked again. They gave me a smoke. Hey don't they know that smokes can kill? I wish the other prisoner here in the Pot wasn't so silent. I cried to him earlier but he wouldn't reply. Must be covering his ears like I did when the Shangaan man howled through the night. The other thing I wish is that I was a kaffir. If I was a kaffir, other kaffir prisoners from other corridors would all sing me through tonight. They do that you know. Those lovely kaffir songs. They lullaby you like when you were born. I'd like that. This silence is a bit of a hell you know. I'm missing my Dylan so much it's giving me heartsore. He'd have got me through tonight. Without him I have to reach around in my head. Another man called Dylan says to me DO NOT GO GENTLE INTO THAT GOOD NIGHT. He also says TIME HELD ME GREEN AND DYING which is unbelievably wise. God gave all the wisdom of this century to 2 Dylans. One is undead, the other's death date is, I don't know. I mean I DO know, I DO fucking know, I just can't fucking remember. It's this fucking silence. Anyhow, it won't last. Any minute now you're going to bring in my dadda, like he was when time held me green, and he's gonna come dancing in, legs going like mad sticks, dancing like he's got a whole klopse band there, fearless of allah today because he's had a few doppies, and he's going to give us those pink, yellow and mauve cookies, and he's going to sing a bit and say all his soft old sayings, salaam alaikom and happy new year, the old one is bygones now, my chommies, Januarie, Februarie, Maart, April, Mei, let the good times roll, daar kom die Alabama, oh danny boy, don't get wet in the rain.

It's 2.13 deep into Monday morning in my bright upright coffin in the valley of the shadow of death. I've just lost control of my bodily functions I'm afraid. I've always tried to keep myself clean even in my years on the long long road I tried to keep my bodily hygiene tip top. So I'm very ashamed so I'd prefer if you didn't tell ma. It really gave me a fright. Just everything came out from all ends and all at the same time without warning. The supper was there too. The last supper. They brought me a whole chicken. Boneless. Because you might stab yourself to death with a chicken bone. Or you might choke to death on a bone. They don't want you to choke to death. Not till 6.30. This is their game and we've got to play it their way. Anyhow you know what the most worst thing about the loss of my bodily functions was? They had clean fatigues standing by. They KNEW it was going to happen.

4 o'clock exactly. Where are you? I think you'll still come. I just made them go and check there wasn't a letter from you. This is the dozen most time I've made them check. They say there's no post at this time. I say go fuck go fuck do you think I'm a dumb cunt just because I sound like a dumb cunt? My letters don't come by POST. They come by MAGIC. Magic can come at any time you cunts you cruel cunts. I can come at any time too because I'm a male of the species and I need to procreate the world. Adrian. The last letter from you was in the Kruger Park. Were you eaten by an animal as you lay kaalgat there in the bush. Which happened to a German I knew. Maybe I told you. Did the selfsame happen to you. Or can the truth be that you just stopped writing. You are a cruel predator my friend. You or our postman. WHO THE

FUCK IS HE? It can't be Knipe because he didn't start work here till after our first letter. So it's either Major Steenkamp or fat Fourie or brandy Adams or Dominee van Zyl or his brother Doctor van Zyl or who is it? Please somebody tell me please. I need to know so I can call out to him and ask him when you're coming.

I don't know what the time is and I've made a new decision not to ask. It's best for me not to say anything as a matter of fact because I fear I'm not making sense. Every time I speak they have to say sorry what pardon come again. So for the sake of dignity I must be very quiet now. So I can't ask the time so sorry. But it's getting light I'm afraid. You've let me down I fear. Still you never know. A reprieve can come at the last moment so maybe you can too. In case you don't I have something to tell you. The judge was right to reject my affidavit. I did do these terrible misdeeds I fear. I did do them all. 45 to 48. Plus the Jewboy singer. Plus you. And I have something more important to tell you. I hoped to say it to your face. Into your light. In any case, here goes.

That time with you in the hotel room I didn't show mercy or CHOOSE to stop. As you know while you were in the shower I mixed up two cocktails of drink, dagga and pills. But I made one of them very very strong. After I mixed up the cocktails I got mixed up too. I must've been a bit loose-brained roundabout then. Because of my life and blah blah. Anyhow I gave myself the wrong one. The strong one. Halfway through pumping you, and holding down your head, and holding it, holding it, holding it, I blacked out. Next thing I knew I was in hospital too and a machine was sucking my guts raw. That's what happened. You're here today because of a dumb mistake. Yes the dumb cunt was just a dumb cunt in the end yes I'm afraid so. In any case, I thought you'd like to know.

So I've made my peace now so please can you come now please. If I close my eyes long enough you'll be there. Or someone. Someone I know. Jesus look brandy Adams and fat Fourie are already back on duty. It must be very late. Knipe's here too. He's looking at me with kindly eyes which isn't like him at all. Oh look how kind people can be. Oh all the kindness lying in people is such a pity hey?

THIRTY-FOUR

Craigrownie Rd.

Mon. 13th Nov.

I've just reached home. The house is very quiet; Mum is gardening out in the front, Dad asleep in the back yard. He didn't wake when I stole a kiss, but snored on, his breath smelling from earlier infidelities with Johnnie Walker. The builders aren't working alongside the house any more – apparently they ran out of funds and have abandoned the project for now. The half-finished chunk of concrete hangs in the sky, a great, lopsided skeleton gaping with holes, sunlight finding its way through here and there.

I flew in from Pretoria about an hour ago. Last night I decided to travel to the prison, after all. Going by road was the only way from where I was, in Ladismith. I don't know what time I set off – I deliberately didn't look at my watch – I didn't want to know if it was already too late to attempt the 1200km journey. I *had* to do it. I *had* to reach you. Nothing else. My body was functioning without my mind – no censorship, no words of warning – 'it's silly' or 'be careful' – I just became this animal pointed north, every instinct forcing it on.

I borrowed the tour coach (for which there'll be trouble, big trouble ... yes, well, probably time to change careers again), but on the first leg of the journey, on the R29 from Oudtshoorn, it became clear that the vehicle would never do it in time – the speedometer was straining at 140km. I'd have to find something else. Hitch a ride, or borrow a car – pay for it or steal it – anything was possible. Our morals are only in our minds, and I was travelling without one, travelling

232

light. I pulled off into the Caltex Service Station at Beaufort West (wasn't Beaufort where you stole your first car? – which you used to 'do' your first person, that black woman walking along the roadside). There was only one car at the petrol pumps, a big blue Toyota. Crossing the forecourt, I suddenly noticed the name of this chain of Restrooms (though I've used them a thousand times) – 'White Rabbit' – and then, as I wondered what to say to the Toyota's driver, I heard an odd, high-speed voice in my head, suggest: 'I'm late, I'm late, for a very important date, no time to say goodbye, hello, I'm late, I'm late, I'm late!' Praying that I wouldn't speak this out loud, I opened my mouth and eventually heard my own voice: 'Good evening, sir, I wonder if you can help me . . .?'

He was a bloated, purple-faced white man, Italian or Jewish stock, with dandruff, and a listless manner. Perfect. He barely bothered to check my ID, or credit cards, which I offered as proof of respectability. When we set off now – he was going as far as Kimberley – he started a long, dull homily about failure, citing his work, his marriages, his commitment to the Old S.A. I hardly listened. I didn't really want to know who he was or why he was driving through the night. The reason was obvious anyway. He was here to drive me. Trouble was, he didn't drive fast enough – he drove like he talked – listlessly – and again this thing, this frenetic jabber, bubbled up inside me: 'I'm late, I'm late, for a very important date . . .!' It lodged in my skull now, like a jingle, and nothing would budge it – not by shaking my head, not by flexing my jaw, like to unpop the ears – nothing. Eventually I sang it, without the words, hoping he wouldn't recognise the tune. So we went on, him talking, me humming under my breath, 'I'm late, I'm late . . .!' When, many hours later, I saw the White Rabbit sign again, as he pulled off into the Kimberley Service Station, I was thinking about killing him. Not just knocking him out in order to take the car, not just driving away if he got out to have a pee, but killing him. We were more than halfway to you now, and death was in the air. The desire to kill him was very confusing, but very strong. So I was surprised to feel my body lift itself out of his car, to listen to myself thanking him, and to watch him drive away.

It was past midnight now, probably well past. Without looking at my watch, I slipped it off and smashed it under my foot. There were no customers at the petrol station. The black attendant peered at me from behind the bullet-proof glass of the Caltex office. I paced round, muttering 'I'm late, I'm late', aware that I could lose this race – this mad race against the night, against the dawn, against 6.30 a.m. I went into a phone booth, I found change, I rang Lt. Gen. Venter's home number. I wasn't sure what I would say to him. Maybe it would come to me when he answered. Maybe: 'Sorry Oom Kobus, I've woken you, I'm sorry, please help me, there's an execution tomorrow morning . . . no it's *this* morning now . . . please, can you . . .?'

(*What?* What was I dashing through the night for? What did I want?)

Venter's answer-machine was on. I burbled into it, calling for him, or someone (the bodyguard/driver?) to pick up the phone if they could hear. This went on for a minute or two. Then a car drew into the petrol station. I dropped the phone, leaving it dangling, and hurried over. Now it was all or nothing. If the driver refused to give me a lift, I'd take the car by force.

But God was on my side. The driver was a big, wealthy Afrikaner farmer; cheerful, fearless, and impressed by how well I spoke his language. 'My friend,' he said, courteously switching back to mine; 'I'm only going as far as Klerksdorp, to an early morning stock-auction nearby, but hop in, I'll drop you at the White Rabbit there.'

His car, a silver Mercedes, smelled of brandy, and veered around the highway a bit, hitting the cat's-eyes in the middle, sending little shockwaves through me, again and again. I offered to take over the driving for a while. He was delighted. We changed over, he put back his seat, and fell asleep almost instantly.

Now at last, that pure animal instinct, the thing that had sent me on this journey, now at last it was free.

First, without looking at them, I scrambled the numbers on his dashboard digital clock. Next I put on some music – his tapes were all Country & Western – to lull him into deeper sleep. Then I put my foot on the accelerator, until we were doing 230, slicing through the night. The car had a phone, so I tried Venter again, whispering into his answer-machine: 'Pick this up, please . . .!' Nothing. Though this time I had a sense of Venter there, Venter and his driver maybe, both naked, both whisky-drunk, gazing at the phone, smiling, as I called and cried into it.

There was light in the sky now, a faint purple colour coming through the black, nothing to speak of, but it was starting . . .

I pushed the accelerator harder. The car coughed. The farmer half-woke, muttered, 'Easy, easy,' with a chuckle, and went back to sleep.

Now I dialled the prison. It rang and rang. What would I say? Please stop the execution? Please hold it till I get there? Please, just tell Yusuf I'm on my way, I *am* trying to reach his side?

In the sky, the light grew.

Nobody answered the phone at the prison. I suppose there must be a different, special number for those miraculous last-minute phone calls which always happen in the movies, and occasionally in real life, halting the procedure, the routine . . . which must've started last night . . . I imagined the hangman before he went to bed, carefully setting his alarm clock ('Early start tomorrow'), the chaplain too ('Leave time for a quick coffee and a cigarette'), his brother the doctor, and the others.

Now, as soft colours gathered on the horizon, turning land and sky into a picture-postcard view of Africa, now it struck me that I really was losing this race, seriously losing it. It was probably about five o'clock. We weren't even at Klerksdorp. My frustration burned inside me. What more could I do, what more could I fucking well do? Then I saw her. A lone black woman walking along the roadside with a basket on her head. Where had she come from, where was she going? She started to raise her hand in greeting. They're very polite out here. (So the world isn't empty after all.) And then I knew how I could be with you, be at your side, definitely and forever. The idea timed itself to my heartbeat. The rhythm was like

'I'm late, I'm late'. I turned the steering wheel fractionally – automatic steering, us travelling like a bullet – and in the split second when she realised what was happening, in that same split second the farmer half-woke again, chuckled 'Easy!', and touched the steering wheel, sending us back into the middle of the road.

The woman had dropped her basket, and fallen backwards. In my rear-view mirror, I watched her climb to her feet and stare after us. I sighed. I had wanted to do that ... really wanted it ... for no reason at all, or every reason ...

The farmer was sound asleep again, and stayed like this as I took him past his destination, Klerksdorp, and then past Joburg, the golden city in a golden sunrise, hitting some traffic now, not much, but enough to slow us down – to waste more time! – and finally on the R101 to Pretoria, stopping just outside, at the prison. At last the man woke, and I heard him start to say, 'Wat die *fok* ...!' – but I'd left the car, and was running to the reception block, aware that the morning sun was already high enough to warm my neck, and then I slowed down, and then I stopped. There was a notice board in front of me, with an official paper: 'For general information it is hereby made known that the condemned person named below was executed at 0630 hours on the morning of Monday the 13th November ...'

I leaned on my knees. Silence. Then I heard a noise I'd never heard before. I couldn't believe it came from me. A howl. So long and free it was like a kind of prayer. My whole body shuddered ... as though two halves were coming together, healing at last ... at last letting me grieve properly for what had happened ... to me, to you, to us.

The blockhouse guards strolled forward, drawn by the racket. They must've seen people like this before, on the morning of executions, bent over, hugging themselves, howling like they're praying ... but those people aren't usually white, young, well-dressed, all that. They watched for a while – like the farmer, standing open-mouthed at his car – then everyone dispersed, shrugging and muttering; the guards back to their duties, the farmer back to Klerksdorp.

I took a long time to let it all out. Eventually I mopped

my face and straightened my clothes. Then I leaned on my knees again, just to breathe . . . before the next task.

I walked the rest of the way into the city, into downtown Pretoria, to the Mine, a bar which is open round the clock, probably illegally – if it wasn't frequented by so many policemen. Also other night-time workers, security guards, armed-response gunfighters – and prison staff. It's in a basement: a tunnel of neon and smoke, packed with serious drinkers – dominated this morning by a group in the far corner. Among them, the fat sergeant (Fourie?), into whose office I was summoned to show my ID when I came to visit you, a middle-aged Coloured man with red eyes and a tiny shiver (brandy Adams?), and three men who turned out to be the chief executioner and his assistants, one a trainee: the young chap with freckled, hairy hands, who had measured you on Friday. Everyone had done a hard morning's work (awake since before dawn), and now, although only about ten or eleven, their working day was over, and they were unwinding – unwinding at a ferocious pace – it made me giddy just to be near them – snatches of talk and laughter, threads of smoke, drink, saliva. This morning's job might be one that they had done many times before (except for the trainee hangman, and he was paralytic by the time I arrived), but it had, apparently, lost none of its horror or excitement. These were like men straight from battle.

The chief executioner himself was, at first, sitting with his back to me, deep in discussion with one of the young ladies who frequent this bar and help the men unwind – so I didn't see him, face to face, until half an hour later, after I'd already bought two rounds of drinks for the group. He's a small strong man of about fifty, balding head, big ears, and unremarkable, almost blank features. This blankness (regulation-boredom?) was unaffected by any adrenaline or booze swimming around inside him.

I asked if I could speak to him alone. In exchange for R25 passed under the table, he agreed, and we moved to another table.

My question to him was straightforward – it's one which

I've pursued throughout this correspondence – 'Just tell me exactly what happened.'

He took a long drink, a deep breath, and began.

At 6.a.m. Dominee van Zyl came to your cell, and asked you to accompany him. With Sergeant Fourie and Warder Adams on either side, you followed him to the chapel. It is situated, I was surprised to hear, beyond the lawn with flowers, where I had stood on the day of my visit, before meeting the nun, and being directed into the non-white visiting room.

To everyone's surprise, you knelt and prayed with Dominee van Zyl. He and the warders positioned this carefully, with him facing the door, you with your back to it, and the warders standing on the threshold, so that they could signal to him when it was 6.20, then 6.22, etc., enabling him to wind up his devotions at the right moment. At 6.27 precisely the following things happened simultaneously: the dominee finished praying, the warders secured your hands behind your back, and the chief executioner entered the chapel with Major Steenkamp. You were apparently alarmed by the sudden fastening of your arms, but offered no resistance. Dominee van Zyl stayed behind (his brother, the doctor, would supervise the rest of it), as you were quickly taken up the forty-two stairs, which you had seen during your time on breakfast trolley duty, and into the room with the gallows. Here you were puzzled, like prisoners before you, to find an ordinary policeman waiting to take your fingerprints.

'A bit late in the day to be checking for mistaken identity,' I said jokingly to the executioner, and he joked back (I think), 'Aagh, but you know how they all look the same.'

Now you were told to strip. In the old days, the executioner told me, prisoners were hanged wearing their green fatigues, but in the mid-eighties, when the number of executions increased dramatically ('Worked off my feet,' my informer grumbled), so did complaints from the prison laundry – the violent shock of hanging causes a flood of excretions – and so some new methods are being tried; either making the prisoner wear his own clothes, in which he'd arrived at prison, or, where these aren't available, hanging him naked. Women prisoners are strapped up between their legs. I asked why, but the executioner shrugged – almost shyly – and declined to answer. I suppose he and his all-male team are squeamish about the discharges that occur in certain cases (menstrual blood, miscarriages?), and prefer this strapping-up precaution. However, it seems to be a Catch-22 situation. The strapping procedure disturbs some women so much that they have to be straightjacketed. These straightjackets are then, of course, badly soiled during hanging, and the laundry department starts complaining again . . .

The straightjacket has to be used on some men as well, but you weren't one of them. Having stripped, you allowed your hands to be tied behind your back. Now you were facing a row of seven nooses – one specifically reserved for you – the one tested with sandbags after they'd weighed and measured you. 'Number three for prisoner 83143118,' the executioner said, reading from his notebook (he confesses this is the only part of the job which still unnerves him – mixing up the nooses – so he likes to have it written down) and you were led onto trap door no. 3, which is made of reddish metal, shiny with wear. Now your feet were tied too. You will have caught a glimpse of the handle which operates the ratchet system, and of course the noose, made of thick, hairy rope. Had you been a white prisoner, the rope would've been white also – new and clean – but it's seldom changed for non-whites, so you will have caught a brief terrible smell of its history, even as they put a white canvas hood over your head. The flap was still open, still allowing you to breathe. Then they fastened the noose round your neck, and closed the flap. The last sight of your face showed it frowning with shock. The executioner allowed the trainee to pull the handle – it was his first time; hence his excitement today in the bar – the trap opened and you dropped through.

Doctor van Zyl immediately conducted an examination – him on a ladder, you still on the rope. It might have been necessary to haul you up and drop you a second time, had you not been, as the executioner put it, 'made extinct' on the first go. This is why it was so crucial to get your weight precisely right, and not to mix up the ropes or trap doors; if there'd been any inaccuracy, you might have been either strangled slowly, or completely decapitated. However, because of the care they took in weighing you, re-checking it on Sunday, and because of the executioner's diligence with his notebook, you were made extinct on the first drop.

You were left on the rope for one hour. This was to allow all automatic muscular activity and irritation of the nervous system to cease; what the executioner called your 'death dance'. When he said that, I pictured your naked body – erect with shock, and twitching – and again I remembered your description of yourself: 'I come into a room hips first, I come to dance or pump pussy.'

Towards the end of the hour, as you hung in mid-air, completely inanimate now, you were hosed down, to clean away any blood, urine, faeces and, yes, sperm ('It's the only thing people ask about,' said the executioner bitterly), before you were lowered. Now the white canvas hood, which was no longer white, was removed. Your whole head had ballooned, your eyes and tongue protruding, both badly discoloured. As the noose was loosened, there was what the executioner called 'a helluva blow-out'. This was from the accumulation of air in your stomach and lungs during the hour while your windpipe was held closed. The 'blow-out' was terribly foul, like it always is; so foul that no-one ever laughs at its assorted, protracted noises – and, in fact, the executioner has to keep two electric fans down there to disperse the air as quickly as possible.

Doctor van Zyl examined you again, and now officially certified you dead. The cause of your death was 'Fracture of the 3rd and 4th cervical vertebrae during the course of judicial hanging.' You were put on a stretcher, this was conveyed to a simple wooden coffin, you were tipped in, the lid was immediately nailed up, and undertakers, whom I think the executioner called Saffas (South African . . . something? . . . Federation, Friends . . .?) took you out of death row, through the black steel gates where I'd waited on the day of the visit, and down the hill to the main gate (where I finally parked today, after my drive through the night), and onto the R101 highway, and to the Coloured graveyard at Eersterus. Here an earth-mover had dug your grave, and, once you were dropped in, promptly pushed back the soil. Your name is not on the grave; only a number on a little metal cross. It's not the same number as the one you had in Maximum Security. Apparently I can apply in writing after a month, and the grave number might be supplied, along with a death certificate.

I won't do that. I've got a different idea. I'll collect all our letters together (mine have been returned from your old Beverly Hills cell), adding these pages, which you won't have seen, post them all up to Pretoria in a sealed bundle, and arrange to have them buried in your unmarked grave. It'll round things off; not sure why . . .

As the executioner got up to rejoin the party in the corner, I asked if he'd do this service for me — bury our letters in your grave.

He smiled — for the first time — and opened his palm. I put R25 into it: the usual fee.

He was our *postman*, you see. The man who delivered my letters to your cell during shower or exercise time, and collected any that you had left. Major Steenkamp suggested him originally, because, apart from mornings like this one, and the tests with sandbags beforehand, his workload is lighter than most of the prison staff; particularly these days . . .

V. POSTSCRIPT

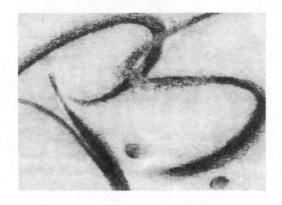

Thirty-Five

Thought about Y. today, for the first time in a while – the day Mandela was released. Watched it on TV with the folks. When it took forever for Mandela to appear on the driveway of Victor Verster Prison, Father said, 'You know why he's so late, don't you? – he's tipping the staff.' Mum said it reminded her of sitting up through the night, watching the first moon landing in '69 (they were in the UK, visiting relatives): 'The whole world glued to their TV sets, staring at a piece of ground, waiting for one man to walk across it.' And actually, when Mandela did appear, there *was* something odd and weightless about his walk; some commentator said he walked like he didn't trust the earth. If Y. was still in Beverly Hills, he'd be a happy man. Two weeks ago, in preparation for Mandela's release, the death penalty was suspended. But in fact all executions were halted long before. The last one was actually on Fri. 17th Nov., four days after Y.'s. *Four* days . . .! I know because I bumped into Father's ex-pupil, Lt. Gen. Venter (that man who's seen the worst of human nature, and rather likes it), in the interval of *Don Giovanni* at the Nico last night. He suggested we have supper sometime. I still don't know if he's after my body or my soul. Anyway, I pulled his leg about the Dept. of Prison Services letting Mandela out, and how it could put him out of a job, make him part of the Great Unemployed, like I am – and he just laughed warmly and said, 'Who knows what the future holds? Last year, when President Ceausescu was asked about the changes elsewhere in Eastern Europe, he said, "Won't happen in my country.

245

Not until pears grow on poplar trees." And you know what? The next morning, some students had hung pears on all the poplars in Bucharest.' Now Venter's smile grew more serious; 'But I suspect *I'll* be here whatever happens in the Republic – civil war, coup, or change of government – I'll be here. Show me a regime that doesn't need its prisons. So give me a call – if you want a job?' Before I could answer, and as the interval bells rang, he began scribbling down his numbers. Remembering that crazy night in November, driving through the small hours and phoning him, I said, 'You've already given me those . . .' He ignored me, finished writing, then pressed the piece of paper into my palm, as he'd done once before, with a Bible. 'No, I don't believe so,' he said, and winked. I understood. Our previous relationship had never existed, but if I wanted to start a new one, he'd be there.